TONGUING THE
ZEITGEIST

Lance Olsen

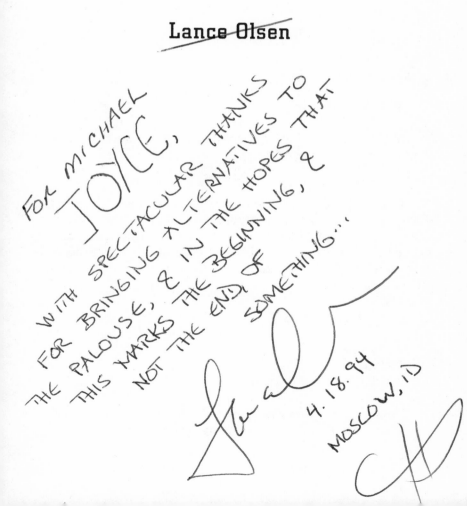

FOR MICHAEL JOYCE, WITH SPECTACULAR THANKS TO FOR BRINGING ALTERNATIVES TO THE PALOUSE, & IN THE HOPES THAT THIS MARKS THE BEGINNING, & NOT THE END OF SOMETHING...

4.18.94
MOSCOW, ID

To Andi, my 24-hour music station

"They say that heaven is like TV."
—Laurie Anderson

Part One

KAMA QUYNTIFONIC

1

They send in the underfed girl, thirteen years old, maybe fourteen if you really stretch your imagination, bald except for that filthy yellow Plughead tassle dangling from her forehead, to pull off the final-dining.

Only the camera fails to record her as it spirals down through the darkness toward the white flash of stage below in the Royal Albert Hall on one of the hottest nights of the year, almost thirty degrees C and here it is November 30, atmosphere gray and close and damp. The camera fails to document her elbowing toward the nearest bodyguard like some little expressionless animal, canister cradled in her arms.

Instead it chronicles the radiant sense of promise spreading over these people, a sheet of flames over a pool of jet fuel. They stand in aisles. Perch on seats frothing foam rubber. Teeter on friends' shoulders, waving at the lens recording this event, making it part of global memory.

They're used to being filmed from above, these people, earth from the space shuttle or GSA station, riot scenes from police VTOLs, football throngs from low-gliding blimps. The guy lapping air, diamond stud flickering on his tongue. The couple, lawyers from nine to five, sporting lilac Aramis head-injury makeup, spinning in some magical private dance down front. The woman with two black eyes, a human raccoon, hoisted between two tall thin boys dressed as late-stage AIDS victims, laughing and rolling back her gray-knit t-shirt to reveal the startling alabaster scars of her cosmetic mastectomy.

Post-verbalists primped in golden nose rings and prosthetic neck burns toast the camera with Dixi-Cups of warm brown lager. Techno-goths tricked out in crimson contacts and white sunscreen, SPF 65, swig whiskey from plastic bottles smuggled

8

in strapped to their ankles. But those in the know realize pills are the future. Shiny pills in fluorescent colors and useless shapes. Lime triangles. Poppy-red hexagons. Lemon squares. Passed from palm to palm in a chain of secret handshakes. So you can *see*, actually *see*, every note float into being at this concert, *feel* each one clap your eardrums.

Everyone's talking at once, a rumble of language through the crammed auditorium as the electrical crew crisscrosses the stage, checking the relays, checking the computer terminals and projectors. As bodyguards gather in the wings, plump hairy arms folded across chests, black teardrops tattooed at eyecorners. As bobbies in plastic-visored helmets, flak jackets, and 50,000-volt stunguns on their belts line the back of the hall by the main doors, legs slightly apart, hands on hips, fifty ominous reminders of what can always happen.

The huge ventilation system convulses, shivers on, a monstrous fan stirring up soggy heat, tangy perspiration and urine, fruity perfume teenage girls wear, strawberry and cherry, diesel exhaust drifting in from Kensington Road, moist hair, alcohol vapors.

These people are the faithful. They've tubed from the Docklands. Hitchhiked from Birmingham. Trained from Newcastle. They've stayed awake the last seventy-two hours straight through a series of crashing headaches, bouts with low-grade hunger-nausea, chemo-fatigue, oil-scented rain clattering on the upper decks of ferries and car bonnets, making connections from Amsterdam, Berlin, Corfu, finagling credit from strangers, finessing rides from acquaintances who've owed them favors for years now and never thought they'd have to pay up this time around.

They're a nation for which it was never a question *of if* they would make it, only *how*. In a sense theirs is a journey that's been underway for months. They are the unwavering, working nowhere jobs to eke out a small line of credit, cleaning tables in a Camden Town pub, collecting fares on an Edinburgh bus. They've been part of this process for so long it hardly seems believable they've finally arrived, they've finally stood in the last queue, passed through the last gate, collected with others in this one prodigious body. They're finally where they've been imagining themselves all this while.

And they're ready. Hooting, whacking their hands together,

stamping their feet.

The camera flies in, unable to capture the stark density of this congregation, the neophilic energy swarming at its center, the passion, the manic vortex, the bright suspense.

And then the stage goes black.

Impulses are coded, transformed into a gray haze of electricity and computerized garble, shot into the sky. They leap toward the Hendrix I, satellite for Air Pyrate Muzzik rotating in geosynchronous orbit twenty-two thousand miles above Nairobi, capitol of the United States of Africa, hurtle down into widescreen HDTVs across the world. Midafternoon into Toronto, sun glistening off cool cobalt blue towers, pith of the financial district. Past midnight into an arid village thirty minutes outside Milan, not a drop of precipitation in the last five years, stars and space debris busy in the night. Late morning into Mexico City, stagnant sulfurous fog already brutally hot, businesspeople in respirators crabbing down streets jammed even on this Saturday in November, lungs aching, telltale pollution sores sprinkled around their nostrils and on their tongues. Excited electrons teem. Cathode-ray tubes oscillate. Video amplifiers fire. Circuitry scintillates, decodes, transfigures white noise into pattern and shape, chaos into cosmos. Snowstorms bloom across screens. Ghosts flare and die. Double images roll, stabilize, wed.

Twenty-five meters above the stage the holounit unfolds marvelous forms and applause lurches through the hall.

A beautiful naked woman with dark red hair and pale freckled skin, sixteen meters tall, the mad Pre-Raphaelite dream of a haunted Rossetti, floats over the crush. Two delicate batwings, blanched flesh and cartilage, extend from her shoulders. She lifts her right hand, opens the palm in which blinks a crystal blue eye, surveys her surroundings.

The eye closes. Her palm folds. Lowering her head, hair spreading over her shoulders like wind, she curls into herself, rotates, loses age and size, dissolves into a fetus, becomes a plant with short parrot-green stems and swollen wet flowers shaped like the plum-colored lips of a vagina. These separate slowly and release a swarm of tiny transparent fish with blueblack wings and scarlet hearts pumping rapidly in their chest cavities. Thousands of tiny orange bubbles swell from their gills.

They morph into copper snakes, purple geckos, angels with monkey faces, transparent fish again, and then a young man in an olivesheen business suit and derby sitting in the lotus position under a banyan tree.

He is speaking to a naked tanned boy with white hair and four arms who sits across from him, also in the lotus position.

"The black box represents the small secret moments, a sense of peace, a sense of wonder," he says.

Around the man and boy grow Venus flytraps, ferns speckled with diamonds. With the slender fingers of his third hand the boy toys with what appears to be a ruby hose on the ground.

"The dream works like this," he says in an Indian accent. "You hold a cat on its back in your arms. Its head wobbles and falls off. You stoop, pick up the head, try to attach it. But it falls off again. This is a process. You are part of this process. This is how the process functions."

"The end of the world is a temple," the businessman says.

The hose is an umbilical cord connecting them. It pulses softly like the tentacles of an anemone.

The tanned boy with four arms squeezes it.

Rich blood surges.

The first computer-enhanced chord reverberates, numbing as the blast from a tactical nuclear warhead.

A spotlight zaps Tango Deltoid, lead guitarist for Dr. Teeth, who launches into a speed riff. The holounit throws his image far above the mob, cuts to his right hand sheathed in the Fender electronic glove that metamorphoses his gestures into complex synthetic sounds. Cycla Propain, female percussionist, kicks in with a power roll. Right behind her come bassist Kupid Zitch and keyboardist Rheum Goldbug.

The decibel level soars like fourteen military jets taking off in unison in a one-room flat, shakes like the LA Shudder on Black Tuesday.

People don't *hear* Dr. Teeth. They *feel* them. They lean into the shockwaves, surrender to the tempest of static bursts slapping their spleens.

And they send up a great unified howl.

Begin to ululate into soundjolts.

And then she appears.

First as a sixteen-meter head levitating over the multitude, blond hair teased like Monroe's, features dipped in shadow like the Virgin's.

Then the face tilts up, huge and glaucous as a geisha's, to reveal the black-and-blue splotches around her browless methyl-yellow eyes, across her left cheek, the dried-blood look at the corners of her carmine lips, and that world-famous patented smile aglitter with teeth filed to wickedly sharp points.

The clamor increases.

The gigantic mouth opens and a thirty-meter-long gold-leafed cobra springs across the ceiling. Slithers down a wall. Disappears into the audience as on stage the real Kama Quyntifonic swoops in with the vocal, part primal-scream, part haunting melody, part tribal chant, camera riveted on her spectacular lingerie, raven corset rimmed in red, on those shiny Mylar thighboots, real nazi, that brass chastity belt with the medieval lock and that sexy nail-studded dog collar that just cries out *Wake up you Quayles, I'm a marketing strategy!* while caving in the heart of every male and every third female in the place.

Dancers in tattered army pants and body suits, shoeless, skin blotched with ersatz scabs, flood around her, crawling on their knees, wriggling on their bellies, hobbling on wooden crutches, and Tango Deltoid, velvet hangman's noose around his neck whipping crazily back and forth, blue hair spattering sweatbeads, leads into the chorus with a compu-guitar solo electronically altered to sound more like frightened rapidfire human cries at two am on some mews in the East End than any musical notes anyone on this planet's ever heard.

Burn this place
Burn your face
Burn this case
Cuz I don't care
I don't care
Cuz I been here
and I been there

Rotten has left the building
Buddha's forgot to pray
My melanoma's spreading
And I'm not even gay

Fans charge the stage, throw themselves at the bodyguards who now begin doing their work, unused to the sheer *numbers* of the devout, the sheer *concentration* of their zeal.

They catch torsos in midflight and catapult them back into the rabble that's become a living version of a stuntman's air mattress, but the fans keep coming, they keep massing in.

Some carry brass knuckles, some sand-socks, some offerings—jewelry, credit slabs, cans of mace—and they scrabble over each other, dive from each other's shoulders, cast themselves headlong at the strong-armed men who are breathless, nonplussed, increasingly agitated in the face of this assault.

At the rear of the auditorium bobbies shout into two-way radios, secure those flak jackets, lower those plastic visors, adjust those chin straps.

The holounit zeros in on the woman dancer whose eyes seem to have melted into myriad epicanthic folds, the scrawny Arab guy in seizures on the floor, then (*keep the camera on the credit, keep the camera on the credit*) Quyntifonic again who's begun shoving her way through these invalids, pushing them onto their sides, kicking their crutches out from under them while she begins the bridge to "Happy Daze" and behind her a ten-by-fifteen-meter screen drops and a black-and-white film, shaky, deliberately amateurish, loops images from Epidemics Hostels around Britain. Rows upon rows of beds. Skin stretched mummy-like over skulls of the dying. Arms the thickness of pencils. Legs the thickness of cricket bats. Specters in wheelchairs. IVs pumping in the morphine, keeping the flow heavy and steady. Quick cuts to the South American war, military jets defoliating what'd been left of the rainforest, tunnels of napalm seething. Remains of LA the morning after the Shudder, megalithic shards of concrete and steel and cable heaved into smoky streets, flames from ruptured gas lines blooming around public housing projects, water spewing from fractured mains, shirtless people in ragged jeans staring into the camera as they stagger through the radioactive wreckage, muddled and embarrassed at what has gone on around them, at what part they took in all this, not even *beginning* to figure out yet things only get worse after this.

But the camera fails to record the underfed girl, thirteen years old, maybe fourteen if you really stretch your imagination, bald except for that filthy yellow Plughead tassle dangling from her forehead, eyes the color of Wedgwood, right ear vangoghed, hovering at the corner of the stage, just a meter away from the nearest bodyguard, an Iraqi who's struggling with another girl who's trying to shinny over him and deliver a cluster of artificial roses to Kama Quyntifonic's feet. He's holding her by a fistful of lavender hair as she writhes and snaps at his face like a Diacomm Doberman-tiger chimera. The underfed girl cradles the canister in her arms, some metallic doll, rocking it gently, scanning the situation around her, patiently taking stock as the lavender-haired fan bites down on the bodyguard's hand, fiercely, for the count of three, seven, and when he screams she bursts by him and almost attains her goal. Four more guards sweep her over their heads before she can reach Quyntifonic, and they toss her into the free-for-all in the orchestra pit. The camera catches her body spin awkwardly through the smoggy air and land at an unnatural angle on a suddenly bare patch of concrete.

Quyntifonic's holographic head releases a ten-meter-long rat.
A bat.
A scorpion.
These creatures dive at the spectators, who send up a communal shout of delighted horror, and then engage in fierce battle on the vaulted ceiling, stinging, gnawing, sucking, while the film keeps looping images of destruction behind the authentic Quyntifonic standing among staged corpses and carving crosses and circles into her right arm with a dagger.
Dr. Teeth's in a frenzy.
Tango Deltoid's sunk deep into soundfields reminiscent of the mumbles and fumbled words you hear during the hypnagogic span just before sleep.
Cycla Propain and Kupid Zitch're pounding out an electronic seizure, wet hair slicked to temples.
And the temperature in the hall is rising, the air thickening, and Rheum Goldbug's zipping along the keyboard in rill after throbbing rill of sick sonics that're just pure clicking mega nazi.

The thirteen-year-old twists a valve at one end of the canister.
She eyes the spectacle before her, raises the bullet-shaped capsule above her head.
Throws.

Thin blood zags down Quyntifonic's right arm and Dr. Teeth has never played better than right now, this very second, and a Virus Baby's upper torso loops on the screen (it'd fit comfortably in a shoebox, silently opening and closing its mouth like some goldfish) and the bobbies enter the rabble to retrieve the lavender-haired girl with the injured spine and the dancers lie motionless at Quyntifonic's feet and a line of gas jets opens at the rear of the stage freeing a hundred plumes of brilliant combustion.

Burn this place
Burn your face
Burn this case
Cuz I don't care
I don't care
Cuz I been here
and I been there

We're talking situation zero
Nothing more to lose or gain
We're talking Krishna's left the disco
And my progens gave me AIDS

And then: the silver glint wobbling like a football in the fracas of laser lights, halting at the apex of its flight for the shortest period of time you can imagine, revolving, then plummeting among the dancers and musicians, mist from its nozzle spraying a wide white V and, just like that, a vast wave of people rolls back from the stage and Quyntifonic's down.

Kupid Zitch and Rheum Goldbug too.

Tango Deltoid's twitching, grand-mal-style, hugging his guitar, his glove generating a brain-splitting screech, coiled into himself like worms when you touch them with something hot.

Cycla Propain sprawls forward into her drumset.

The dancers try standing but are flat and still all at once. The bodyguards and roadies go to their knees. The holounit shuts off. Deafening feedback shoots through the speaker system.

For three heartbeats the audience falls silent.

Then a colossal animal sound of fear rises into the hot atmosphere, and the stampede begins.

The bobbies barely have time to lift their stunguns before the mass belts into them, the momentum kicking them back, someone on the PA system pleading for calm. Feedback rams through the hall. Shouts for help go up everywhere. The press of wild-eyed fans slams against the exit doors. A Datacidist wearing small nails through her ears trips and her ribcage implodes; her lover's elbows crack as he bends to wrestle her up. A guy in LA Gear desert camouflage propels into a wall and hears his own lower jaw disengage; a disoriented boy yanks on the complicated blue scarab-and-iron jewelry jangling around the downed guy's neck. An Überthrasher who's just lost her tongue attempts clambering over a hill of people but slips back into the fray. Some suffocate in the immense army of bodies surging forward. Others lose fingers to the dying who struggle to the very end, only dimly aware of the explosion somewhere above and behind them as the gas jets on stage touch the screen, and the screen ignites and touches the holounit, and a cloud thick as burning tar churns along the ceiling, flames tonguing fuschia and tangerine, the sprinkler system cutting in only to make the smoke thicker, like inhaling battery acid, like drinking lye.

And all across the globe dead-channel ash rains on television screens.

Part Two

BEAUTIFUL MUTANTS, LIMITED

2

I'm major bummed," Dobie Gillis-Snekvic announced from his computer terminal to no one in particular, then adjusted the decorative Genera electrode nubbing out the left side of his neck.

He wore a matching one on the right side, Frankenstein-like, sign of his allegiance to the Tech-head Union, the pair of which cost him slightly more than a week's credit, but it was always the left one that jimmied loose by lunchtime. Which toxed, because Dobie hated having to tinker with anything even remotely connected to his overall appearance once he got to work. It gave people the impression he was basically narcissistic. A bad impression to create, since Dobie was basically narcissistic.

Every morning he rose at five am so he could spend nearly an hour and a half gluing on those damn electrodes, shaving the right side of his scalp, dying the fuzzy left side a kind of orchid pink, plucking eyebrow stubble, applying fake Halston cuts to his forehead over a white Hyperion sunscreen base, slipping in his purple Optikon contacts, making sure his fingernails hadn't started growing back yet, administering various fragrances to various swatches of skin across various parts of his body and, needless to say, standing in front of his closet quarter-hours on end while restructuring his wardrobe in complex combinations before arriving at something even minimally respectable, though his clothes always trailed at least two months behind current fashion and hence continually teetered on the very edge of outdatedness.

At work, though, everything was different. At work every time someone complimented something he wore, Dobie contemptuously peered down at the object in question and responded "Oh, *this*?" as if his whole sense of choosing and matching, rejecting and sorting, was really a matter of uninteresting cosmic whim.

Which was pretty funny, because nearly everyone at Beautiful Mutants, Ltd. knew Dobie pretty well and enjoyed toying with him on this score just for the heck of it. Like Mitzy Weenis, the Israeli who sat at the next terminal over in the antiseptically white corridor lined with identical Sanyo stations. Mitzy's skin was the unhealthy color of old newspapers and her hair of margarine left on the counter a month too long because she refused, simply refused, to go in for that trendy nineteeth-century consumptive look, even if it *would* save her epidermis from those ultraviolet rays frying down. She spoke with an artificial southern accent she'd picked up as a child from 1950s westerns recycled on the Tel Aviv tube at horrible hours each morning. Yet she never quite got the inflection right, so her accent tended to take small tours of the southern United States, sometimes stopping in Atlanta for the pronunciation of a verb, Charlottesville an adverb, Baton Rouge a noun. Consequently she sometimes sounded like the big rooster in the Daffy Duck cartoons, sometimes like Scarlett O'Hara, and sometimes like the family in the *Texas Chainsaw Massacre*.

But she always dressed like Dale Evans, from the cowboy hat to the pearl-rimmed bluejean blouse and skirt to the jazzy rattlesnake-clone boots in tribute to an America that never existed and yet had lines of force capable of drawing her from her homeland to the one that did.

Firmly convinced she could read the future through people's hair designs (an old Kabalistic ritual), Mitzy'd look up from her monitor as if a thought'd just crossed her mind and lean back in her black-plastic-and-chrome chair and glance at Dobie and utter something like "Say, isn't yaw left electrode a lil crooked?" which invariably sent him scurrying toward the restrooms, trying to appear like he was thinking of going in that direction just about now anyway.

"*Ev'rahone's* majah bummed, you lil dickhayed," Mitzy replied. "Ev'rahone across the whole ruckin' *arth* is majah bummed."

"I didn't say they *weren't* major bummed," Dobie said, a little defensively. "I just said *I* was major bummed, which I am, in fact. Mine wasn't a general statement about the state of the world, but a specific statement about my own specific situation which is, well, specific."

"*You* not cayah about otha people? Ah find that hard to fathom." She tapped in an order coming from Calgary, BC, pressed <<<ENTER>>>, and turned back to Dobie. "Ya'll know somethin'?"

"What?"

Dobie was busy entering an order himself.

"Yaw hayah spells trouble today, cowboy."

Dobie half-lidded her in mid-stroke.

"What you mean, 'trouble'?"

"T-R-O-U-B-L-E. Trouble. You know."

Dobie just looked at her, one purple eye a tad smaller than the other.

"You know what yaw hayah's doin' behind yaw back? Yaw hayah's sayin', 'Watch out. Just watch out. This cowboy below me done got up on the wrong side of the bed today. It's gonna be a bad haul. Ya'll might not wanna come along.'"

"My hair isn't saying a goddamn thing," he said, surreptitiously touching the top of his head.

"Yaw hayah's sayin', 'Ah'm givin' a sign. Ah'm payin' witness. STAY AWAY! KEEP YAW DISTANCE! AVOID THIS BEIN' ATTACHED TO MAH HIND PARTS AT ALL COSTS!" Mitzy leaned toward Dobie and asked in a low voice: "Want me to read yaw follicles?"

"You're sick."

"Ah shudder to think what Ah might discovah."

"Get away from me. Shoo. Scat."

"Tell me somethin'."

"Not on your life. I got work to do. *You* got work to do. Let's do our work. Look at me working. Here I go."

"Ya'll got the kind of hayah stands up by itself after eleven pm?"

"What?"

"You know the kind Ah mean. As if it got some kinnah min' of it's own? Go on. Tell me *that* if you ain't scayahed."

"I most certainly *don't* have the sort of hair that stands up by itself after eleven pm. And I'm not listening to you anymore. I'm working. Here I am working. Watch me."

"Dream on, cowboy." She turned to Ben Tendo who was sitting at the station on her other side and asked: "Ain't that right, Benny?"

Ben didn't look over from his screen.

"I guess so," he answered, typing, his earphones and mike making him look like an air-traffic controller.

He was in the middle of taking an order from Burlington, Vermont, for *Greek Plays*, this month's special starring Candi Cain and Rommel Reagan that concerned the secret torrid sex lives of a pederastic acting troupe, and he failed to look over, not because he was concentrating on what he was doing, nor because he was apathetic about the topic of hair in general and Dobie's hair in particular, nor even because he was generally a little quiet around his co-workers, though in reality he was, a little.

It was just that he was *so* bummed, so downright depressed, so out and out wretched, he could hardly speak.

This was because, for starters, Ben wore thick prescription sunglasses since he couldn't afford colored Optikon contacts at a point when colored Optikon contacts were the only thing you wanted to wear when it came to your eyes. And even though he sported a burgundy prosthetic AIDS scab on his cheek and greased his black hair flashback-style, and wore his black Van Heusen button-shirt backwards with his black 1001s and black Nike techno-sneakers trimmed in scuffed white, he nonetheless felt, if the truth be known, a smidgen dorky.

He was almost twelve centimeters taller than the average guy these days who stood at a hundred and seventy-three. When he looked at himself in the mirror he couldn't help stooping, feeling like a caricature of somebody he didn't especially want to meet.

And of course there was the sobering fact that he was already twenty-one years old, already on the shady side by the standards of many in the circles he frequented, yet was still stuck playing in a relatively good (though never-to-be great, or even *really* good) band called the Lithium Breed, doodling on acoustic guitar because he was almost wholly ignorant about compusoundgear and had never practiced enough to perform all those speed riffs you had to if you wanted to impress the bar crowd these days and attract the sluggish attention of the music biz.

In a word: he had no prospects.

None at all.

And the scary thing was he simply couldn't imagine himself doing anything different from what he was doing now when he was thirty.

Or forty.

Or fifty.

Which caused a small uncontrollable tremor to warble through his hypothalamus, a fairly regular event in his life lately. His fingertips tingled, his scalp itched, and he briefly beheld green and red organic shapes swimming away from him.

He saw himself, as if through a zoom lens at quite a distance, hunching over his Sanyo terminal in a low-slung red glass office building on the eastern outskirts of Spokane-Coeur D'Alene, what all the guidebooks these days referred to as New Seattle, in the fifty-first state of Columbia, just six years after the Secession, breathing other people's toxins and viruses in this hermetically sealed workplace, punching in credit numbers and addresses and stock information as part of his McJob at Beautiful Mutants, Ltd., a mail-order factory that specialized in sex toys and interactive holoporn vids featuring, among other eccentricities, handicapped teens, cosmetically enhanced hermaphrodites, and blackmarket films of sports personalities and congresspeople in a multitude of compromising positions, all carrying titles such as *Oral Minorities, Knights in Red Satin,* and *Blow Bi Blow.*

He had exactly fifty-three seconds to take each call, enter each order into his computer, and sign off. More than that, and small bits of credit would be chipped away from his weekly wages. To make sure he was working at full capacity, the company mainframe counted the strokes made by his fingers on the keyboard. At the end of each fiscal year all the employees received a readout recording and ranking their stroke-counts. Those attaining the lowest figures and highest sales, hence laboring most efficiently, won a credit-bonus. Unfortunately Ben always hovered somewhere at the top of the scale and bottom of the ranking since he had this habit of jacking into sundry networks across the globe instead of taking orders, chatting with pretty much anyone who'd listen, Blipverts and Neurocores, Plugheads and Bone Dancers, in order to pass the time and stop those tremors.

His zipperhead boss, Bob Buob, a dwarfish Latino with a virtually square head and monochrome smile you'd never want to trust your kids with, didn't take kindly to this. He'd threatened Ben more than once with JT, or Job Termination. So Ben's aim at this stage in his career was to creep as close to stroke-underload as possible without actually crossing the border into the arid state of unemployment.

All this was discouraging, it went without saying, from Ben's perspective. It was bleak. Plain gloomy. Only what really got him, what really undermined his feeling of connectedness and galactic sense of well-being, was the realization that his idol, his reason for getting up every morning for the last three months (not to mention her whole band, several roadies, and upwards of a hundred and fifty fans) was currently mysteriously dying in New St. Thomas's Hospital in south London.

He simply couldn't fathom how this sort of thing could occur. Couldn't get it through his head someone could just pogo into an internationally televised concert and take down *the* hyperstar of the season, just like that.

Snap.

A politician at a rally he could see. Happened all the time. A labor leader, say, or an ambassador. A corporate executive. People with beliefs. People emblematic of important concepts. Sure. But *Kama Quyntifonic*? Kama Quyntifonic was emblematic of nothing except some pleasure, some fun, escape from crapulent gray Sanyo monitors like this before which he sat eight hours a day, five days a week, three hundred and fifty-one days a year, slightly more than four hundred and twenty thousand minutes so far, give or take.

What could anyone possibly gain by doing this?

What could anyone possibly think they'd accomplish?

Mitzy was presently in the process of prognosticating follicle mayhem, complete hairloss followed by universal calamity brought down upon Dobie's head like some black judgment: failed love, decreased sexual proficiency, financial disaster, fashion suicide, the works. Dobie's face, Ben noticed, was sweating. His eyes were bloodshot. He was trying to counter Mitzy's psychological siege by mounting an epic and alphabetical catalog of Mitzy's personality disorders. Still among the c's, somewhere around *castration anxiety*, he was clearly on a roll.

"It all boils down to one thing," he was saying. "Some people have penises and some people don't."

"People shall talk about you behind yaw back," Mitzy was replying. "'Are mah eyes deceivin' me, or is that lil dickhayed goin' bald?' they shall ask themselves. 'What a terr'ble thang. How just terr'bly *pathetic.*'"

"No penis, no genuine castration anxiety. No genuine castration anxiety, no chance for a complete introjection into adulthood. A full half the population doomed to infantile paralysis. Ugh."

"'But saddest of all,' they shall say, 'is his choice of pants.'"

"Which says nothing of compulsive behavior. Bizarre, irrational, uncontrollable needs."

"'Picasso painted them,' they shall whispah amongst themselves. 'But he'd nevah, nevah *weah* them.'"

"Let me tell you something about control freaks, okay? An ugly, ugly business. I shiver at the very, well, thought."

But Ben didn't want to hear about control freaks, and he didn't want to hear about dead artists. He had his own problems. And the last thing he needed right now was to be exposed to more apocalyptic predictions. So he reached over and connected with another customer, this one from Sante Fe, who was searching for a backlisted copy of *Cunning Linguists* starring Ken Dahl, Stefani Lappér, Velvet Tong, and Bonny Delta and concerning the secret torrid sex lives of an old-time English department. Ben really had to push it to snakebelly in under the fifty-three-second wire, grepping the archive file to see if Beautiful Mutants, Ltd. still carried the tape.

Done, he signed off and jacked into Teeth & Co., Kama Quyntifonic's fanclub. He wasn't all that surprised to find no one on-line. A dark angel had rushed through the system almost at once after the attack yesterday, and then, instantaneously, everyone'd gone silent, struck dumb by some existential aphasia. No one had anything useful to say anymore. No one could find any words worth uttering. All the syllables in the universe just crinkled up and vanished before the absolute horror of the deed.

Ben stared at the Sanyo monitor for a while, then typed a single sentence into the void.

WERE ALL MAJOR BUMMED.

It floated on the screen briefly and disappeared.

Ben checked the digital clock pulsing in the upper righthand corner and rose. Stretched. Bent and touched the toes of his black Nike techno-sneakers trimmed in scuffed white. Straightened. Pushed his glasses up the bridge of his nose.

Decided he might as well check out the Shure Beta liquid crystal HDTV he'd brought in today to keep abreast of the latest on Kama Quyntifonic. It was at the bottom of his knapsack under some ancient socks, a stiff yellow t-shirt, a box of Fender guitar picks, a tube of Elmer's cosmetic adhesive, a blue plastic jar of Noxzema sunscreen makeup, a Walkman, a shiny royal blue Visa slab, and what may have been last Tuesday's lunch: a brittle farm-shrimp roll under a layer of Reynold's shrinkwrap.

He set up the Shure Beta next to the Sanyo monitor so he could study its seven-centimeter display while taking orders, careful to half-cover it with his knapsack to make sure Bob Buob couldn't spy it unless he was really intent on looking.

A man who couldn't spell in Iwa Sity, Iwa, was waiting to purchase Karli (née Karl) Gamick's *Just Busted*, in which the elderly glam made his long-awaited comeback with armless Sharon Lipps and legless Randy Chimer after Gamick's much-heralded sex-change operation and two-year vacation at a youthing spa in the Swiss Alps, while a woman with a gorgeous first name in Caracas, Brazilia, waited to purchase an assortment of Sin-Tillating Sex Tools including Wanda's White Lace Body Suit with ruffled neckline, lattice back, and snap crotch; Cathy's Designer Cuffs with padded wrist bands; Thelma's Thumbscrews with quartz pressure gauge; and this month's hottest item: the GE Sensorium Low-Voltage Cattle Prod, whose very name caused a ripple to whisk through Ben's already vulnerable hypothalamus.

MTV mostly cycled slo-mos of the silver canister twirling above the stage, white spray radiating from its nozzle, Kama Quyntifonic lurching and crumpling to the floor, Tango Deltoid jerking into that fetal position beside her an instant before the cameras blacked out in the flames. Sometimes, too, there were external shots of the Royal Albert Hall taken from Kensington Gardens across the street as the first police cars, ambulances, and fire engines twirled into view, emergency personnel axing through the jammed entrance doors, and, of course, stunned faces of the survivors stumbling into the spotlights over heaps of corpses, thick sooty smoke churning around them.

Ben got used to these. It was as if there'd never been a second when they didn't exist. It was the same sensation he got when he heard a top-of-the-charts song the first time and felt as if he was remembering it, as if it'd always been around some-where, maybe lurking in some alternate universe and that now it hadn't just been created so much as simply squeaked through some wormhole into this one. He got to know that look of as-tonishment in Kama Quyntifonic's eyes as if it was his own.

Every so often an anchorperson appeared for a live update. Usually this took the form of either Jared Marîd, the young Iraqi with the African tribal scars on his cheeks, or Martha Quinn, the purple-haired vee-jay who'd returned to the airwaves from two decade's retirement in London just to cover this. Currently Scot-land Yard had entered the investigation and rumors were circu-lating that the attack'd been the work of the IRA. But, whoever the guilty party turned out to be, the fact remained thirty-two fans had been crushed in the riot that came on the heels of the attempted final-dining. One hundred and forty-eight people had been injured and taken to area hospitals. Another seventy-three had been treated and released. Though there was still no word on Quyntifonic and Dr. Teeth & Co., five thousand devout fol-lowers collected in the streets outside New St. Thomas's to hold an around-the-clock vigil. Footage showed blocked traffic, hordes pressing police barricades, countless candles twinkling against the London twilight like an aerial shot of old LA at night.

"Many foreign leaders have already sent messages wishing the hyperstar a speedy recovery," Marîd reported as out the cor-ner of his eye Ben noticed the <<<MAIL WAITING>>> signal bleeping on his monitor.

Reaching over, he punched it up.

3

The Sanyo informed him the person who'd sent the message was still on the Teeth & Co. board which'd unexpectedly come back to life.

<<<DISPLAY>>>, Ben typed.

YO MAJOR BUMMED, the computer came back, IT SO RUCKING *HURTS* MAN DONT IT?

Quinn appeared again on the tube. She was talking about something with grim solemnity. Ben sort of wanted to listen to what she was saying but was also drawn to the communiqué with which he felt instantly simpatico. It *did* so rucking hurt. That was the thing. It so rucking hurt that the words *it so rucking hurt* didn't even begin to cover it, seeming as they did like some rank understatement of some exceptionally dull banality.

DAMN STRAIGHT, he clacked into the void.

The console whirred.

LIKE A HOLE IN THE HEART came the reply.

LIKE SOMEONES JUST TAKEN AWAY SOME VITAL ORGAN FROM YOU.

YOUR HANDS MAN. YOUR EYES.

CAN U BELIEVE THIS THINGS REALLY HAPPENING? I MEAN IM SITTING HERE WATCHING THE NEWS, OKAY, WATCHING THIS FOOTAGE OVER AND OVER AGAIN AND I STILL DONT HAVE FAITH IN THE IMAGES IM SEEING. SITTING HERE THINK-ING, ITS ONLY TV YOU KNOW? ITS ONLY THIS ELABORATE SHOW. ITLL BE A DIFFERENT ONE TOMORROW, ONE THAT DOES BETTER IN THE RATINGS.

ONLY ITS NO SHOW. ITS REAL. SAME DAMN THING NEXT WEEK. SAME DAMN THING WEEK AFTER THAT.

ONLY IT DOESNT CLICK. I KNOW ITS OUT THERE ONLY I CANT GET MY MIND AROUND IT.

IT CLICKS MAN. IT CLICKS ROYALLY. THATS WHATS SO
NAZI. CLICKS ONLY TOO WELL.

HEY YOU GOT YOURSELF A NAME?

Some expert's head flipped onto the Shure Beta. A gold nose-stud connected to a gold earring by a gold chain dangled down to the guy's jawbone. His name, Dr. Jonathan Manhattan, and his affiliation, University of London, King's College, was printed below him on the screen. Dr. Manhattan was pointing to a cut-away view of what looked like an aluminum thermos bottle filled with a number of sinister-seeming colors.

CALL ME JESSIKA.

JESSIKA?

?

THOUGHT YOU WERE A GUY.

HOW BOUT YOU MAJOR BUMMED? MORF?

MALE. BEN TENDO. BENNY.

SO: WHATS A BEN TENDO?

The goat-cell and collagen injections hadn't helped Quinn much. Neither had the hair transplants nor the operations to prop up her sagging nose. Her SPFless skin was puffy and red-dish. The flesh under her brown eyes drooped in multiple folds like a basset hound's. Her neck was as thin as one of her anorexic arms. She'd never really made the transition from one century to another. The fin de siècle hadn't been good to her.

BEN TENDO IS A GUY WORKS FAR TOO HARD AT BEAUTI-FUL MUTANTS LTD TAKING ORDERS FOR SOME TRULY STRANGE SHIT.

COULD DEFINITELY HAVE DONE WORSE IN LIFE.

KNOW THE PLACE?

WHO DOESNT?

LIVE IN SPOCOEUR?

WEST END OF TOWN. KNOW MADISON?

ME TOO. SPRAGUE. HEY LISTEN. JUST WANNA SAY ITS
NICE TO KNOW SOMEONE ELSES OUT THERE.

CANT BELIEVE THERES NOT MORE TO THIS MAJOR BENNY
THAN WORK AT A HOLOPORN CO.

GUITARIST IN A BAND CALLED LITHIUM BREED.

HEARD YOU GUYS PLAY. CLUB FOOT. YOURE *GOOD*
DUDE. REALLY *GOOD*. ADORE THAT 12-STRING. NO ONE
PLAYS ACOUSTIC ANYMORE. YOU GUYS DO A LYSERGIC
COVER OF "DEMOLISHED MAN." REALLY. // GOT A FAMILY?

PROGENS FINAL-DINED IN THE SHUDDER. SISTER IN SAN LUIS OBISPO.

CLOSE?

HOLIDAY TALK. EXCHANGE INAPPROPRIATE GIFTS. LISTEN TO DIFFERENT BANDS. SHE DRESSES LIKE A BANKER YOU KNOW? YOU?

SIBLESS. PROGENS IN TORONTO I THINK.

THINK?

KICKED ME OUT WHEN 15. SAID I WAS LIKE TOO WILD TO DEAL WITH. TRIED TO GET ME LOCKED UP IN ONE OF THOSE PSYCH FARMS DOWN SOUTH. WHICH WAS WHEN I

<<<INTERRUPT>>>

SOMETHINGS JUST COME UP MAN. GOTTA FADE.

<<<DISCONNECT>>>

HEY JESSIKA? YOU OUT THERE?

<<<YOUR PARTY HAS DISENGAGED>>>

Ben pondered this, then hit QUERY MODE.

ADDRESS?

<<<UNKNOWN>>>

FULL NAME OF SENDER?

<<<UNKNOWN>>>

SEARCH MODE

<<<ENTER SEARCH WORD AND FILE>>>

JESSIKA. ***SPOCOEUR PHONEBOOK.***

<<<1327 ENTRIES PRESS "ENTER" TO LIST>>>

CANCEL ***SEARCH MODE***

<<<ENTER SEARCH WORD AND FILE>>>

JESSIKA ***WEST SPOCOEUR PHONEBOOK***

<<<243 LISTINGS PRESS "ENTER" TO LIST>>>

Ben contemplated two hundred and forty-three Jessikas wandering the streets of western New Seattle and got even more depressed, if that was possible. For about thirty seconds he toyed with the idea of calling all of them. Then he gave up and punched out.

Just in time to hear Martha Quinn on the Shure Beta using a word he didn't want to hear.

She was interviewing a clean-shaven thirty- or thirty-five-year-old man in mirrorshades and a snappy slate-colored business suit and Jell-O green tie. He was identified as Quentin Gifford of Scotland Yard.

"...consistent with a bomblet designed for dispersion of biological agents," he was saying. "Diffuser vanes located on top. A breaker disk next. The upper portion of the bomblet typically loaded with toxic particles, the lower with compressed air."

Cut back to Quinn.

"The compressed air propels the poison into the environment?"

Cut back to Gifford.

"Right. The toxic particles are released in aerosol form from a height of seven to ten meters above the target. This for maximum dispersal."

He touched the knot on his tie, straightening it, unaware the camera was still on him. Behind him in the brick-walled studio was a plastic mockup of the bomblet and a blackboard with a blueprint of the Royal Albert Hall drawn on it.

"Is there any information available about what *kind* of biological agent or agents were used?" Quinn asked.

"The doctors involved in the case have informed us that the victims' symptoms are compatible with those associated with exposure to a botulinus toxin—severe nausea, vomiting, extreme muscular weakness, vision disturbances."

"Can you say anything at this point about the prognosis of the victims?"

Gifford's face hardened almost imperceptibly.

"I'm not a medical doctor, Ms. Quinn. I shouldn't want to speculate upon such matters at this time. All I can do at present is assure you Scotland Yard are following all leads in this case and shall keep the public fully apprised of the situation as it develops."

"Thank you, Mr. Gifford," Quinn said. She looked up at the camera which rolled in for a closeup. "Quentin Gifford, special agent with Scotland Yard, confirming that the canister set off on stage last night during the concert at the Royal Albert Hall was indeed a biological bomb. Now back to you, Jared."

"Thanks, Martha," Marîd said, the ridges of his scars catching the intense mobile television lights.

He was standing on the sidewalk before a late Victorian red-brick building somewhere in London. Above the wrought-iron gate behind him was a sign reading KING'S COLLEGE.

"I'm speaking with Dr. Manhattan, an expert on the history,

manufacture, and use of biological weapons," he said. "Dr. Manhattan, can you fill us in on what we're dealing with here?"

The camera panned back to include the doctor standing patiently with his hands clasped before him.

"Surely," he said. "I suppose I should point out that, while many of us think the use of biological weapons goes back no farther than the second half of the last century, in fact it is at least as old as warfare itself.

"During the Middle Ages, for instance, bodies of plague victims were thrown over city walls to hasten the end of a city under siege. In the 1800s American soldiers made so-called 'gifts' of blankets from small pox hospitals to hostile Indian chiefs.

"But—may I have my photos, please?"

The screen filled with grainy black-and-white images, a series of what appeared to be warehouses in a tropical forest, some kind of military base surrounded by tall barbed wire fences and watch towers.

Next followed the bust of an oriental man with mad eyes and a Fu-Manchu mustache.

"But contemporary biological warfare really has its roots in the experiments of a Japanese army surgeon named Ishii Shiro. I believe your audience is viewing a photograph of him now? Right. Well, shortly after the conquest of Manchuria in 1931, Shiro set up the infamous Unit 731 at Harbin to conduct the first methodical exploration of biological weapons. There over three thousand Chinese, Russian, and American prisoners were infected with plague, typhus, anthrax, and a number of other toxins, then left untreated to determine the course and KR of the diseases."

"KR?"

"Kill Rate. Many prisoners were also murdered with morphine during the course of their illnesses in order to study the diseases' progress. Then, between 1940 and 1944, full-scale experiments using data collected at Harbin were tried on at least eleven Chinese cities."

Rows of army cots filled with the dead and dying tripped into jittery footage of oriental women, dead babies clenched to chests, sprawled along dusty roadways.

"I should add it wasn't until 1976 that evidence of what went on in Unit 731 became public, although the Japanese had in actual fact revealed their findings to the Americans thirty years earlier in exchange for immunity from prosecution in the ensuing war trials.

"Meanwhile, the Allies set up their own experiments at the Microbiological Research Establishment, MRE, at Porton Down in 1940 and, in 1941 and 1942, tested an anthrax bomb on the island of Gruinard off the west coast of Scotland. Which island, by the way, remains contaminated even today."

A megalithic windowless gray building, green hills unfurling into the distance. Men in Mylex suits wandering thorugh patches of scree and chunks of grass stretching across a treeless terrain. Cut to Marîd, holding his mike and nodding. Cut to Dr. Manhattan, mobile lights sparkling off the gold chain connecting his nose stud with earring.

"Although Churchill ordered five-hundred thousand similar bombs to be assembled for use on German cities, the Allies ultimately employed biological weapons only once during the war, when they supplied Czech partisans with grenades filled with botulinus toxin—similar to that used at the concert last night, if Mr. Gifford's information is correct—in an assassination attempt on the man destined to become Hitler's successor: Reinhard Heydrich.

"Heydrich's car was hit with a single grenade on May 2, 1942. He died a few days later of septicaemia, a generalized infection, although he'd received only minor injuries from the bomb splinters."

Black-and-white photos of Heydrich in his slick uniform, his car tilting half in and half out of a ditch after the attack. Planes defoliating rainforests in Brazilia. More dead civilians in the doorways of whitewashed houses and near broken fountains. A well-dressed man in his fifties dropping behind a podium.

"The later use of biological weapons by the United States in Vietnam, Iraq upon its own people and those of Iran in the 1980s, Venezuela upon the Brazilian civilian population during the South American war, and the Red Army Brigade against the President of Germany, are all well known, although perhaps I should —"

Dr. Manhattan continued speaking but Ben lost his concentration as it slowly dawned on him he wasn't the only one viewing his Shure Beta.

Dobie and Mitzy were leaning over from their respective Sanyos, checking out the news with him. Mitzy gave one of those little don't-look-now nods over her shoulder and Ben realized that behind them, standing on his tippy toes, virtually square head and monochrome smile and all, was Bob Buob, his midget boss.

The interesting thing, though, was that Bob wasn't yelling, wasn't stooping there sinisterly like Bela Lugosi waiting to pounce on his unsuspecting prey.

Nope.

Instead, he was balancing on his tippy toes.

And crying.

Sobbing was more like it. Weeping copiously at the reports he'd just been watching, snot running freely from his nose and making his froggish lips shine. His eyes were tiny puckered crimson jellies. His shoulders flexed up around his ears as if they were trying to eat his large head.

And at that instant it struck Ben he'd made two really big mistakes about human nature.

First, he'd misread Bob for years. There wasn't just a dwarfish fascist zipperhead standing beside him, slobbering on the sleeve of his sports coat and snorting like a fallout shelter door on rusty hinges, but another soldier in Teeth & Co.'s army, another one of the faithful.

Ben's heart softened like a wad of Trident on a stretch of August asphalt.

Simultaneously, however, there was this idea not one quarter as appealing as the first.

The attack on Kama Quyntifonic and the others in the Royal Albert Hall didn't mark the end of something. It didn't mark some final step in a long and elaborate plot by who knew who.

Uh-uh.

Not at all.

The attack on Kama Quyntifonic and the others marked only the gunshot that announced the start of the sprint.

The monstrous birth of something Ben knew he couldn't even *begin* to grasp.

4

A hundred and eighty pounds of iron were crushing Uriah Ovulteen's chest and he was really getting into it.

So was Andrea Dorthea, who was squatting next to him, admiring his vein-webbed biceps and graphite-smooth chest while shouting "Push, *push*, PUSH, *PUSH!*" into his cosmetic cauliflower ear.

Lithium Breed's latest demo, *Industrial Culture Handbook*, played on the Yamaha sound system. It'd been recorded last month in Ben's loft and the band had been pretty happy with the hybrid results that welded neo-punk lyrics and gentle folk melodies on keyboard and guitar with grinding rhythms on bass and electronic percussion in songs with titles like "Spiky Permaculture," "Illuminati Papers," and "Schrödinger's Cat."

The idea now was to start sending it around to music companies via Lithium Breed's manager, Mona Lisa-Dreyfus—if, of course, Mona'd ever start returning their calls. Which was getting to be a real question these days.

When they'd started all this stuff five years ago, Mona'd actually searched *them* out, dogging the band from club to club till they'd finally relented and allowed her to take things over. For maybe the next six months she worked like a Technogoth getting them gigs and peddling their wares at two or three places. Only as soon as it became apparent Lithium Breed wasn't due for instant stardom, her nuclear reactor'd just sort of shut down. *Mercedes Nights*, their second demo, sat on her desk unlistened to for four months, at which time the band paid an unannounced visit to her office atop a thirty-story gold-glassed building overlooking New Seattle, just to have her lean back in her alligator-clone chair, a very tall grasshopper with a very black beret, and declare: "I don't love it, guys. You need to find someone who

34

loves it. I *like* it. I'm not tearing my hair out over it. You need someone who's tearing their hair out over it, banging their foreheads against a wall, ripping up little kittens, emotional-impact-wise. I'm not ripping up little kittens."

That was the last time they'd seen her in person. Afterwards it was all secretaries and assistants to assistants. Unless you count the time Uriah swore he'd seen her duck into the women's restroom at the Club Foot. She'd never come out again.

Uriah was convinced she'd climbed through the back window and fled.

The bar on the FlexMach inched up. Uriah bore down. Muscles in his face stretched unnaturally as if he were in a shuttle trying to attain escape velocity.

"*Hiroshima!*" he wailed. "*Nagasaki!*"

Uriah was one-eighth Japanese. Mostly he was Irish. There was also a dash of Native American in there, some French, some Spanish, more Iranian than he'd care to admit, Brazilian, Danish, Hungarian, even a pinch Polish too, which was great, the Poles being a romantic breed, gallantly if fruitlessly charging the Russian tanks on horseback during the Second World War. The Japanese genes were bullies, though, when it came to Uriah's appearance and his sense of cultural identity. His dark brown eyes were Japanese eyes, his light brown skin Japanese skin, his silky black hair kept knotted atop his head Japanese hair.

Ever since he was five, and discovered different people from different places looked different and this seemed to matter to them, he wanted to learn Japanese. He'd never had enough money to take private lessons, and, still protesting the Japanese manipulation of world markets at the turn of the century, Columbia didn't offer the language in high school. So, as compensation, Uriah'd taken to memorizing and then citing names of various Japanese cities whenever he was upset or otherwise in need of an expletive. Which he was in the process of doing right now, Andrea pushing him toward one more set on the weights.

They'd been muscling two hours in the living room (which also served as dining room, bed room, studio, and weight room) of their weather-worn, worm-eaten, tumble-down Alzheimer's victim of a log cabin tilting imperceptibly starboard somewhere in a pine grove on the edge of the dead lake almost an hour northeast of Sandpoint, repeatedly listening to *Industrial Cul-*

ture Handbook while taking turns spotting for each other on what looked like an elaborate Inquisitional device, all the time sweltering in what the vee-jays in the area had taken to calling a WINGEVE, or Winter Greenhouse Evening. Already nine o'clock, the temperature outside had yet to beetle below thirty degrees. The intense sun from the late afternoon was still trapped inside, and had mixed with Andrea and Uriah's own body heat.

Which Andrea and Uriah thought was just great.

Watching each other sweat, smelling each other's musky pheromones choke the air, beholding each other's pleasure-pain face-strains and endorphin punches—it was enough to turn anyone on.

Andrea concentrated on her drummer's arms, though she also did her fair share of inverted situps off a straight-bar and not an unimpressive number of leg thrusts while sitting in what seemed the cockpit of an old-fashioned biplane. This last had given Uriah a continuous erection.

He'd only gotten around to his upper torso twenty minutes ago and knew he should tear some more fiber before quitting but also knew sex was going to be fantastic tonight. Something Andrea, aware of his erection like a cat is aware of a farm-shrimp burger on the counter, knew as she picked at her molar with her forefinger, thinking.

She had the worst set of teeth Uriah'd ever seen. The front ones were okay, if you didn't mind the crusty plaque buildup and blotchy caffeine stains. But the back ones were a nightmare. They were carbon around the gums, crammed with fillings, sensitive to the slightest touch. Last month one'd fallen into her hand while she was toying with it on stage between sets. She kept saying she had to get to the dentist one of these days yet Uriah remained dubious. And anyway, bad teeth were Andrea's trademark in Lithium Breed. That and her fetish for head-injury manuals and makeup. The band's small but devoted group of fans saw her rotten mouth as an endearing feature, an extension of those black eyes, artificial bruises on the side of her half-shaved purple head and neck, bandage she always wore like a bandana. Certainly Uriah did. He found it all erotic as hell.

"Four reps," Andrea said, extracting her finger.

"I can't."

"Just four. Even *I* can do four more reps at a hundred eighty."

"I see a long white tunnel. At the end are people I know."

"Three reps and I'll shut up."

"They're beckoning me to join them. I'm saying, 'I'm on my way. Here I come. Don't go anywhere till I get there.'"

Andrea curled her nose, then leaned over and kissed him on what was left of his earlobe.

"Okay, tiger," she said. "You win. It's Elektra time."

She said this with a tone that suggested she was eating her broccoli after hours of pouting at the family table. The truth, however, was she was as excited as Uriah, who immediately clamped his palms together and sat up.

"*Elektra's Complex?*"

"Picked it up from Ben this weekend."

He struck his Indian mystic pose, legs crossed, arms raised and cocked at elbows, little okay-signs formed with thumbs and pointers.

"I'm feeling better even as we speak."

"I'm sure you are," Andrea said, reaching for his erection through his royal blue gym shorts. "I'm just sure your are."

Squeezing.

They had a dim recollection of meeting six years ago during a Secession Night party at Ozzy Mantis's. People in eastern Washington, northern Idaho, and western Montana had been talking about consolidating their leftist political power for more than fifty years, only things had gotten serious over the last decade. First came the marches, long and loud and mean, followed by the protests on the steps of the Court House in Spocoeur. In a poorly planned move that led to violent riots in Moscow and Missoula, not to mention the beginning of the end of her presidency, no-guff Fonda sent in the National Guard. Armed skirmishes erupted between tekked troops and rag-tag Columbian militia comprised of hunters, loggers, forestry service personnel, elderly hippies, animal rights activists, and generally pissed-off students looking for a good fight. Tanks rolled through downtown New Seattle, fighting severe in the north. Government soldiers leveled Gonzaga University, the old Sheraton Spokane Hotel, the Convention Center. Rebels mined and sunk the floating golf course at the resort and blew up the three major runways at the airport. Nearly five hundred people were killed and nearly two thousand injured in what amounted to a three-week civil war.

By the time Redford made his bid for the White House on the Demopublican ticket during the impeachment hearings, it was clear the only thing left to do to save the country's soul was to allow the fifty-first state to come into existence. Redford thus made the announcement in his famous "Heal Our Wounds" inaugural address.

The Secession Night parties across Columbia were brain-sizzlingly crazy. The new state government ignited a massive fireworks display every evening for a week. Techno-pills flowed freely, as did such Nostalgia Drugs as LSD, Ecstasy, and Nazarene. In Spocoeur revelers overturned cars and shattered store fronts. Bars opened early and stayed open around the clock and citizens of the fledgling state Brownian-motioned from one to another, drinking and carousing, duded in bizarre costumes that made Mardi Gras appear yawningly predictable.

Which was what Uriah Ovulteen had in mind when he turned up at Ozzy Mantis's in his samurai outfit replete with sword and simulated leather shield. He was nineteen, already blitzed, and out to have the kind of night he could still tell his friends about when he was seventy without repeating himself. Only when he strolled through the front door and reached into his pocket for his credit slab, vaguely contemplating whether he should start slow with six beers or dive straight into a row of double vodkas, he felt the first concussions from the band's electronic percussionist whomp him and promptly fell in love.

Women were fine, had been his way of looking at it, but nothing to get all bent out of shape about. He'd slept with a lot, had some damn good conversations with a few, and had even been friends with one when he was fifteen. Only he'd never before felt the crackle of static among his ribcage, the scalding hot itch in his groin, that he experienced at that very instant. Maybe it was the way she throbbed out those rhythms that pulverized his heart. Maybe it was her sixteen-year-old body, bee-bite breasts, long purple hair with the square shaved into one side. Maybe it was that nazi mouth or those mega greenish brown marks running up and down her neck. Whatever, he knew this was it. This was the Big One.

He ran right over, some tin and metal things clanking around his knees, and asked the bartender her name. The only thing the guy behind the counter remembered, though, was that the group was called Tachyon D'Eath and they were getting paid pretty well and the lead singer's name was Ludwig Fun Beatoffen. So Uriah realized he had to take matters into his own hands. He moved to the front of the dance floor and began whistling, gearing in his samurai suit, and otherwise acting like an asshole. Before long the percussionist was sneaking peeks at him, a good sign, and between songs Uriah ordered a beer sent to her. Between sets he decided to hunt his dreamgirl down. She was sitting by herself at a table in back of the bar, eight Buds lined up in front of her, picking at her left rear molar. He took a seat across from her and began telling her how much he loved her and how he wanted to marry her and then—well, and then things got substantially more nebulous. Uriah thought he remembered sitting and talking to her for a long time, perfectly in tune, then walking arm-in-arm to a nearby motel where they performed eardrum-shattering sex with the tube blaring. Andrea, however, recalled it differently. While she couldn't piece together all the fragmented images misfiring among her synapses, she clearly recollected Uriah and her huddling in a stall in a nearby Wong Yan Silver's restroom, the presence of a Great Dane, and the smell of toothpaste, probably Crest.

Neither memory apparently jibed very well with what actually transpired, since both of the rockers clearly remembered waking several days later beneath a spruce in River Park, temples whanging with acoustic pulsations, vision quadrupled, aches in places that'd never ached before, amid a crowd of polite Boy Scouts carefully setting up a pup tent.

Andrea, smitten by the samurai keyboardist with the great biceps, quit Tachyon D'Eath. Uriah introduced her to Ben Tendo and Helmer Skelter, two buddies with whom he'd been jamming at his cabin just for the heck of it for a couple of months. And, before anyone could exactly put their finger on it, Lithium Breed materialized along with its pseudo-flashback-style music that tended to mass-induce a low-grade sense of bittersweet memory in its audience.

Using Andrea's connections with Ozzy Mantis, they booked themselves there and into about half a dozen other places around town. At the end of their first gig a very tall grasshopper in a very black beret, black body suit, and crimson army boots approached them and asked to be their manager. Her name was Mona Lisa-Dreyfus. They said they had to think about it. She said fine. But behind her back Helmer, a member in good standing with Paranoids Anonymous, said he definitely had bad feelings about her. It was just too coincidental for his taste that she showed up so quickly on the Saturday night that also happened to be Friedrich Nietzsche's birthday. Nor was Helmer's paranoia quelled when Mona proceeded to dog them from club to club for a month before they finally relented.

But they *did* finally relent. Mona finally became their manager partially, they hated to admit, because they'd simply had no other offers.

Meanwhile, Andrea and Uriah moved in to Uriah's ramshackle cabin nicknamed The Monastery. They hit it off magnificently, both sure this was something chemical. And they lived together pretty much happily ever after, leaving the place less and less, convinced as they were that the new Dark Ages were upon the world and that the only hope was for individuals to hole up in tiny Zones of Safety and tend their own affairs as environmentally and ethically soundly as possible. This notion was reinforced when they looked at the news every night and understood that, after the Shudder, Seattle had become the reborn LA, and that, after the Secession, Spocoeur was well on its way to becoming the reborn Seattle. Subsequently, they appeared in the city only for gigs and the occasional Chicago-style pizza on Sprague, just around the corner from where Ben lived. Otherwise they lived quietly, eking out enough to afford the mortgage and satisfy their basic food and drug requirements. They slept till one-thirty or two every day, practiced every afternoon, worked out on the FlexMach every evening.

And, of course, explored those mind-expanding holoporn vids Ben provided as much as their bodies humanly allowed.

Andrea slipped *Elektra's Complex* into the Mitsubishi while Uriah foraged through the pharmacy in the cabinet above the grease-smeared microwave and extracted a translucent plastic bottle with a green label. He raised it so Andrea could see and she in turn barked like a terrier, panted, rolled over on her back amid a pile of over-sized artificial Mideastern pillows, and stuck her arms and legs in the air.

The national anthem suffused the cabin smelling of timber, coffee and several scent strips Andrea'd had fun scratching and sniffing while bottom feeding in some recent issues of *Underground Drug Library* and *Hardcore California*. She'd really gotten off on Redford's Fetish, not tox at all for the old fart, though she had to admit Brooke Shields's Estrus was *deadly*. No doubt that woman was on her way to Congress, child abuse allegations or no.

The White House and other key Washington monuments levitated in the middle of the room as the First Amendment promo accompanying each vid spun. Mind blank, Andrea hit FAST FORWARD and tested how long she could keep her eyes open without blinking till Uriah joined her with four tekked Piracetams and two Flintstones glasses filled with Welch's brown semi-organic apple juice laced with choline.

He sat beside her.

Andrea popped the pills and chugged some juice, shut her eyes, and enjoyed a few seconds of anticipation as the drugs glided down her esophagus.

"I can hear the mouse the owl is holding in its beak in the tamarack down by the lake," Uriah said after a time.

"Cool."

"Its voice consists of a three-note chord. B-flat. B. C."

Andrea attended carefully.

"Oh yeah," she said. "I gotcha. I gotcha. Hint of a C-sharp in there, too."

"And lower notes behind that. The owl's thinking about how *good* this thing's gonna taste. You can just *feel* it."

Propping himself up king-fashion, he languidly reached over and hit PLAY on the remote control panel.

The radical Indian feminist holoporn queen hovered two meters off the floor, grinning sexily, part Buddha, part Himmler, part your mom on ludes, and gazed down on the couple. She wore her patented Robomatrix simucort exoskeleton through whose braces you could see her finger-thin arms and legs, Auschwitz hips, wide white scar where her left breast had been, and huge tumorous bulge of her superimplanted right.

Behind her appeared a burning bush that dilated into Ramon Codd, the Caribbean renowned for his dreadlocks which reached to his waist and salad of self-inflicted body scars, mostly razor- and glass-cuts on his face, neck, and shoulders. He sported four-centimeter golden rings through his nose, nipples, and testicles, and a diamond stud through his tongue which now glistered among saliva as he stepped up behind Elektra and unfastened the nylon and velcro straps holding her exoskeleton in place.

41

Elektra leaned back into him and groaned.

Andrea was busy massaging her small breasts with one hand and poking around in her mouth with the other. Every time she came in contact with a particularly bad tooth she flinched, the Piracetam increasing her awareness of the pain.

"Do it," Elektra whispered, first to Ramon, then to Andrea and Uriah. "Do it. Do it."

Ramon lifted the quadriplegic out of her last braces, which dissolved like Alka-Seltzer in water as they fell away, and lay her horizontally in the air like a magician his assistant.

The light in the room turned velvet red.

Elektra parted her lips and a cloud of miniature doves fluttered out, transforming into whips, nooses, blindfolds, and finally meter-large roses that twirled slowly like balloons, bumping into the ceiling, merging with the furniture, fracturing as if they'd been stuck in a vat of liquid nitrogen, each shard forming a new rose. Ramon licked her neck with his diamond stud, teased the misshapen nipple of her superimplant with a lock of tightly-wound hair.

Next he launched a maddeningly gentle exploration of Elektra's thin brittle limbs while beginning to rub his own member. Every once in a while he'd look over his shoulder at Andrea who dropped her right hand and buried it between her thighs, head falling back, low guttural noises bubbling from her throat.

Elektra twisted her neck from side to side in pleasure.

Uriah pumped himself slowly at first and then started picking up speed.

"You look so *good*," she said to the couple. "Oh, yes. *Yes*. You look so beautiful."

When a part of Ramon's body strayed too close to her mouth, she bit hard, drawing blood. Scorpions scurried from her vagina and scuttled up her abdomen, stinging her taut yellowish brown skin as they went.

"Yummmmm," Uriah said.

"You like this?" Elektra asked. "I bet you do. I bet you like it almost as much as I do. Ohhhhhhh. *Yes*."

"Pinch me," Andrea said, sighing.

Uriah did.

"Oh, *yes*," Elektra said. "Oh, *yes*. Bring it home, baby. You know you dig that pain. You really click on it. Yeah. You want more, always just a little more each time. Sweet as the snap of a whip on your thigh, out-of-reach as trying to kiss your own spine. You want it bad. You want it *so* bad. Love my teeth on your arm, fingernails across your neck. Come on, baby, bring it home to Elektra. Bring it home to Mama Pain..."

Uriah had managed to stay pretty much in synch with Ramon to this point, thinking about other things, that owl out back, the oppressive heat, the sticky pine fragrance liquifying the atmosphere, only he kept returning to visions of sex he'd seen in those bleached-out two-dimensional vids made in the days before The Epidemics, full intercourse, an idea that forever boggled his consciousness in aboriginal wonder, to Andrea's and Elektra's incredible moans, to how they were both whispering *do it do it do it* now as Ramon slid back and forth along the dent in Elektra's shoulder, faster and faster, how Elektra's blue blue Optikon eyes began rolling up inside her head, how without warning a burning sensation gathered presence and speed between his own legs, and how the wood-walled room instantaneously swarmed with green frogs bearing golden eyes, a flurry of obese rats in tiny plastic human masks, foamy-mouthed police dogs, shimmering two-meter-tall crystals, a rain of pearls, a thundershower of milk, light turning bright white like a nuclear detonation as Ramon released in the crevice separating Elektra's withered bicep from the bone in her arm and then gasped and Elektra gasped and Andrea gasped and air caught in Uriah's chest.

"*Kanazawa,*" he croaked a few minutes later as he stood over the ceramic kitchen sink, plucking at his cauliflower ear while waiting for the pump to bring up some cold water. "*Oku-fucking-shiri.*"

"*Listen to this listen to this listen to this!*" Andrea shouted from the over-sized pillows.

She'd flipped from the holounit to MTV's coverage of the attack on Kama Quyntifonic. Martha Quinn's face pervaded the screen. There were tears in her eyes.

Andrea cranked the volume.

"...has disavowed the bombing," Quinn was saying. "The Rock Commission and Scotland Yard have now turned their investigation toward the possibility of a lone assassin. They are currently searching for Quyntifonic's ex-lover, Uncle Fester Ziff, for questioning in connection with the singer's murder."

"Oh *SHIT!*" Andrea hollered.

Without thinking Uriah opened the cabinet above the microwave and took out a bottle of barbituates and ticked six into his palm.

"To repeat, then," Quinn was saying, voice quavering. "Kama Quyntifonic died at 4:13 am London time of complications stemming from exposure to biological agents. Billboard Stocks have begun to plummet on the Tokyo Exchange."

Uriah lay three pills on his tongue and reached down to test the water.

Initially he thought it was steaming even though he'd turned on the cold tap. For several moments he just couldn't understand what he was looking at.

Then he realized the skin on his hands was fizzing as it melted.

5

<<<MAIL WAITING>>>
<<<MAIL WAITING>>>
<<<MAIL WAITING>>>
<<<MAIL WAITING>>>
<<<MAIL WAITING>>>
<<<MAIL WAITING>>>
<<<MAIL WAITING>>>
<<<MAIL WAITING>>>
<<<MAIL WAITING>>>
<<<MAIL WAITING>>>
<<<MAIL WAITING>>>

SECURITY MODE
         <<<SECURITY MODE ENTERED>>>
VIRUS SCAN
         <<<VIRUS SCAN NEGATIVE>>>
DISPLAY
MAJOR BENNY. HOWZ THINGS CLICKING?
JESSIKA? THAT YOU?
NONE OTHER.
GOOD TO HEAR FROM YOU. // HOWD YOU FIND MY
LINK?
GOT MY HACKER WAYS. HOW YA DOING?
NUMB. WHEN YOU CALLED I WAS SITTING BY THE WIN-
DOW IN MY LOFT ALL THE LIGHTS OUT JUST LOOKING.
WHAT AT?
BIG CITY WERE LIVING IN YOU KNOW?
PEOPLE ARE PLATHING THEMSELVES TEENAGERS CLIMB-
ING INTO THE FAMILY CAR IN THE GARAGE TURNING ON THE
ENGINE DOWN THE STREET FROM ME THESE KIDS TOOK A

JUMP OFF THE DAM 7 OF EM HOLDING HANDS.

DELTOID TOO?

PROPAIN ZITCH EVERYONE.

ALL OF A SUDDEN I CANT REMEMBER A TIME THEY WERENT GONE. WHAT WAS IT LIKE WHEN THEY WERE ALIVE? IT MUSTVE BEEN INCREDIBLE.

DONT *YOU* START GETTING ANY IDEAS.

CANT EVEN PLUCK MY OWN EYEBROW HAIRS. BUT ILL TELL YOU SOMETHING. YOU EVER GET THE IMPRESSION THINGS ARE I DONT KNOW *SPEEDING UP?*

THINGS?

LIKE YOU TURN ON THE NEWS AT SIX OCLOCK & ITS COMPLETELY DIFFERENT FROM THE NEWS AT FIVE OCLOCK. SONG THAT WAS NUMBER ONE LAST MONTH WHEN YOU HEAR IT AGAIN YOU CANT REMEMBER HEARING IT BEFORE?

LIKE MAYBE YOU DIMLY RECOLLECT IT FROM WHEN YOU WERE 4?

YOU CRACK A JOKE & PEOPLE OVER 25 LOOK AT YOU LIKE MAYBE YOU HAVE A BRAIN TUMOR & HAVE 3 WEEKS TO LIVE.

LIKE *THIS* IS THE FUTURE & WHAT COULD POSSIBLY COME NEXT?

SO TELL ME SOME MORE ABOUT YOUR SISTER.

SISTER?

SAID YOU HAD ONE IN SAN LUIS OBISPO.

MIKKI.

YEAH. MIKKI.

GREW UP TOGETHER IN EAST LA. PROGENS WORKED AS RESEARCHERS FOR DIACOMM LABS. MOSTLY LIVED IN COM-PANY QUARTERS SO WE SAW EM LIKE ONLY A COUPLE TIMES A MONTH. MIKKI & ME WERE HOUSED IN THE CHILDCARE COMPLEX. SHE WAS 6 YEARS OLDER THAN ME SO I COULD NEVER FIGURE OUT EXACTLY WHO SHE WAS OR WHAT HER RELATION TO ME WAS SUPPOSED TO BE WHEN WE SAW EACH OTHER. WHICH WASNT VERY OFTEN.

SHUDDER DIDNT CATCH YOU?

COMPANYD TAKEN THE KIDS INTO THE MOUNTAINS FOR FIELD TRAINING. ALWAYS TREATED US REAL WELL. LAB WHERE MY PROGENS WORKED WAS 2 MILES DOWNWIND OF THE DISNEY NUCLEAR REACTOR. JUST VANISHED IN THE DEBRIS RADIATION OILFIRE CLOUDS. COMPANY DIVERSIFIED

IMMEDIATELY AND SET UP SATELLITES IN NORTHERN CALI-
FORNIA ARIZONA PHILIPPINES.

HOWD YOU END UP HERE?

DIACOMM SENT MIKKI TO COLLEGE IN TUCSON.

SHE WAS 1ST CHILD.

RIGHT. SHE MAJORED IN CHEMISTRY & BIOLOGY & AFTER
HER MS MOVED HER TO SLO. PART OF THE COMPANY RE-
CONSTRUCTION CAMPAIGN. I WAS 2ND CHILD SO THEY
EMANCIPATED ME WHEN I WAS 17.

YOU FOLLOWED THE NORTHERN MIGRATION.

ALWAYS LIKED MUSIC. BEEN PLAYING GUITAR SINCE I WAS
EIGHT. FIGURED THERED BE LOTS OF OPPORTUNITIES IN
SPOCOEUR. MET URIAH HERE. THRU HIM HELMER & ANDREA.
DIACOMM TRAINED ME IN COMPUTERS SO WHEN THE JOB
AT BEAUTIFUL MUTANTS CAME ALONG I APPLIED. DIACOMM
STILL HAS RIGHTS TO 10% OF MY EARNINGS BUT THE CREDIT
AT BEAUTIFUL MUTANTS IS REAL GOOD.

MISS YOUR PROGENS?

LIKE UNCLES AND AUNTS.

GOT AN IDEA.

?

HOW BOUT GETTING TOGETHER AT THE LOST IN SPACE
TOMORROW NIGHT FOR A DRINK? WE CAN TALK MORE.

CLICKIN.

SO LETS SEE IF I GOT THIS STRAIGHT OKAY? YOURE
SITTING ALONE IN THE DARK LOOKING OUT YOUR WINDOW.

JUST THE LIGHT FROM THIS SCREEN. WHOLE LOFTS
SORTA GREENISH LIKE THE BOTTOM OF A SWIMMING POOL
AT NIGHT WHEN THE FLOODS ARE ON.

WHATRE YA WEARING?

WHITE T-SHIRT. PAIR OF JEAN CUTOFFS. SOCKS. NO
SHOES. AIDS SCAB.

T-SHIRT SAY ANYTHING?

USE JETS WHILE YOU STILL CAN.

NICE.

LINE FROM HOLY TERRORS.

WHY DONT YA TAKE EM OFF?

WHAT?

YOUR T-SHIRT AND SHORTS. GO AHEAD. // WHAT YOU
GOT UNDER EM?

UNDER THEM?

YOU HEARD ME.
NOTHING.
TAKE EM OFF.

<<<<u>INTERRUPT</u>>>>
<<<<u>INTERRUPT</u>>>>
<<<<u>INTERRUPT</u>>>>
<<<<u>INTERRUPT</u>>>>
<<<<u>INTERRUPT</u>>>>
<<<<u>INTERRUPT</u>>>>
<<<<u>INTERRUPT</u>>>>
<<<<u>INTERRUPT</u>>>>

OKAY.
GOOD.
YOU?
ME?
YEAH. WHAT YOU WEARING?
NOTHING. ;)
SERIOUSLY?
WOULD I KID BOUT SOMETHING LIKE THAT?
;)
CLOSE YOUR EYES AND TELL ME WHAT YOU SEE.
SEE YOU SITTING AT YOUR CONSOLE.
YEAH?
YOURE TOUCHING YOURSELF.
MEGA.
GETTING INTO IT. SMILING.
YOU GOT THE HANG OF THIS THING PRETTY QUICK
HUH? // ONLY YOU KNOW SOMETHING?
WHAT?
IM NOT AT MY CONSOLE ANYMORE.
NO?
IM LIKE ON MY KNEES IN FRONT.
YOUR HANDS ARE ON MY THIGHS.
YEAH. AND IM USING MY TONGUE. *LOVE* USING MY
TONGUE. SO SENSITIVE YOU KNOW?
RUNNING MY FINGERS THROUGH YOUR HAIR.
ITS BLACK BENNY. REAL DENSE.
YEAH. AND IM GUIDING YOUR HEAD UP AND DOWN.
ONLY I PULL BACK ON YOU TEASING. LICKING LONG AND

SLOW.
    I SHIFT FORWARD IN MY CHAIR BRUSH YOUR HAIR BACK SO I CAN WATCH YOURE REALLY PRETTY JESSIKA.
    HEADS BETWEEN MY LIPS. HARD AND SOFT AT THE SAME TIME. SMOOTHEST SKIN ON THE WHOLE BODY YOU KNOW? OUR EYES MEET.
    WET MY FINGERS. CIRCLE YOUR NIPPLES WITH THEM.
    WORKING FASTER NOW FULL STEADY STROKES DOWN TO THE BASE.
    I REACH BETWEEN YOUR LEGS AND

    <<<WARNING: ELECTRONIC TRESPASS IN PROGRESS>>>
    <<<WARNING: ELECTRONIC TRESPASS IN PROGRESS>>>
    <<<WARNING: ELECTRONIC TRESPASS IN PROGRESS>>>
    <<<WARNING: ELECTRONIC TRESPASS IN PROGRESS>>>
    <<<WARNING: ELECTRONIC TRESPASS IN PROGRESS>>>
    <<<WARNING: ELECTRONIC TRESPASS IN PROGRESS>>>
    <<<WARNING: ELECTRONIC TRESPASS IN PROGRESS>>>

    JESSIKA?
    NO.
    WHO IS THIS?
    ///////
    LINK?
    //////
    SEARCH MODE
    DATA READS: **SKY FILLED WITH DETRITUS**
        <<<SEARCH MODE INOPERATIVE>>>
    COMPUTER LOCK
    THINGS ARENT ALWAYS CLEAR IN THE BEGINNING.
        <<<COMPUTER LOCK INOPERATIVE>>>
    THE WHIRLWIND. THE VIOLENCE OF THOSE WHO ARE ALONE.

        <<<VIRAL INFILTRATION IN PROGRESS>>>
        <<<VIRAL INFILTRATION IN PROGRESS>>>
        <<<VIRAL INFILTRATION IN PROGRESS>>>
        <<<VIRAL INFILTRATION IN PROGRESS>>>
        <<<VIRAL INFILTRATION IN PROGRESS>>>
        <<<VIRAL INFILTRATION IN PROGRESS>>>
        <<<VIRAL INFILTRATION IN PROGRESS>>>

SHUT DOWN
<<<<u>SHUT DOWN INOPERATIVE</u>>>>
ALL AROUND ME IS

BRIGHTNESS

AS IN THE INSTANT

LIGHTNING BLASTS YOU.

A CHORUS OF

WHITE NOISE.

HOW CAN WE
(THINK?)

WHAT YOU WANT?

HOW CAN WE

(REASON?)

SOMETIMES THE PRISONERS

REMEMBER WE ARE THE

SHIP

THE COORDINATES
THE BLUEPRINTS

WATCH US

WATCH AS THE

LIGHT TAKES US TO   **PIECES**
ALL THE
             LEPTONS

                    SCREAMING.
TELL ME WHATS

          <<<<u>EMERGENCY POLICE INTERRUPT</u>>>>
          <<<<u>EMERGENCY POLICE INTERRUPT</u>>>>
          <<<<u>EMERGENCY POLICE INTERRUPT</u>>>>
          <<<<u>EMERGENCY POLICE INTERRUPT</u>>>>
          <<<<u>EMERGENCY POLICE INTERRUPT</u>>>>
          <<<<u>EMERGENCY POLICE INTERRUPT</u>>>>
          <<<<u>EMERGENCY POLICE INTERRUPT</u>>>>

MR. BENDIX TENDO?
?
HOME LINK CODE?
ZZT71492.
     SERGEANT ROSWALD OF THE SPOCOEUR PD. CALLING
ON BEHALF OF MS. ANDREA DORTHEA AND MR. URIAH
OVULTEEN. PLEASE MEET US AT DEACONESS HOSPITAL ASAP.
     WHY? WHAT HAPPENED?
                    <<<HANG UP>>>

6

This was Helmer Skelter's idea of a nightmare, the kind of thing he flopped awake thinking about at three in the morning, face beaded with sweat, heart gushing, body shaking, pillows sopped, sheets wadded and strewn across his tiny room in the Davenport Hotel. The kind of thing that stopped him dead in his tracks as he squidded past oxygen booths in River Park on spring afternoons, sky the tone of asphalt, breeze pungent with fossil fuels and ammonia, temperature already in the high thirties, and sent him slinking into Café Gone on Spokane Falls Boulevard to huddle in the back corner behind a newspaper, hoping to god his pulse would slow down, his fingers quit trembling, his lungs return to something like a human rhythm.

It embodied all the horrific prophecies he'd always almost convinced himself were nothing more than juvenile delusions, those footsteps he just *knew* he heard speeding up behind him as he hurried by the Amtrak station at eleven in the evening, the electronic pips across his phone line as he tried talking in earnest to his friends during lunch breaks as a mechanic at Les Schwaab's, those strange hieroglyphs he found carved into the wooden walls of every gas station restroom stall from Berlin to Paris if he simply looked for them hard enough that autumn he decided to leave the EEC and come to America to start his music career.

The kind of thing he'd spent years, *years*, whimpering about to his support group at Paranoids Anonymous, only to be told by people with terrified eyes it was all in his head, nothing more than a loveless childhood mixed with a healthy dose of rampant German guilt for the first half of the twentieth century. The kind of thing that prompted him to join televangelist Joey Taboo's increasingly popular Cult of Aloneness based in Las Vegas when he turned eighteen, reading *Pathways to Lessness* daily, embracing celibacy and autonomy at all costs, heading into the Nevada desert on bimonthly solo retreats to dodge poisonous snakes and get in touch with his singleness, eschewing the concept of all long-term relationships, reconciling himself to diminishing expectations of sexual, interpersonal, and material wealth.

Only *now* it was all real. Only *now* it was nipping at his heels like a pack of rabid coyotes.

He paced from the large plate-glass window covered with white aluminum blinds, where he peeked through at the frightening city on the other side, to Uriah's bed, where he gazed at his buddy lying unconscious, hands bandaged à la Claude Rains's in *The Invisible Man*, to the two suits standing by the door, arms folded across their chests, eyeing Helmer suspiciously, to Ben and Andrea Dorthea whispering to each other in bedside chairs, though Christ only knew what about.

"Hey, man," she said, catching his glance. "You got to dumb down. You're not gonna accomplish anything except a blown vessel, you keep doing that."

"Einfach for you to say," Helmer said, still on the move. So blond he was almost albino, chalk hair nearly touching his ass, he wore white sunscreen, black lipstick, black shirt, black 1001s. "We haf a keyboardist who can't play, a bassist who's living one drawn-out anxiety attack, and who knows how many rockers somewhere on the other side plotting who knows what. Yeah, sicher, I might as well just sit down here and take a little Lessness Meditation, nicht?"

"Nobody's plotting anything." The green-and-blue makeup around her eyes had smudged with the tears, making her look a little out-of-focus. "And don't count Ury out yet," she added. "He's just burned his *hands*, is all. It's not like the end of the world or something. He'll be fine, just fine. Dumb *down*, man."

"What makes you think other musicians are involved in this, Mr. Skelter?" one of the suits asked.

It was hard to tell which, though. Neither moved their mouths when they spoke. Their baggy gray coats and pants, latex gloves, pollution sores peppered below their nostrils, and flashback short-spiked strawberry hair were identical. Because the air-conditioning in the building only wheezed on briefly every twenty minutes or so for two in a feeble attempt to save energy, both perspired heavily. Large wet cusps bled along their armpits.

They'd been asking questions since first appearing around midnight, less than forty-five minutes after Uriah'd twisted the faucet in his kitchen. They'd gone over the details of the event and a list of Uriah's enemies, which consisted of the rocker's mother's name and that of his mortgage company, as well as his daily regimen in an effort to pin down when someone could've tampered with the pump.

"Who else would go through all the trouble of casing The Monastery, figuring when Andrea and Uriah'd be gone or busy, unsealing the well, and filling the lines mit acid, eh?"

"You think it's the competition?"

"Our band out of the way means a hole in the schedule for gigs. A hole in the schedule for gigs means an opening for a new band. That's all I know. What else?"

"Someone out to scare Mr. Ovulteen for some reason. Disgruntled fans. Gangs in from Seattle looking for a good time. You remember Mark David Chapman, guy who final-dined John Lennon? Patrice Keane, girl who took out Rachel Origami? There's a long history of rock'n'roll crazies intent on getting themselves into the limelight, one way or another."

"I *knew* this would happen," Helmer said. "I had dreams."

"It might be a good idea if you guys took some time off."

"'Off?'" Andrea repeated, piping up.

"From playing and all," the suit said.

"It's all in my head, they said," Helmer whined, pointing. "It's all up here."

"Like in laying low?" Andrea asked.

"Like in a vacation. Just till things sort themselves out."

"For how long?" Helmer asked.

"We got jobs here," Andrea said. "We got lives we're in the middle of trying to live."

"Oh, I don't know. A while."

"A *while*?"

"Yeah. A while."

Ben took the elevator down to the luminous white lobby and collapsed into a black beanbag chair across from the two-meter-wide HDTV, shut his eyes, and concentrated on making the tremor in his hypothalamus go away. Only he didn't have much luck. No matter how hard he struggled to fix his thoughts on something neutral, a tiny army of termites continued to gnaw away at his brain stem. He searched his pockets for some Ephedra, Phenylalinine, anything, but all he turned up was a minuscule knot of fly wings and dust.

So he reached for the remote control panel half hidden under a pastiche of *Androgemorphy*s and *Hardcore California*s on the plexiglas coffee table in front of him and began flipping channels.

Eventually he came upon *Stretto*, the weekly vid magazine. He skipped over the written parts and went for the brief film interludes. At a news conference, a woman from the Global Space Administration with bobbed brown hair and candy corn Going Private contacts was saying the space program, which had virtually ceased after the Shudder because of redirected allocations for cleanup, was back on track and setting its sights on reaching Mars within the next thirty years. On *Crime Deterrent Digest* an execution was in progress; somewhere in Wyoming a tall scared Thai man in leg irons, one of the serial-killer pack called the Cannibalists, was being shuffled toward a gas chamber at the end of the long gray cement hall, the audience and talkshow host in the prison bleachers riveted by the sight. An aluminum speedtrain shot into the recently opened Tunnel of Prosperity connecting Alaska and the Chukchi peninsula in Kolyma. On board President Redford, cheeks pruned with age and amoebaed with olive spots, pumpkin-colored shoulder-length hair thinning, smiled widely at the camera and toasted the celebrity passengers with a glass of champagne. A docublip chronicled the thousands of voluntarily sterilized Japanese being redistributed into less populated areas of the United States of Africa by the World Population and Community Development Organization. A special focus on communication satellites showed paraplegics working easily in zero-gravity.

Ben flipped again and the televangelist Joey Taboo's face overran the screen. An intense closeup accented the pores and blackheads on his chubby nose, the individual follicles in his bushy slaty beard, the golden stitches in his navy blue GO YANKEES baseball cap. A pair of wire-rimmed reading glasses balanced over a pair of regular black plastic ones. Behind these, his sun-staring visionary iron-blue eyes were unblinking.

Here was a guy with oceanic power who really knew how to

use it. It didn't take much to understand what Uriah saw in him. Taboo'd started thirty years ago on the floor of the Tokyo Exchange, an indentured boy from just outside of Hattiesburg, Mississippi. He hustled his way up through the ranks toward freedom, dropped from public view five years (claiming later that he'd entered the Nevada desert to meditate, though other reports hinted at insider-trading scandals), then unexpectedly flashed into the big time as CEO at Air Pyrate Muzzik. Over the next decade he spent his energy gobbling various media concerns and building a small communications empire, then launching his Cult of Aloneness out of Las Vegas.

"...honest with you, so help me God," he was saying. "I ain't gonna lie to you. I ain't gonna tell you no falsehoods. No, friends. I'm gonna tell you God's holy truth. I need another car for my estate. I need another vehicle."

His face faded into footage of rolling spray-paint green pastures laced with fog, a scarlet sun burning through dawn haze, Arabian horses cantering along white fences.

"I'm thinkin' Cadillac," he said. "I'm thinkin' pink. I'm thinkin' circa nineteen hundred and fifty nine. You know the one I mean. You know the one I'm thinkin' of. Close your eyes. Lower your head. You can see it too if you try."

Zoom on a white-trimmed red barn. Inside, row upon row of antique automobiles: beach buggies and land-rovers, golf carts and racers, a metallic silver 1970 German Volkswagen next to a matte black 1925 English Daimier Limousine next to a nail-polish red 1998 Alfa Romeo.

"Those fins on the rear. You've seen them. Smooth and sharp. Can you imagine runnin' your hands over their polished surface? Feel the curve. Feel the tensile strength. Feel the sacred sense of grace and line and shape."

Between an ivory 2013 Sendai Electric and a pale yellow 1899 Packard was a space waiting for the new arrival.

"Feel those decorative silver strips running up the sides. Feel the magnitude, the hope. Here is a car that speaks of purity, seamless form and love. Here is a car that cries out for humility and praise from us. Before it we are small. Before it we understand our finitude."

Closeup of those iron-blue eyes.

"But let me tell you something, friends. Let me share with you the truth. Such cars don't come cheap. Uh-uh. They aren't

God's little giveaways. They demand generosity, a good credit rating. You have to *pay* for these things just like you have to *pay* for all things in life. Because life is a stock market, friends, and that market is forever in flux.

"And, God knows. God knows: I simply don't have the credit. I simply don't possess the wherewithal to purchase such a beauty. So I come to you.

"I'll be frank. I'll be fair. I need your help. I need your compassion.

"Praise the Lord of Solitude. Praise the Lord of Loneliness."

Pan back to include the cigar in his right hand aimed at the lens like Uncle Sam's big finger.

"I need seven-hundred thousand credits by next Wednesday and I'm lookin' to you to provide it."

Warm avuncular smile.

"I'm givin' you the bottom line. I'm givin' you the brass tacks. I'm givin' you the respect you've always given me.

"I'm readin' you the fine print. I'm warnin' you about the cosmic clause. This credit ain't destined for my church. This credit ain't destined for some highfalutin charity.

"Uh-uh.

"This credit's destined for my new Cadillac. This credit's goin' for my new vehicle.

"And I know I can count on you to help me out.

"Put the credit into my account, friends. Put the credit into Nixon Savings. Let me be able to say, along with the woman in Luke 15:9, 'Rejoice with me; for I have found the piece which I had sought.'

"You're standin' up right now to git a pencil and paper to write down my number. You're walkin' into the kitchen as we speak, gettin' ready to dial 1-900-GOD-SQAD. That's 1-900-GOD-SQAD. Ten credits per call, plus five credits per minute, seven minutes minimum. You must be eighteen to lift that receiver. Operators are standin' by.

"Bless you. Bless you all.

"I can see each and every one of you out there. Your pure hearts. Your crystal souls.

"I can see you *call*.

"There you *go*!

"*THERE YOU GO*!

"*Praise the Lord*!

"Our switchboards're LIGHTIN'!"

Then "They're going to tell you something," he said gently, voice low and slow as if on a cassette whose batteries were running down. "You need to notice things you didn't notice before. Single strands of hair in the keys of your computer board. That fingernail caught in your mouse. They'll blame it all on AJAKS."

"Hey," Ben said, instantly flushed with sensory alertness.

"They'll blame it on Anarchists for Jesus the Anointed King and Savior. But look elsewhere. Watch for worlds behind you."

Joey Taboo closed his eyes and opened them again. The intense color had drained out of them. Now they were fluorescent disks.

"It's like my head is teeming with electrons," he said.

He opened his mouth and brilliant white light shot out.

"My heart is a cathode ray tube. My mind is a satellite receiver. It's beautiful, Ben. It's so beautiful I could die."

7

The Lost in Space was a popular retro-theme bar located between a grungy blackmarket cosmetic boutique and a graffiti-slathered Epidemics Hostel on the swarming outskirts of Shanty Town, a tangle of meter-wide alleys lined with shacks made of old aluminum cans, shards of grease-stained translucent plastic, and huge soggy appliance boxes, where Brazilification had taken root with a vengeance. Campfires smoldered in doorways and the air stank of rotten vegetables, foul meat, and astringent petroleum distillates.

From outside, the bar looked like any of the storefronts along the street: large blacked-out windows, peeling green wooden door, shivery orange lettering spray-painted along the sidewalk. Inside, however, was a different story. When you stepped through that peeling green door you entered a glitzy universe featuring characters and settings from various space-related tube shows and vids. Waitresses dressed as Rotwang's sexy robot in *Metropolis* took orders. Bartenders outfitted as Flash Gordon mixed your drinks. And the bar itself had the feeling of the bridge from *Star Trek*'s Enterprise while individual tables took the plastic form of Klaatu's streamlined saucer from *The Day the Earth Stood Still* and chairs assorted monsters from hairy Dr. Zaius out of *Planet of the Apes* to *War of the Worlds*' Martians. The walls oscillated and poinged with 1940s' versions of computer panels, thick rubbery purplish-brown tentacles hung from the ceiling in place of potted plants, and dry-ice machines pumped a four-inch layer of B-film fog across the floors.

Pushing his glasses up on his nose, Ben stood in the doorway and looked around for an empty seat. The place was already crowded and loud at nine thirty. People were standing everywhere, cradling drinks and laughing, something with a computer-fabricated melody by Kill All Redheads hammering on the powerful digital sound system. Ben had to hold his arms unnaturally close to his sides as he wedged his way toward the bumpy lap of the Hideous Sun Demon near the stage.

Two women at the flying saucer next to him spoke French and nuzzled. They were apparently Canadians. One with her left eye sewn shut rubbed her cheek against the neck of one who'd shaved a tonsure atop her violet head. At first Ben imagined they were speaking about sexual things, they seemed so turned on by their subject, but then it occured to him they were meditating aloud about the holdings of Jerry Lewis-Foozebane, the powerful Saudi who owned the place. Lewis-Foozebane'd inherited titanic sums of credit from his father, who'd inherited titanic sums of credit from *his* father, who in turn had made his fortune helping to cap those more than six-hundred oil wells Saddam Hussein torched in the final days of the Gulf War. Lewis-Foozebane had invested wisely and presently owned a number of retro-theme bars across the Northwest. Although he specialized in SF jobs (radioactive mutants and galactic travel were his most successful leit motifs), he'd also branched out into horror and near-death experiences. Since he lived nearby, he often hung out in the Lost in Space, though tonight he was nowhere to be seen.

Ben ordered a Choline Enhancer from what must have been a very short techno-hippy inside a Robby the Robot costume and watched Granger Glitter and the Peptic Ulcers, a Portland-based group, set up. The amps and mikes were already on stage, the band in the process of wheeling out their percussion system, synthesizer, and guitars. Which was a problem for Granger Glitter himself because, being an Ozone Baby, he couldn't do much with those flippers of his. So he spent most of his time testing the microphone, which fit over his throat like an antique pilot's radio, admiring his shirtless chest ashimmer with metallic gold sunscreen, and unselfconsciously scratching his side with a flap of cartilage while exchanging words with the lead guitarist, a toothless guy named Gonzo, and the chemo-look woman on synthesizer whose name, if Ben heard right, was Ratfuck.

"Nazi scab, Major Benny," a voice behind him said.

He turned to find this real cute black girl, maybe fifteen or sixteen, irises and lips white, tribal scars grooving forehead and cheeks, grinning at him. Her beaded dreadlocks rustled down the back of her inky Versace tank suit all the way to the white cordless phone snapped to her velcro belt.

"Jessika?" he said.

"Gonna ask me to sit down or what?" Not waiting for a reply before sliding into the lap of a Metaluna Mutant from *This Island Earth*, huge exposed brain, bug eyes, crab claws, colors rubbed off here and there. She surveyed the bar. "Future sure isn't what it was cracked up to be, huh? How you clickin', man?"

"Lysergic. Real lysergic."

"Such as?"

She picked up the drink menu and grepped.

"Such as I'm talking to you on the computer, right, and all of a sudden this virus comes along and starts cracking up on my screen."

"Cracking up?" she said from behind her large laminated card cut in the shape of a raygun.

"Ranting about light and shit and then plathing itself."

"They're going around."

Granger Glitter and the Peptic Ulcers started with a rockabilly number called "Higher(An)archy." The Canadian women at the next saucer stood and began bonedancing. Some Überthrashers and Technogoths joined in. The panels on the walls began pulsating in earnest, linked as they were to the percussion set, casting people in ghastly greens and yellows.

Jessika leaned forward, elbows on table.

"Tried calling you right back when we got cut off, only your link was busy. I waited a couple of minutes and tried again, but you were gone."

Ben explained about Uriah. He had to shout because Granger was on a long refrain.

"Don't matter if you black or whu-whu-whu-white," he was singing, slapping time with his flippers, "just matter if you got the muh-muh-muh-might."

Eskimos at the bar raised powerfists.

Ben finished his Choline Enhancer and a busty Jane Fonda from *Barbarella* appeared. Jessika ordered two Hemophilias and a basket of farm-shrimp crisps.

"He's doing okay, though," Ben said. "You know, in general. Hands are in bad shape. Doctors say he won't be playing any more synths."

"What about the band?"

"Had to cancel our gigs. Now we've got to decide whether to go on without Uriah or start looking for a new keyboardist."

They paused to watch Ratfuck's hyperbolic solo, in the midst of which she began wagging her tongue. The skin on it was hot pink and slick as a plastic raincoat, tastebuds cauterized as part of the new Oprah Winfrey Diet.

"You got a clue who'd do such a thing?" Jessika yelled after a while.

"Police think it might be a rival band. I don't know. I'm blank."

"You guys got yourselves some enemies?"

"Who doesn't?"

The Jane Fonda returned and set bright red drinks and farm-shrimp crisps on the table. Ben handed her his credit slab and she disappeared.

"That isn't the end of it, either," he said. He took a swallow of Hemophilia. It tasted of medicinally artificial strawberry juice, rum, and something vaguely tarry. He followed it with a handful of crisps and said with his mouth full: "So I'm in the lobby after-wards, right, and I flip on the tube."

"And?"

He raised his hand to signal hold on a sec and finished chewing.

"And there's Joey Taboo talking to me."

Jessika leaned back in the Metaluna Mutant's lap and stared at Ben.

"Listen. I wouldn't believe me either," he said. "But there's Joey Taboo, and he's talking to me. Telling me stuff."

"What kind of stuff?"

"Nothing that makes a whole lot of sense. Stuff about AJAKS. About his heart. Weird stuff."

"You were dreaming, man."

"I wasn't."

"You were tired. You were stressed. You had to've been. Sometimes dreams seem awfully real when you're in the middle of them."

She reached over and popped a crisp in her mouth, assessed him.

"Hey, you okay?"

Ben parted his lips to answer and had the impression he was rushing backward through a long dark tunnel at an unbelievable speed. At the other end was Jessika, sailing farther and farther away from him.

"Yeah, well," he said, dazed.

"You're looking real blank."

"My head's sort of light all of a sudden."

He stood and then sat down again. "Oh boy," he said. He put his hand on top of his head and leaned back.

Jessika rose and walked around the saucer toward him. Her journey took hours.

When Ben shook his head to clear it he jumped outside his body and saw himself speaking with her. Only someone had turned down the volume so he couldn't hear what she was saying. Her lips were moving. She touched his forehead. Then she took his arm in hers and helped him stand.

On the sidewalk he inhaled deeply and his lungs seized. It was scorchingly humid and the night air was ripe with burning rubber. Wisps of yellow mist churned in headlights along the teeming street. Car alarms clashed with horns, police and ambulance sirens with squeaking brakes, huge exhaust fans with the cries of tuk-tuk drivers trying to maneuver through the continual traffic jam in this part of the city.

Jessika hustled Ben through the throng. He tried to slow their pace but skidded in a puddle of orange liquid and fell. Before he could take in what was happening she'd already hoisted him up and begun shunting him forward again.

They rounded a corner into one of the narrow alleys of Shanty Town. The reek of feces hit him. They passed rows of ramshackle huts thrown together from strips of corrugated aluminum and plywood, rusted paint cans, old shopping carts, plastic jugs, milk cartons, cardboard boxes. In the doorways people sat around campfires. They watched the couple hurry by.

A man in a tattered trenchcoat and insectile goggles scuttled toward them, the diseased skin on his face flaking off as he moved, making it appear his body was snowing. He instinctively flattened himself against a shack, letting Ben and Jessika pass unhindered.

Then Ben was lying on his back in stagnant darkness, feeble gas lamp hissing in the shadows, bitter smell of vomit searing his sinuses. Jessika was kneeling over him, examining him without emotion. Behind her on the floor lay a kid, eight or nine, so black he appeared purple. The boneless flesh of his hands jellied over his groin. Telltale pink and white sores blistered his lips. His spine and ribs were gone. Unable to move his head, he stared at Ben out of his peripheral vision. Ben'd heard about this happening in Shanty Town, people who either couldn't get the polycarbon simucort exoskeleton on the government's Emergency Health Plan because they didn't have a North American ID number, or did get them but had to sell them for credit.

"Lie still," Jessika said. "You'll be all right. Relax. Think of happy things. Think of that great autumn we had last year. Remember? All that coolness in the Big Room?"

The cordless phone on her belt beeped. She leaned back on her haunches and unhooked it. For a while she listened. Then she said something.

Ben tried to concentrate on what she was talking about but the words kept skewing away from him.

He tried to raise his hand and found he couldn't. All the muscles in his arms, legs, and neck had become pulpy. He could no longer close his eyes. Soon he sensed his bowels loosening.

So he stared at the light sputtering across the ceiling like a multitude of butterflies and waited for the hallucinations to begin.

8

Andrea Dorthea twitched awake at four in the morning with a mouthful of bees. She opened her mouth to free them but they wouldn't leave. Mostly they stung her along the gums at the righthand corner of her jawbone. Some targeted her upper wisdom teeth, others her left canine. A fat furry one tunneled behind an incisor.

She scrambled out of bed and rifled through her drugstore in the cabinet above the microwave. Phenylalinine. Ephedra. Three pouches of choline powder. Pamprin. Percodan. Ex-Lax. But all the Nembutals, Seconals, and Amytals were gone. She rummaged under the kitchen sink, in the refrigerator, even beneath her mattress, but knew she wouldn't find anything.

A heavy grayish lethargy had settled over her the night Uriah entered the hospital. No matter where she looked all she saw was her lover lying there in that wide white bed, hands bandaged, staring into space and trying to take in the idea that his hope of playing with a band was over. It was as if he'd had this vacation as a musician and now reality had fussed back onto the scene to tell him it was all a joke, get back to work. The result was Andrea began sleeping fourteen hours a day, taking two baths every morning and three every evening, and getting real well acquainted with what the satellite dish had to offer by way of home shopping networks.

So somehow she never quite got around to leaving The Monastery in search of pharmaceutical supplies, let alone things like food and drink, the outcome being she found herself standing topless in her tiger underwear in the middle of the shabby cabin in the middle of a WINGEVE, fragrance of timber and coffee in the air, clutching her jaw and sweating freely.

She examined her face in the bathroom mirror, pissed off

because it didn't look half as bad as it felt. She wandered into the living room and tried to read a new head-injury manual. She tried *Greek Plays*, the new holoporn with Candi Cain and Rommel Reagan, hoping the endorphin rush would shortcircuit her pain centers. She returned to the kitchen, emptied an ice tray into a ziplock bag, wrapped the ziplock bag in a washcloth, and held it at various angles on her face while she paced back and forth and witnessed the greenish pink sun rise over the dead lake through layers of carbon monoxide, methelene chloride, and kepone, waiting for a dentist, any dentist, to get off his butt and answer the phone.

The first who did was Mel Greco, Mexican oral surgeon extraodinaire and ex-tattooist specializing in cheap but durable dental ornamentation. Andrea explained through a web of swollen tissue what the problem was and Mel told her to come right in. She drove to the outskirts of the city in her rust-flecked flat-olive Geo Tracker, parked at one of those megalithic Ride'n'Save lots, and rode a tin-canopied three-wheeled tuk-tuk navigated by a man wearing goggles and respirator through Shanty Town into the core.

A December inversion had descended with pollution so thick it could take the place of mousse in styling your hair. The city swam in a sienna fog. A stench of nitrobenzene and bad chicken from the paper mills along the river permeated everything— clothes, sheets, upholstery, towels, skin. Even tap water smelled of it. Andrea became dizzy as she moved through the narrow dirt lanes and, worse, she found when she finally reached Mel Greco's walkup there was no air-conditioning there. No waiting room, either. Just a dark steamy office the size of a large bathroom cluttered with metal shelves and surgical tools.

Mel himself was in his fifties. He'd shaved his elongated cranium and vangoghed his ears so his head was smooth as a fleshy lightbulb. Across it he'd tattooed blue and green circuitry. He'd had his lips amputated, which accented his Jantzen teeth. He met Andrea at the door and ushered her over to a large foamy dental chair.

She lay back gingerly and he moved to a shelf, slipped on his latex gloves and gauze mask, clanked among his tools, picked out a tiny mirror on the end of a brass stick, and, setting the rubber damn in place, began examining her.

"What's flossing?" he asked as he stroked her gums.

On one of the shelves was an ancient boom box tuned to a twenty-four-hour news station. Currently there was a report airing about the food shortages in New York. The analyst predicted another round of riots for January unless the Russian congress voted in favor of another massive grain shipment.

"Flossing?"

"And brushing," he added. "What are they?"

Andrea looked past him at the yellow fishbowl light on the ceiling, dust motes rotating in its orbit, and said: "I guess I haven't been very good, huh?"

Mel snuffled in derision. His face was dewed with perspiration. His fingers tasted like the memory of farm-shrimp.

"'Not very good,'" he mimicked. "'Not very good.'" He caressed a canine. Andrea winced. "They're *tattoos*, Ms. Dorthea, no? They form a semiotic system that presents you to the world. They make proclamations about your selfhood. They announce your goals. Your past. Your beliefs."

Mel had too much of his hand in her mouth for Andrea to respond. She felt a drop of sweat squiggle down the back of her neck.

"You know what teeth are?"

"...?"

"Teeth are your body's AT&T Telephone Network. They reach out and touch everyone."

He wielded what looked like a long shiny pencil with a hook on the end. Andrea closed her eyes and tried to think of Uriah.

"Sick teeth, sick body," Mel said. "Sick body, sick mind."

"A new infestation of bubonic plague has broken out in the San Diego area, scientists at the Atlanta Center for Disease Control reported today," the voice on the boom box said.

The shiny pencil skipped off a tooth.

"*Aaaagh.*"

"Sorry. Wider. You know what tattoos are?"

Andrea heard a police VTOL pass low overhead on its way into Shanty Town. Her internal organs vibrated in time to the rotors. Then in the hallway she heard what sounded like a nine-year-old boy threatening one of his progens with a fork. "You want me to see if you're fucking *done*, mama?" he shouted. "You want me to see if you're fucking *cooked*?"

"The Egyptians used tattoos," Mel said. "Romans too."

He removed the hooked pencil and began to stroke Andrea's teeth and gums again. He leaned into his work, exerting gentle pressure. For a moment Andrea thought she would faint.

"Black spots beneath the skin," the radio announcer stated. "Swelling of the lymph glands or *buboes* in the groin, armpits, and neck. Open sores, chills, fever, headache, body pains. A shortness of breath."

"Go on, you fucking animal," the progen shouted back. "Stick me! Stick me! Go on! I dare you!"

"They used them to identify slaves, criminals, and heretics," Mel said. "Tattoos became the sign of the social outcast. Early Christians took pride in wearing them. You feel this?"

"*Ugh.*"

"Okay." He massaged her palate. "Ever have trouble moving your jaw?"

"Uh-uh."

"Then they dropped out of sight for over a thousand years. Captain Cook's sailors rediscovered them in the Pacific Islands in the eighteenth century and brought the idea back to Europe. How about here?"

The radio announcer was telling people with the symptoms he'd just described to report to a local Epidemics Hostel immediately. Next came reports about a three-hundred-and-twenty-seven-car pileup outside smoggy Seattle and a possible strike by air-traffic controllers angered at being required to take smart drugs. Tears welled up in Andrea's eyes from the pain. The yellow fishbowl light above her wavered. Mel's head became longer and thinner. He straightened, put his hands on his lower back, arched his spine. His lipless mouth caught the light and twinkled.

"Our bodies are our canvases, Ms. Dorthea," he said. "We paint upon them. We address them to the Big Room. Your teeth are rotten. Some are going to have to come out."

"You fucking *zipperhead*," the boy in the hallway was shouting. "You fucking Quayle." Andrea heard sobbing but couldn't tell if it was the progen or the boy. Then came the smack.

Mel remained oblivious.

Andrea's mouth ached so much she didn't even have the energy to *try* haggling down the credit.

"When can we start?" she asked.

"Right now, if you're ready." Mel ran a palm across the circuitry atop his head, picked at something with his forefinger.

"Okay, fine," she said. "Let's do it."

Mel climbed a small ladder and groped around the penultimate shelf, coming down with a stubby syringe and an unlabeled vial of clear liquid. He cleaned the needle with bleach and dipped the tip into the vial.

"Valium," he explained. "It'll help you rest. It's all I could get my hands on this month. Sorry. Open up."

Only she knew it wasn't Valium almost right away. A tidalwave of azure light crashed through her brain and then she began falling.

She tumbled through the large foamy dental chair. She dropped through the office floor. She plunged through the blackmarket cosmetic boutique below Mel's walkup and headlong through the building's cement foundation, able to make out the individual grains of sand, stone, and glass as she went.

People were locked in the soil before her in fetal positions. Her progen, naked, over a hundred years old, smiled as she sped past. President Redford waved, hardly able to move his frozen hand. There was Mona Lisa-Dreyfus wearing that beret and Julio Ramirez, the Venezuelan resistance commander in the South American war. Old-time rocker Morph Allah G with his plucked eyebrows, silver skirt, and spangled blouse, and her tuk-tuk driver in those goggles and respirator.

And, of course, there was Uriah. He was in a dark blue double-breasted suit with golden buttons. His silky black hair was knotted atop his head and his black wingtips shined. His eyes, which were the only part of his anatomy he could move, blinked, filled with tenderness.

She plummeted past her second-grade teacher, Mrs. Barnett, who still believed in books and brought a different one tucked in a ziplock plastic bag to class every week for show and tell, and past a small green dragon with red eyes. She tore by Elektra Geestring in her patented silver simucort exoskeleton, a growing ball of fiery orange magma, a grouper with bubbles trickling up from its gills, an angel with a bloody wing, and a complete matte black police VTOL, pilot and copilot transfixed in the cockpit.

And then, as in cartoons, past Uriah again.

She shot out of the earth into a vast black sky misted with stars and heard her heart stop. Only then did she realize how loudly it had been beating. Someone was speaking in the distance. It took her a while to figure it must be the announcer on that ancient boom box on Mel Greco's shelf. He was saying Uncle Fester Ziff had been exonerated of all charges and released, that AJAKS had now taken credit for the assassination. Then he was saying: "The flesh between your breasts. The thenody. The outlines. The shapes in time. The stars. The sky. The stars. The stars."

9

The sun flared through a couple of rips in the black plastic they'd taped over one of the high windows. Ben thought it was a sunrise he was looking at, but he figured it also could have been a sunset. Girders and vents crisscrossed above him. He tried to rub his eyes under his sunglasses and it came to him he was in restraints, his wrists and ankles bound with nylon straps to aluminum rails running along the sides of a hospital bed in a cavernous warehouse. He lay on a thin air mattress, a kerosene lamp winking on a small aluminum stand next to him.

When he tried to concentrate he lateraled into a dream where ballerinas with spikes through their heads were dancing in a parking lot. The sky was purple, the sun green. Chunks of cracked concrete thrust up all over, revealing shorn pipes, cables, iron mesh. The ballerinas in frilly lilac tutus leapt gracefully into the twilit air. Then one of them went limp in mid-jump and fell to the ground with the lifeless impact of a large piece of rotten fruit. Another dropped, and a third, and soon they formed a pile of ballerina corpses, and there was only one left: Mikki, Ben's sister. Blood seeped from her mouth and ears. Her hair slipped off her head in ragged clumps. She looked at the green sun, her shoulders became wings, and she began to fly. Ten meters, twenty, into the emerald light, wet wads of hair and scalp slapping the pavement below her.

Somewhere a metal door creaked and Ben heard footsteps echoing toward him. A short dark figure with long frizzy hair leaned over him.

"Jessika?"

"Someone wants to talk to you." It was a guy. "You ready?"

"Where's Jessika?"

"Don't know no Jessika."

Baggy cream Japanese pants shushing with each step, he walked over and turned up the lamp. The pool of harsh light spread across the floor. Scars from the poorly performed muscle grafts networked his upper arms and shirtless chest.

"She was with me last night," Ben said.

"Last night?"

"In the Lost in Space. Yeah."

The guy shrugged and shushed away. A metal door creaked again and banged shut.

The sunflash blinked out and was replaced by an infrared glow. A steady *thump-thump-thump* came from the roof. Windmills. That'd place him to the east, over by the airport, near the Zone. Assuming, of course, they were still in Spocoeur. The glow'd make it sunset, which'd mean he'd been out at least a full day.

"Ever hear of the Rabids?" another voice asked.

Ben opened his eyes. His tongue tasted like tinfoil. The guy with the muscle grafts tugged on some latex gloves and undid his restraints. In a flimsy wooden chair next to the aluminum stand sat another guy, hands folded in his lap, one leg crossed over the other, duded up in black-rimmed Buddy Holly glasses and a gray Gottex zoot suit with navy blue pinstripes. He wore a neatly wrapped blue turban. It was Jerry Lewis-Foozebane.

"Dominant gang in this part of the Zone," he said, picking a piece of lint from his trousers. "Hate to fuck with 'em. Replaced their saliva glands with sacks full of rabies shit. One bite and you're history. Slo-mo history."

The guy with the muscle grafts moved over and took his position behind Lewis-Foozebane. He folded his thick arms and Lewis-Foozebane reached back and unselfconsciously stroked the guy's left thigh as you might the haunches of a great dane curled at your feet.

"Even the police don't visit this place if they can help it. Gotta copter in just to avoid the mess in the streets."

Ben sat up slowly. He removed his sunglasses and massaged his face, remembering the Jane Fonda, the bright red Hemophilias.

"Anyways, door's always open," Lewis-Foozebane added. "You can leave any time you want."

He laughed.

Something whirred under Ben's feet and shot into the shadows. It was a Panasonic mobile alarm system, an aqua plastic bubble on wheels. The high-pitched noise it made was almost out of Ben's range.

"Where's Jessika?"

Lewis-Foozebane looked at him.

"Jessika?"

"Girl I was with last night."

"Blank on me."

He reached into his suit and pulled out a pack of Gauloises.

"Mind if I smoke?"

"I was at your place with her. Someone nuked the drinks. Then I was outside, in Shanty Town."

"We live in fuckin' sensitive times, man. Can't smoke here, can't drink there. Gotta be so fuckin' *careful* not to offend anybody."

He tapped out a cig, produced a matchbook, lit up; took a long toke, savoring, and exhaled two blue vapor trails through his nostrils.

"Want one?" he said, offering Ben the package.

"Someone had to've brought me here."

"Someone did." He drew in another lungful. Let it out. "You ever get the impression we've maybe gone too far? I mean, you have to be so goddamn *fastidious* these days, you know? If the anti-racists don't get you, the anti-ageists will. If the anti-ageists miss you, the animal-rights people won't. Might as well just sew your mouth shut and throw away the needle and thread for all the good it'll—"

He began to hack wetly, as though his lungs were aslosh with mud, and brought up a mouthful of flem, which he reswallowed. Ben waited till he was done, then asked: "So who was it?"

Lewis-Foozebane reached into his suit again and extracted a gold oxygen inhaler and took a hit.

"Who was it who what?" he said.

"Who was it who brought me here?"

"Listen, man. All this is just some business with me. See? I'm not out to dumb this all down for you. I got some work to do."

"What kind of work?"

"Following instructions, doing what I been told to do, is all you gotta know."

"I thought you were the guy in charge of all this."

"I'm *never* the guy in charge of all this." He examined his cig and looked up at Ben. "How you feeling?"

"Okay, I guess. Head's sort of clogged a little."

"Marc, why don't you go and get our friend some inhalant? Perk him up a bit." Marc nodded and jogged across the warehouse. Lewis-Foozebane watched him disappear, turned back to Ben. "Otherwise you okay?"

"Yeah."

"Good. We like to deliver the merchandise in one piece. Long as the merchandise cooperates, that is." He stubbed out his cig. "Sorry about your band, man. You guys had some nice tunes."

"The band? It's okay. We'll survive."

Lewis-Foozebane stood up and, brushing off his suit, said offhandedly: "No. You won't."

Marc returned with some Vassopressin and Ben took a hit. He put on his sunglasses and the world spun into focus. Everything glinted.

"You stand?" Lewis-Foozebane asked.

Ben realized it wasn't a question.

Marc hoisted him up and as his Nikes tapped the cement floor the mobile alarm system whooshed out of the shadows and began circling him, uttering tiny agitated squeaks.

"Doesn't recognize your pheromones," Lewis-Foozebane explained. He gave a short whistle and the squeaks ceased. The bubble scooted toward him. He kneeled and punched in a code and the alarm system wheeled silently away. "It's such a cute little shit. Wouldn't think it'd have the chutzpah to laser your legs in half?"

They crossed the warehouse, Marc in the lead with the kerosene lamp. At the south end they entered a stairwell smelling of mildew and iron filings. Ben was hungry. And thirsty. His lips were chapped. When he reached up to touch them he also discovered his prosthesis was gone.

"How'd you know where I'd be?" he asked. "How'd you know where to find me?"

Lewis-Foozebane put an arm around his shoulder and gave him a little squeeze.

"There's lots of things we know about you, Benny."

"But you couldn't have known I'd be there. Nobody could. *I* didn't even know till the last minute."

"You know anything about statistics?"

"Statistics?"

"Decision theory, point estimation, posterior distribution?"

"Uh-uh."

"You take this mainframe, okay? Feed it all the biological, social, biographical, and chemical data you have on somebody. Let it work for a second. And you know what you come up with?"

He let his arm drop as Marc opened the heavy metal door to the roof. They passed into viscous air, foul as an old dog's breath. Lewis-Foozebane began coughing a moist-with-flem cough again. He took out his oxygen inhaler and squirted some gas into his mouth.

Behind them were three windmills, eight or nine meters tall, each blade the size of a man. Even in the faintest of breezes they were spinning.

Across the roof was a Cub VTOL jet-chopper, rotors circling slowly. Two men in fluorescent orange vests were waiting by the hatch. When they saw the trio come through the door one turned and shouted and the engine revved, rotors picking up speed. It sounded like a small tornado had just touched down. Everyone leaned forward into the stinging wind, pellets of grit biting their faces.

"What you come up with is a statistically accurate psychological profile," Lewis-Foozebane yelled.

"I could've been anywhere," Ben yelled back. "Could've decided to go to Vancouver, Hong Kong."

Lewis-Foozebane hacked meatily.

"You only think so. That's what's so fuckin' wonderful, Benny."

"What is?"

Ben looked out over the city, the intricate maze of scintillating circuitry smearing toward the hazy horizon, the ghost of communication stations and guarded fortress suburbs flickering across the mountains.

"You're acting just like you're supposed to act," Lewis-Foozebane said. "You're playing yourself perfectly."

One of the men in orange vests gave them a thumbs-up sign and grabbed Ben's arm to boost him into the VTOL. Lewis-Foozebane touched his shoulder.

"Hey, wanna hear a joke?" he called.

"Where are we going?" Ben hollered back.

"The Rabids, Benny? Mainframe came up with that. The doors really *were* unlocked. You weren't going anywhere, though. Computer said so. You have a nice flight, now. It's been real."

"You're not coming?"

"Can't stand flying. Those things are always coming down."

"Tell me what's going on. Tell me what's happening."

"What's happening is you're taking a little trip, Benny. Journey of a lifetime, you know?" He let go another mucoidal cough and reached for the inhaler. "Take care of yourself."

He turned and started walking back toward the door. Marc joined him and slipped an arm around his waist.

Ben made a half-hearted move to break free but was already up through the hatch into the air-conditioned cabin, the VTOL was rising, the involved city beginning to glide away.

Part Three

NIGHT MOVES

10

Y our first time up?" an English-accented voice asked as the force of acceleration pressed him into the lush gray upholstery and tugged back the corners of his mouth.

Two women were strapped in across from him and, while they obviously weren't related, the surgery'd made them look surprisingly alike. Both had sharp noses, no chins, and cinder-colored sharkskin grafts rorschached like birthmarks down the left sides of their faces. Their eyes and three-centimeter plastic fingernails were blood red. It seemed as if someone had sewn delicate female heads onto massive male torsos bulky with biceps, triceps, pecs, deltoids, and glutes, the appearance of which was enhanced by the stitches tattooed across their necks.

"You're not looking so well," the one on the left said. "Do you think he's looking well?"

"I should think he's looking a bit under the weather, actually," said the one on the right. "A little off his feed."

"Time for a derm, perhaps."

"Precisely. Time for a derm." Then to Ben: "This sort of thing happens all the time. A little shock to the system. We're traveling rather quickly."

They were dressed in sleeveless gray flightsuits with black ammo belts, holsters, and small sonic grenades around their waists.

The one on the right unsnapped a pouch and produced a flat peach-colored square. She undid her harness, leaned forward, peeled off the Vicks derm's backing, and smoothed it carefully into place on the inside of Ben's wrist.

"Sedative," she explained.

"Helps you rest," said the other.

"Calms your stomach."

"We've used it a hundred times. We absolutely swear by it."

"We do."

They smiled pleasantly.

"Where *are* our manners?" said the one on the left all at once.

"Oh goodness!" said the one on the right.

"We should introduce ourselves."

"By all means. We're your hostesses."

A warm comfortable density crawled up Ben's arm and radiated through his chest. He sensed himself coasting into a trance and let himself slide.

"I'm Emma," said the one on the right.

"Emma Kawasaki," clarified the one on the left. "And I'm Mary."

"Mary Jane Air. Cheers. We're the X-Smith twins, products of British Telecom & Scientific-Atlantic Cosmetic Technologies & Securities."

"SEPBOGs."

"Somato-Enhanced Prototypic Body Guards."

"All SEPBOGs are sisters, in a manner of speaking."

"In a manner of speaking, they are."

"We share a belief, for instance, in neuroelectronically refined nervous systems."

"We're members of the Church of the Techno-Hippie."

"We believe in turning inward and discovering the Apple in us all."

"Macintosh is a state of mind."

"Our reflexes are top-notch."

"Our hearing's first-rate."

"We've been together three years."

"Three and a half, really."

"Forty-one months. Yes."

"If you want something, by all means you simply *must* let us know. We're here to serve and protect you."

"Make your journey more enjoyable in every way we can."

"Unless, of course, you try to escape."

"Right. Well, there's always that."

"Right. Well. Sedative works like a charm, doesn't it?"

"Marvelously. I don't believe I've ever seen anything quite like it."

"We most certainly shouldn't disturb him, then, should we?"

"No, most certainly not. Let him rest."

"Get on his feet again."
"Catch forty."
"He does look so peaceful."
"Just like an angel."
"An angel. Yes."

They crossed another vast rooftop toward chrome elevator doors in the side of a small concrete bunker next to a private desalinization unit and air-conditioning compressor.

One of the SEPBOGs halted near the roof's edge. The other came up short beside her. Ben stopped too. They all took a moment to survey the hazy silhouettes of tube aerials and satellite dishes, radio antennae and generators, high voltage lines and barbed wire fences that thorned buildings all the way down to the waterfront.

"She certainly *has* gotten ugly, hasn't she?" the SEPBOG on the left said.

"Who's that, dear?"

"Seattle."

"Oh, my word, *yes*. Pity, isn't it?"

"One face lift too many, I'm afraid."

"Hearing isn't what it once was."

"Sight's not really worth talking about."

"A shame, isn't it."

"Nothing if not that."

While Brazilification had struck Spocoeur thirty years ago, dealing a deathblow to the middle-class, it had plowed full-throttle into Seattle almost fifteen years earlier. The street-level now belonged to gangs, packs of dogs mated with coyotes down from the deforested Cascades, and mutant cockroaches with the mass, intelligence, and shading of baby mice. When it rained, it rained fairly high-quality battery acid laced with lead. Which was like a breath of fresh air compared to when it didn't rain, because then that warm mineral wind blowing off Elliott Bay carried with it the stench of gas, rotten eggs, brackish sludge, dead detergents, methanol, cordite, mercury, mothballs, paint remover, pesticides, sulfur dioxide, and tar.

And that was the part of the city where living was relatively easy. Dead Plan Alley, the southern half, was out-of-bounds completely. Twenty years ago the EPA had unleashed a heavy dose of *Citrobacter* into this industrial pocket with the intention of having the bio-engineered bacteria designed to eat cadmium freshen up the cadmium-contaminated area, hence making way for a plantation of condos. The problem, it turned out after four years of use in the field, was that over time *Citrobacter* got horny to share its genetic data with other, less goal-directed bacteria it encountered, gradually transmogrifying into a strain that often could (and often did) infect humans.

Accordingly, the only truly safe enclaves in the city these days were hermetically sealed penthouses whose inhabitants, remembering a kinder, gentler Seattle, were wealthy enough to cement shut their doors, run a private elevator to the roof, feed themselves on air-dropped food, and oxygenate their immediate environments with imported canisters of the stuff affixed to their ventilation systems.

It was into one of these enclaves that Emma and Mary elevatored Ben. The cool lush sunken living space was fashioned after an ancient Roman villa rich with pocked marble pillars and floors, involved tapestries and intricate mosaics, holographic red-figure vases and uncircumcised athletic statues from the World Museum (whose motto was "Now everything can be everywhere"), a jungle of vibrant plants and a maze of tarnished bronze mirrors. Across the room one full wall was a window with a view of Bainbridge Island, campfires of the dispossessed dotting the hills. Nearby, steps led down to a sugary blue bath, steam adrift upon its surface, next to which hulked a bank of LogiTech screens encased in rough-hewn rock. And, beside these, a Bang & Olufsen sound system and holounit thin as a slab of slate.

Couch-sized Persian pillows sagged here and there like psychdelic deflating tires, on one of which was presently lazing Elektra Geestring, skin café au lait, eyes Optikon blue. Her Robomatrix exoskeleton hummed almost imperceptibly as she raised a blackmarket orange, flown up, Ben guessed, all the way from one of those Central American NAFTAed greenhouses, to peel with her bony fingers. Next to her lay Holy Ryder, the silver-haired Ozone Baby glam who spoke in tongues during the act, voodoo-ish, and studded each flipper with ten or twelve transistor-shaped earrings. Naked, she was puffing a chubby Dutch Masters, oblivious to everything but the screens before her. A patchwork tan covered her body in a pattern of overlapping squares and rectangles, giving her the semblance of a human cubist painting and partially concealing the penis surgically implanted above her natural vagina.

Now these were two of Ben's most treasured goddesses in an admittedly large pantheon who, up to this point in his life, had been nothing other than polychromatic haze to pass his hand through three or four nights a week.

And at this very second these heretofore spatiotemporal phantasms were actually sitting right there in front of him, watching on the LogiTechs what looked to be a special report on nursing homes ("VR RVs where the elderly embark on the *ultimate* vacation," the reporter was saying); coverage of two more kidnapppings of pregnant women outside a Mobile abortion clinic by AJAKS members who kept their victims in captivity till they delivered the babies and then released them unharmed; Joey Taboo's latest sermon, this one on his need for a mint condition 1994 Porsche, preferably lilac in color; a slo-mo rerun of that nazi execution of the Cannibalist in Wyoming last week; a docublip on the Transhuman movement among paraplegics working in orbit who claimed that, with the help of their artificial limbs and organ replacements provided free-of-charge by the GSA, they represented the next step in evolution; several flashback sitcoms; ten or fifteen commercials; and a very bad Russian-financed soap in which a lacy woman wept on the shoulder of a lacy boy who wept on the quilt of a satin-sheeted bed which hung in the gauzy light of an extremely baroque eighteenth-century room in St. Petersburg. Elektra glanced up as the trio entered, then returned to the screens.

"Who's the Quayle?" she asked over her shoulder, an orange slice slipping between her lips.

But over the course of the next few hours the tone of things gradually lightened. The soap, named *Tapeworm* for its maniacally convoluted plot televised four hours each weekday, two in the afternoon, two in the evening, concluded. Someone soon broke out a plastic bottle of Gallo wine-substitute cut with a mild dose of psilocybin. And Emma and Mary took Ben on a tour of the penthouse while Holy and Elektra put in a tape of greatest hits by the recently deceased Epidemics band Symone and Carbuncle.

Ben spent a good while in the laboratory of a kitchen where the SEPBOGs treated him to the taste of his maiden authentic banana, imported from Biosphere 3000 in Peru, as well as three microwaved McDonald's farm-shrimp burgers on soybean buns and a large glass of purified ice water with a twist of real lemon in it. They showed him his bedroom, almost three meters by two, and provided him with a fluffy towel and pump-dispenser of liquid Dial so he could partake of another first: a long bath in that warm sugary blue sunken tub. When he climbed out he found waiting for him a neat pile of new black 1001s, socks, bright white Disney-Volgada techno-sneakers; a white Bergdorf t-shirt that clicked royally, printed as it was with splashes of what seemed to be actual blood; a replacement Calvin Klein prosthetic scab and package of cosmetic adhesive strips; a jar of Halston sunscreen, SPF 75; one tube of Oil of Olay daily UV protectant moisture replenishment cream and one of Cindy Crawford's Safari Climate Response lip shield.

Emma and Mary retreated into their bedroom to retune and, hair damp, makeup moist, Ben shyly joined the glams back at the LogiTechs busily scanning the vid menu for their favorite performers and genres.

Only the Silicon Underground, local cable pirates, kept breaking into the programming to redirect some vids into other systems and feed unannounced others into this one. Many of these latter had to do either with the holoporn industry or how-to terrorist cookbooks, subjects making Elektra and Holy brain-wrenchingly bored almost instantaneously. So ten minutes later they flipped off the tubes again, slipped in the digital cassette by Oink Blat with the holographic cover of a handsome man in a business suit spontaneously combusting, inhaled a little Vassopressin, sipped a little of that razzed wine-substitute, and magically commenced speaking with Ben like folks you might just bump into between sets one night at Club Foot.

Ben learned, for starters, that these glams weren't in their mid-thirties as he'd assumed. They weren't in their late twenties, either. Elektra was nineteen, Holy eighteen, they'd entered the business half a decade ago, and it'd been a long half decade.

Elektra, daughter of a wealthy Indian diplomat, had been brought to Seattle from New Delhi by her parents to be fitted with the exoskeleton and receive chemotherapy for osteal liquefaction which she'd contracted from multiple mosquito bites when eleven. Her private tutor at the hospital had introduced her to a number of key avant-garde feminist tracts by the Gynorads. A subversive revisionist group when they originally erupted on the Vancouver fringe some seven years earlier, they asserted that pornography wasn't the negative patriarchal power structure it had been alleged to be by the ConservoFems, but a positive matriarchal celebration of the body, especially of the female body. They thus advocated a radical pornographic enterprise that explored the idea of womanhood in ways that made women, and sometimes even men, see the gynecoidal figure with fresh and adoring eyes. To young Elektra, already feeling the first stirrings of pubescent desire locked in a frame she'd come to conceptualize as gargoylishly deformed, this made perfect sense. She asked her father to contact Zabrina Zosima, president of Polyform Videos, and set up an appointment. The next week Elektra's father bought her apprenticeship rights.

Holy, on the other hand, didn't need the Gynorads to teach her the obvious. Ever since she was five, and had seen her first holoporn in her parents' living room in the gray block of a public housing project she grew up in amid the swamps just outside New Orleans, she adored everything about the human body, male and female, short and tall, black and white, well-endowed and not, limbed and limbless, blond and brunette, kinked and straight. Moreover, she was deeply moved by the act of penetration, any sort of penetration, with any sort of apparatus, because for her it symbolized a gesture of primal cooperation and divine visitation. Plus it felt good. So when she was six, and witnessed her first four-way in an artless job titled *American Maid*, she was smitten with rapture and dropped like a chunk of neutronium to the carpetless concrete at her baffled parents' feet where she began speaking a crazy-eyed patois of Haitian Creole, Afrikaans, Latin, Castilian, and Cantonese. Her first film offer arrived two months later. And, two months after that, she traveled to Switzerland for the sex-addition operation.

Over the next several years Elektra and Holy, they continued, learned that the porno industry wasn't all it was cracked up to be.

It was a lot more than it was cracked up to be.

It was no less than an alternative dimension radiant with interesting people, illuminated ideas, gourmet sex, exquisite drugs, fast jets, shimmering accommodations, stunning credit, sweet oxygen, luminous clothes, free medical care, blitzkrieg parties, incandescent glams, timid butlers, excellent security, and every drop of purified water you could ever want to drink, with or without lemon.

"And don't forget the fame business," Elektra added.

"There ain't *nothin'* like the fame business, honey," Holy said, leaning forward and with her flippers crushing the butt of her third cigar in the glazed beige ashtray shaped like a large hollow phallus on the sarcophagus coffee table.

Elektra clipped and lit a new one and placed it between Holy's lips. The area around her pillow was two-tiered with gun-gray smoke.

"But I thought fame was only supposed to *look* great," Ben said. "That under all that greatness was really this tox ungreatness."

"Drug addiction?" Holy suggested.

"Insanity?" suggested Elektra.

"Suicide? Depravity?"

"Spiraling decadence?"

"Yeah," Ben said, surprised.

The air purifier clacked on in the kitchen, extracting nitrates from the atmosphere, retarding the aging process in the penthouse and, in a sense, slowing time.

"See, honey," said Holy, "people want to believe famous people aren't happy people. They want to believe famous people don't *really* fall in love, just into a commercial for love. That they don't *really* experience adoration, just their publicist's commodification of adoration. Photos. PR spots. Media events."

Elektra stood and crossed the room. She replaced Oink Blat with the Enola Gays, all Gregorian vocals. Her movements were slightly rigid in the exoskeleton, as though a strobe light were working on her.

"The tabloid vids tell the public what the public needs to hear," she said, returning.

"And what the public needs to hear is that famous people have sold out," said Holy, "that rich people are less satisfied than poor people, that richness only leads to sadness."

"All of which is absolutely true, of course, except for one thing."

"Which is?" asked Ben.

"Which is that none of it is true."

"Rich people are happier and more satisfied than poor people."

Holy leaned forward and set down her cigar after a long puff and brushed back her short silver hair with an eraser-pink flipper.

"Sue me if I'm wrong, honey, but I just can't help it. Rich feels *good*."

"With fame comes power."

"With power comes control."

"With control comes identity. *Any* identity you want. Just think. You want to be that person you always wanted to be? Be him. You want to rethink that person inside you you never really liked in the first place? Rethink him."

"And that spells freedom, honey."

The warm gravity of imagined contentment pressed down on Ben. He felt the wine-substitute and psilocybin glow like sunsap in his veins.

Holy unselfconsciously scratched her small left breast fuzzy with male hormone treatments.

"That's why they call fame fame, honey," she said. "It makes people famous."

"Not to say it doesn't take work," Elektra added.

"You got to *want* it, honey."

"Early mornings. Late nights. Long days in between. Sixteen, eighteen hours, when business's good."

"Publicity shots. Charity jobs."

"Hours of practice. Filming."

"But it's *worth* it, honey. Nothin' like it in the whole. Big. Room."

They spoke along those lines for a while longer, the glams further outlining the perqs of the fame business, Ben sailing farther and farther into a sense of well-being, asking them questions, telling them about his life in New Seattle, and then Elektra came up short as though an idea had just crossed her mind, studied Holy a minute, turned to Ben and asked: "You know Ramon Codd?"

Holy picked up her Dutch Masters, stood, and walked over to the wall window, penis bobbing between her legs as if it were semiliquid.

"Sure," Ben said. "*Stocks and Bonds*'s one of my favorites."

"Well, there's something else you should know about fame."

". . . ?"

"Fame monitors fame."

"Fame watches out for itself," said Holy, looking over Seattle. "It doesn't take any shit from anybody."

A cumulus of nicotine briefly ate her head.

"It's like this," Elektra said. "Rule of the dance is a biweekly checkup by the in-house doctor. Nice guy named Greco."

"Mel Greco."

"Yeah. Tip to toe. The works. Including but not limited to a regular series of Epidemics tests. Keeps things in the business clean."

"Long as everyone follows the rule, everything's cool," Holy said.

"Only Ramon skipped three in a row."

"And no one fucking even *noticed*."

"No one thought anything about it at first. We all get caught up in the rhythms of the day-to-day."

"Only then we put the pieces together."

"You know Stephani Lappér?"

"*Cunning Linguists*," Ben said.

"Yeah. Well, Ramon'd been filming with her." Holy turned around, flippers clutching the cigar, face hard. "And all of a sudden, a month ago, she's diagnosed with radical lymphosarcoma." The air purifier came on. "*Shit*, honey. We knew her. Stephie was our *friend*. We'd done a ton of vids together."

"She died last week," Elektra said.

Holy turned back to the window.

"So next day some of us hold a kind of meeting, see? People in the fame business. And her and me, we get elected to do the discipline."

"That's why we're here, Benny," Elektra said.

"Waiting till things blow over a little."

"'Do the discipline'?" Ben said.

"See, Ramon's got some problems of his own now," Elektra said.

"Yeah. As in a fucking bad case of SML."

"*Supra mycobacterium leprae*."

"Hyper-leprosy to you and me, honey."

"Fame keeps track of fame," Elektra said after a pause.

"You can count on it," added Holy.

Five-thirty in the morning, sky paling from black to opal-rose, campfires on Bainbridge Island beginning to flitter out, the X-Smith twins bustled into the living room holding another

Vicks derm. One peeled it and applied it to Ben's wrist before he could complain while the other explained he needed to get his rest today. Supported between them, he barely made it to his bed before he began to trance.

Then it was dark again, the derm gone, and he was being hustled down a corridor, up the elevator, and onto the hot sticky roof where the VTOL jet-chopper was waiting, engines whining to life.

11

A tactical nuclear device was detonated late last night in the Tunnel of Prosperity, killing all two hundred ninety-seven passengers aboard the Alaska-Kolyma speedtrain," an announcer reported on the Panasonic newsbox in the kitchen.

"Fuck me harda, *harda!*" urged Ramona Fogazzaro, Bronx chair of the President's Foreign Relations Committee, as Bill Cosby Se-Jin, Chinese VP at General Motors, took her from behind in *Congressional Exposé,* now tracking on the Commodore holounit in the living room / bedroom / bathroom.

"Gonna *push* you 'round, gonna *move* uptown, gonna *do* what I *gotta* to *get* a good *shot at* da Pres-i-*dent,*" rapped Glaisha & His Hitt Teem-2 on the Dolby sound system nearby, old-time hiphoppers from Ghana currently doing life for taking their lyrics a little too seriously.

"Well, Fred, how much do you think this little fella'd go for down at the Labs?" asked the co-emcee on the Home Shopping Network. The Technics screen projected a closeup of a large hand petting a small Doberman-tiger chimera cub: cat head, dog eyes, body of a tiger, coloring of a Doberman.

"Anarchists for Jesus the Anointed King and Savior have claimed full responsibility for the bombing," said the newsbox announcer, "stating it was an attempt on its part to quote 'hasten the glorious coming of the Apocalypse' end quote."

"Harda, *harda!*" cried Ramona. "Oh, yeah, baby, *that's* the way I like it!"

"Wild Life, the eco-terrorist group based in Missoula, Columbia, has also claimed full responsibility, stating it was an attempt on their part to draw attention to quote 'another corporate suicide mission on the environment' end quote."

" . . . *shoot* him in the head, gonna *shoot* till he's dead, gonna *shoot* him and *shoot* him till we change the fuckin' *sys*-tem."

"Seven other terrorist organizations, including the IRA and JDL, have also claimed responsibility for the bombing."

"Lower? Gosh, Sam, I don't know," said the co-emcee's cohort. "Four-fifty? Four hundred? I'm just guessing now."

"Among the dead was Mainline Lady, lead-singer of the successfull band the Infocaines. Clean-up crews will arrive on the scene this afternoon, according to an Amtrak spokesperson, and the mop-up is expected to take fifty to seventy-five years."

The chimera cub purred till a can of Purina Puppy Chow was opened nearby, then it began barking and squirming. Its pinpoint claws emerged on its paws, luminescing under the floodlights.

"Whoah, little fella!" Sam said. "Slow down!"

"I'm comin', baby!" screamed Ramona, pendulous breasts bouncing, dark body drifting two meters off the beige carpet next to the tube, Bill croaking behind her as he raised his hand and began spanking.

"Boy, Sam," said Fred, "you can just imagine what this little guy's gonna look like when he grows up."

"Oh *yeah!*"

"The perfect live security system. Bio-engineered to love kids, imprint quickly on up to sixteen adults, learn fast as the dickens, and disable intruders with a minimum of fuss."

"Gonna *take* down the Man, gonna *make* a Last Stand, gonna *do* it gonna *do* it till people *see* it's a *sham*."

" . . . course, I bet it's accompanied by the famous Diacomm credit-return guarantee. Right, Fred?"

"You're making me *come*, baby!"

" . . . concealed timing device."

"You just hit the nail on the head, Sam. If you're not *completely* satisfied with your purchase, just send it to us within ten days of receipt for your full credit back, minus shipping and handling."

" . . . Quality Board suggests remaining indoors if possible, and make sure to wear your sanitary mask! Remember: if it isn't 3M, it isn't pure!"

"Just the thing for the little lady at Christmas, eh Fred?"

"Oh! Oh! *Oh!*"

"One out of every five children divorces its progens, a report..."

"…not speaking about a hybrid here."

"…*do* it gonna *do* it till people *see* it's a *sham*."

"The tiger and dog tissues will remain separate for the life of the animal, and there's no worry about unwanted reproduction. You will receive *this* product and *this* product only. It won't mate and it won't produce offspring. That's a Diacomm promise."

"…aftershocks expected this evening in the San Diego area. So buckle up, Golden State commuters!"

"…*do* it gonna *do* it till people *see* it's a *sham*."

"…not talking four hundred. We're not talking three-fifty. Nope. Not even two-seventy-five."

"Ooooh, *make me COME!*"

"That's right, folks. You're hearing correctly. We'll *give* this cute-as-can-be furry critter to you for just *two hundred fifty credits* if you act now."

Mikki Tendo cracked a smile and saw her face reflected in her Sense8 computer screen: short pink bob, pink contacts, golden front tooth.

"…outbreaks of a new strain of encephalitis in the LA region last week, the Atlanta Center for Disease Control . . ."

She had to.

"Oh, lover."

"…*see* it's a *sham*."

"…Mars program back on track, President Redford maintained today at the opening of the new Bologoye Wing at the Smithsonian."

She just had to.

Even in the morning info-storm, sorting through the rush of data, Mikki just couldn't help taking a moment to pat herself on the back.

Hell, it was *her* team's baby.

Sitting at the kitchen table at her terminal, simultaneously checking out the news, doing a little shopping, nuking her low-cal cholesterol-free egg-substitute and farm-shrimp bacon in the microwave, relaxing with some music, replaying her favorite scene from the holoporn she'd bought yesterday and already watched four times last night, and catching up on what'd gone down on the Tokyo Exchange while she slept, she just couldn't suppress that trace of pride that'd begun darting through her chest. *Shouldn't*, either. That Doberman-tiger chimera'd been one of hers. Probably Diacomm Labs' most lucrative project back when it originally went into production.

Platinum job, the one that really got her career off the ground. Pure status.

Major rank.

She closed her eyes and remembered the slightly metallic taste of her credit slab.

Success: you could smell it, man, and it smelled like sex.

Funding, funding, funding.

Only real question after initial production was one of marketing. The Home Shopping Network's pitch notwithstanding (though it was good, *very* good, so rucking sincere, with that great patina of nerdish innocence on the interplay between Fred and Sam, a real artform, you had to give it to them), chimeras didn't come cheap.

Sales team, however, did beautiful work targeting wealthy metropolitan dwellers, frightened lonely widows, West Coast police departments. Even the military'd started sniffing around, only the limited imprint potential caused some real probs there and the KR was never high as the Pentagon'd hoped. One good tactical nuclear warhead, and there went the profits.

Shit, though. Even *that* turned out to be a blessing, didn't it, ultimately leading to funding for the current project, mother lode: man-ape chimeras for the US Army and major police forces, genespliced for obedience, strength, controlled aggression, pretty good marksmanship, and, let's face it, one sphincter-splitting ugly face you couldn't do anything with except run from.

If these new babies flew, if they really took off, well, you bet your ass a VP position would be rubbing its snout all over your career, a move to that spiffy uptown Arizona branch. Oh, man, now wouldn't *that* be a kick?

It smelled like Ramona and Bill on the holounit, like electricity and plastic.

Mikki stood, shuffled to the microwave, and extracted her breakfast pouch, thinking, shit, a career move like that'd definitely be a step up from this place, itself just half a step up from some prole tube-room in the company quarters.

Okay okay okay: so it was bright and white and clean and everything. Yeah. Not to say it didn't have its status. Not to say it wasn't expensive as hell. Not to say young professional types around here wouldn't give their left testicles for a piece of comparable real estate. But, god*damn*, the living room / bedroom / bathroom was, what, two meters by three-and-a-half. And the kitchen was a whole bunch tinier than that. A *whole* bunch. And windows, well, windows were just a class-A wetdream.

She centimetered her way to the sound system and changed digital cassettes, replacing Glaisha & His Hitt Teem-2 with a Minskian muzak-grindcore group called the Five-Year Plan just out on the Rough Trade label.

Then she phoned the Home Shopping Network and ordered that clicking pseudo-Picasso scarab bracelet she'd just seen advertised.

She sat down again, peeled open her breakfast pouch, and began eating, figuring sometimes you got the impression that every move you made in this place involved another move. Every turn or bend or stretch tripped this congested chain reaction that led to bruised elbows and scraped knees. You wanted to push the chair back from the table, you first had to push the table back from the chair, make sure the pantry door was closed, inhale and tiptoe over the futon in the living room / bedroom / bathroom. You wanted to unfold the futon, god, you first had to nudge the Dolby out the way, which meant you had to shove the Technics to one side, which meant you had to scooch over the Commodore, which meant you had to lift it on top of the kitchen table.

Plus, only way to keep solvent right now, keep clear of those tube-rooms, was to play the market heavy. Which, let's face it, was always a tox gamble which could backfire any time, undermining even *this* feeble excuse for a living situation and sending you spiraling right back down the prestige ladder into the unutterable horrors of some statusless dimension.

Mikki shuddered and scrolled down, trying to find the data she wanted. Then she moused SEARCH MODE, keyed in some stock names, and the machine whirred, pondering. Up flipped the stats.

Her heart lightened.

"All *right*," she said aloud.

John Updike, Inc., that computer-generated series of clone-texts out of Liberia, was off by a couple of fractions. Okay okay okay. They needed to pump some more hardcore into the merchandise, just hadn't found the right balance yet between romance and triple-X.

But Warhol Enterprises was up, probably because of the increasingly high profile of that Kraut—no, *Dutch*—artist, who was making a fortune signing his name in various pastel colors on blank canvases. What was it again? Hound? Howne? Uh-uh. Something more—Cowne. *Towne.* Yeah. That was it. Hans Towne. Had this incredible eye for what people'd buy, and people'd buy pretty much anything if they thought it had an iota of culture. Culture meant credit and credit meant class. Had to admire that in the guy. Knew how to manipulate the market forces without even a quiver of disingenuousness.

And then there was that never-ending hypertext, *Funhouse Blues*, by the writing team at Disney-Random House, whose first installment was due out next week, hook on every page, already up four points and still rising.

Make me come, baby, she thought as Ramona and Bill's vid began looping again. Make me come.

Oh, and here it is. Here it is.

Spank me till I'm red.

You can smell it, girl. Just look at that: Billboard Stocks for Kama Quyntifonic, Ltd., up another seven points after that initial slump following the final-dining. Nothing increases sales like a good tragedy well-covered by the media.

People who'd never even *heard* of that woman were out there, swarming the music stores, discovering what they'd almost missed.

People only *mildly* interested in her when alive were neophilically *mesmerized* by the public spectacle of her mourning fans on MTV. The anguish market's booming.

And the die-hard groupies?

(Mikki glanced down at her Movado watch. It was six-thirty, thirty-seven degrees. She had to get going.)

Well, the die-hard groupies scoffed up that bitch's cassettes, recently introduced sunscreen and clothing lines, posters, dolls, vids of the actual final-dining, of the reenactments of the actual final-dining, on the conspiracy theories about the final-dining (it was INTERPOL, it was the Global Space Administration, it was the mafia, it was a jealous lover, it was AJAKS, it was the music industry itself), ersatz bootlegs, holographic concert photos, playing cards, bubble-gum, and replicas of the band's musical instruments like there would never be a day when they'd look back on all that shit and feel vague puzzlement trying but failing to recall that weird woman's name and why they'd even bothered to care about it in the first place.

None of which was hurt by the fact that Vologda-Lloyd's had insured her for an amazing amount and were in the midst of a cost-effective scramble to make back their losses.

The thing was this, thought Mikki as she wiped her plate with a brittle stick of farm-shrimp bacon and slurped it into her mouth. The thing was this: a dramatic death, a really wild-eyed death, worked wonders for image-building.

Now you didn't want any of these mysterious disappearances or comas-after-highspeed-race jobs or other such halfway measures. You wanted the real thing, the Coca-Cola thing, the big black thing, and you wanted it internationally televised in high-definition with Magnavox sense-around. The on-stage drug overdose and bone-breaking seizure in mid-strum. The swandive off a skyscraper into rush-hour traffic eighty-three stories below with, needless to say, the flail and fumble at the last moment that signals the honest-to-god breathclenching change of spirit. The point-blank hollow-tip in the belly by the lovelorn groupie in front of a swanky New York club, only to find out later that that groupie: she wasn't a she. Even, if you played your cards right, a tactical nuke aboard a speedtrain (Mainline Lady's stocks were starting to slink up, after all, just look at that, will you?).

But the hard part was knowing when to pull out. When the public'd had almost enough, *almost* enough, but not *too* much. That's where the *real* business acumen came in.

Game was to ride those fads close and long as you could, fast as a two-year-old's attention span, whole hip trip born and growing, aging and dying, in the course of something like a week, then jump the hell off that missile before the trajectory began its inevitable pause, spin, and descent into rapidly deteriorating assets and shell-shocked stock figures.

Humming along with the Five-Year Plan, Mikki put the computer to sleep and leaned back in her chair. Wiped her mouth with the tips of her first two fingers on her right hand and looked at her reflection in the blank screen once more. Pink was her color. It spoke of credit. It spoke of caste.

And those Kodak contacts. They were razzed. Downright tox.

Leaning over, she opened the pantry, took out her cosmetics kit and mirror, and began applying sunscreen.

It was already hot, probably over forty outside.

Inside, on the fifty-fourth floor, the anemic air-conditioning wasn't helping matters much.

She consulted her watch again. It was thirty-eight degrees.

That was one good thing about getting into the Labs early. You could sneak by the crushing heat of mid-day, temps in the high forties, hole up in perpetually cool dry recirculated air. Lots of incentive to stay late, too, since it seldom dropped back into the thirties before nine or ten at night. So the whole business of going to work became very Jap in appearance—dedication to the company family, bizarrely long hours, good overtime that ultimately bought jack shit on the streets because of the Tasmanian Devil-like inflation whirling through Diacomm towns.

And all this climate-produced devotion to the job worked pretty well for positioning for promotions. Or at least it *used to* work pretty well a couple of years back. Today everyone did it. Everyone came in early and stayed late just to find some shade, stretch their limbs in labs almost always larger than their own quarters, listen to the muzak-grindcore pumped over the sound system while they performed their research, eat two free meals a day that you had to admit could always be a lot worse, exercise in the plush gym four times a week, catch some tube in the lounge after dinner with your buddies, if you had any buddies, all the while simpering like old dogs whenever the management strolled by, which wasn't, if the truth be told, a whole hell of a lot.

Everyone knew the moves these days. Everyone knew their lines in the drama.

Which meant, among other things, that rush hour was already going full-throttle in the streets below at six forty-five in the morning, busses, electric cars, gasahol-burners, tuk-tuks bumper to bumper in a vast splay of gridlock and poisonous fumes under a Californian sun made gigantic and orange by the rotten yellow post-Shudder sky.

Meaning the half-mile haul would take just over an hour if she started immediately. Meaning she had to get her ass in gear. Meaning she —

Something caught her eye in the mirror.

Glinting.

She tried to locate what seemed askew in the reflected scene. The bluish biolight strips in the kitchen caught the glossy white paint on the front door which was ajar five or six centimeters. All the chains and deadbolts were smoking, burned right through.

She spun around, knocking her cosmetics kit to the floor, and saw the plastic guns first. Short and stubby and gray. Barrels three or four centimeters across.

They were pointing at her neck.

An instant later she heard her lipstick, eyeliner, rouge, nail polish, greasepaint, and sunscreen clatter around her feet.

Then she saw the two massive women with the tiny heads behind the guns. Sharp noses, no chins, and—what *was* that?— prole sharkskin grafts blobbing across their faces.

They were just *thugs*, for chrisakes, a pair of lousy idiot rucking *thugs* outfitted for a minor gang war, and they were smiling in unison like these two demented aunts someone'd locked in the attic too long. Smelled like aunts, too, what with that low-income Lorus perfume they were wearing. Couldn't the security guards keep the troglodytic riffraff out of the building?

"What the *fuck* are you doing in my apartment?" Mikki said.

The one on the right spoke first.

"I'm Yukia," she said.

She had to speak loudly because of the info-storm squalling around them.

"Yukia Sonnibono," clarified the one on the left. "And I'm Bobbie."

"Bobbie Ann Landers. Cheers. We're the X-Smith twins, products of British Telecom & Scientific-Atlantic Cosmetic Technologies & Securities."

"SEPBOGs."

"Somato-Enhanced Prototypic Body Guards."

"All SEPBOGs are sisters, in a manner of speaking."

"In a manner of speaking, they are."

"We share a belief, for instance, in neuroelectronically refined —"

"Get the fuck *out*," Mikki said. "Get the fuck out of my apartment and get the fuck out of my building, or I'll get the fucking exterminators in here to wipe the fucking floors with you." She glared at them. "You got three seconds. Enjoy them."

She glanced at the red button four centimeters below the light switch next to the door and then back at the twins. It was two strides away, would take her just over one second to reach. A minute later the apartment would be swarming with security personnel in riot gear. And she could still make it to the Labs in plenty of time.

"One," she said.

The X-Smith twins exchanged looks.

"Oh *my*," said the one on the left.

"Two," Mikki said.

"Oh dear," said the one on the right.

Mikki raised her head and studied the twins.

"Fuck you," she said. "Three."

She sprang.

She felt the burn of adrenalin, the sprint of her heart, and then the icy sting of the first dart as it pierced her neck—all before her feet could leave the carpet.

The second dart caught her in the right temple as she was falling. A bitter cold shockwave whammed her skull.

Momentum carried her into the door edge, collarbone detonating, and then, unexpectedly, she was lying on her back at a strange angle, gagging. Blood was skittering down her forehead into her eyes. The muscles in her chest were tightening. It seemed as if someone had tugged a plastic bag over her head.

The X-Smith twins spoke above her.

"We believe in the founders of IBM," the one on the left said.

"We believe in Timothy Leary," said the one on the right.

She kneeled and lay her hand on Mikki's chest, middle fingers spread in some sign. She closed her eyes and said: "Find the Apple within yourself."

"Run a search for the directory."

"Discover the insertion window."

"And know that when the sad Macintosh face appears on the screen it means the computer can go no farther."

"And that often this indicates a hardware problem."

"And then it's time to see your Apple dealer."

"It's time to seek professional assistance."

12

At the same moment the X-Smith twins uttered those words to Mikki in San Luis Obispo, the private jet carrying Ben, Mary, and Emma touched down on a back runway at Gatwick and reversed its engines.

Ben'd been trancing on and off for hours. He'd come alert briefly as the VTOL landed on an abandoned airstrip somewhere in what he took to be Canadian tundra, the twins double-timing him toward the plush Mantra 3000 across the tarmac under a hot carotene sky, and later as they hit some turbulence and he leaned forward groggily, peering out the porthole at nothing but Atlantic glittering through a layer of clouds all the way to the horizon.

Now he leapt to consciousness and found himself slouching alone in the backseat of an air-conditioned electric Rolls with tinted windows. It was crawling past oxygen booths on Knightsbridge Road in a thick silver smog. He'd seen a million vids of this area of London, the part where they preserved all the old building exteriors for the tourist trade, just a few blocks from the Royal Albert Hall. His derm was gone and a Vassopressin inhaler was cradled in his hands. He lifted it to his mouth.

Through the haze he spied the imitation Georgian facade of the Hyde Park Hotel, the flower gardens and the trees naked and black as though a firestorm had swept among them. The Rolls passed Hyde Park Corner, from which Ben could barely make out the red brick wall, two or three meters of barbed-wire skimming above it, that surrounded Buckingham Palace Gardens, then the large stretch of toast-toned grass and more blasted trees dotted through Green Park. A group of professional mourners in robes ululated before the Hard Rock Café on the left. Some stood by the entrance wringing their hands, some sat on the pavement and swayed back and forth. Others wandered aimlessly along the sidewalk amid passersby and teens waiting in line for t-shirts and shouted at the heavens. But who were they shouting for? Kama Quyntifonic'd final-dined ages ago, and mourning—even this kind of choreographed head-banging for a hyperstar like her—usually ran its course within a week or two.

You miss twelve hours of news, Ben thought as the tube station snailed by, and the whole world barrels past you. You miss half a day, and you age a hundred years. You blink, and you're Rip Van Winkle.

"Oi," the driver said over the intercom.

Ben could just discern the back of his head through the smoked-plastic barrier separating the front and rear compartments. It was a big head, a very big head, the size of a basketball, one of the biggest heads, in fact, Ben had ever seen. And yet when the barrier slid down and the head half-turned in its seat, Ben comprehended the lysergic fact that it was the most petite thing about this driver. It was downright delicate compared with the rest of him. The guy in the black turtleneck was huge in a steroidy, hydrocephalic kind of way. He was neckless. His mastadonic head sprouted directly from his shoulders. His short spiked hair was the color of dandelions and he had a cosmetic harelip that accented his left front tooth, or would have, if he'd owned one. It appeared that all his rubiate features— crinkled forehead, conjunctive anally puckered eyes, thumb-sized chin, shiny cheeks, mangled mouth—had gotten together and decided to hold a huddle within a three-centimeter radius from the center of his broccoli-tipped nose.

"Fa'ted themselves to death, they did," he said, facing front again. He wasn't actually driving, just monitoring the limo's progress on the computer screen in front of him on the dash. A green blip navigating a tangled Rube Goldberg contraption. "It's god's honest truth. Been documented and all. World Helf Organization. Let fly all this, what you call it, like *methane* stooff in the air. Fooked up the bloody climate. Know what they do to themselves? Know what they *do*? Jaysus. The fookin' dinosaurs coot the cosmic cheese and blow a fookin' hole in the fookin' ozone layer big as a fookin' *coon*try. Greemhouse Affect. Cosmic fookin' Calamityville Horrors. Yeah cheers. End of the known world as we know it. Death by fookin' cheese cootin', it was.

Death by bloody self-asphryxiation. And you know what it was, then? You know what it was? A scientific certainty and all. Computer projections. Been documented and all. And you know what the current situation in the present foretells? It says *we're* the fookin' *new* dinosaurs on the block. Yeah cheers. Welcome to the cosmic fookin' loo, mate. *We're* the fookin' new cosmic cheese cooters now. *Look* at this place. Just look at it. Fookin' *coast's* disappearin'. Polar caps meltin'. Lake Diftrict turned into a bloody *museum* you *pay* to bloody drive through. Know what we're doin' here, mate? Know what we're doin' at this very intersection in the space-time continuum as we know it? We're fookin' drivin' through our own fookin' dinosaur fa'ts and methanes, innit. We're sniffin' up our very own assholes."

Ben looked through the tinted window.

The guy with the basketball head was right. He definitely had a good point. For as they moved by the Ritz, golden lights blinking its name over the entrance, the smog actually became denser. It darkened, took on the appearance and consistency of television static between channels. It was bad. Fetid. So much so Ben initially assumed it had begun raining. But when he peered up at the sky, or what he could see of the sky, he saw the sun doing all it could, which wasn't terribly much anymore, to burn through this atmospheric mess. Its rays caught particles and glimmered, creating the sensation of moving through a sea of metallic gray paint.

"Used to fookin' need your fookin' gamp and willies just to cross the street this time of year when I was a kid. But not no more. No way. Little buggers don't even know what a bloody drizzle *is*, they don't. Don't even know what a fookin' cloud's'pposed to *do*. Yeah cheers. Used to wear jumpers, the lot of 'em. Now you're looky if you can get by in your unnershirt, it's so fookin' hot. Only you know what we're doin'? We're still bloody *pretendin'*, if you can believe it. We are. Still goin' round like bloody makin' *believe* you don't need like the bloody air-conditioning. Who needs ice in your drinks, eh? Not me, mate. Not me. Oi. We're all like still bloody pretendin' we're not like some fookin' load of fookin' dinosaurs with our noses stuck up our bloody sphincters. And the tube stations? Fook it. The tube stations. Might as well stick your head down a barrel of bloody toxic sludge and have a good hearty sniff around. Yeah cheers. Know why? Simple. Because, mate, our assholes are behind us.

Our shit always comes out the bum-end, don't it? So it was like natural we thought we could leave it behind us. Yeah cheers. That's my theory. What the fookin' tyrannosaurus thought too. Go to the Museum of Natural Hifory and have yourselves a good laugh, innit. Say hullo to your fellow assholes, mate. Nice ta know ya. Yeah cheers. Bloody 'ell."

He didn't stop there. He didn't even slow down. His language had built too much momentum to wait for him to catch up with it. It tumbled headlong into his other theory that the Pakistanis and Russians were somehow responsible for this, that Ben should call him Mondo for short, though Mondo never explained what the longer alternative to his name might be.

Only Ben wasn't listening.

A new bit of data in his environment had snagged his interest instead: those red pinprick lights on the black leather armrests by the release handles were off. Meaning the doors of the smart car were unlocked. Meaning either Mondo had forgotten about them or decided Ben was trancing so intensely when he deplaned that those locks were the last thing he needed to bother with.

They passed the flags rippling outside the Royal Academy on their approach to Piccadilly Circus and the traffic began slugging to a virtual standstill in the semi-roundabout.

Ben heard Lewis-Foozebane back in Spocoeur explaining that chemicals were recombining in his head to form new emotions, that he wasn't about to do anything he wasn't supposed to do. But which choice now presenting itself to him was the statistically predictable one, which the one nobody was expecting?

While Mondo prattled on, Ben contemplated the giant Memorex billboard flaming fuschia and yellow over the biggest McDonald's on earth. The acid-pocked plaster statues of Elvis, Madonna, and Morph Allah G gazing down beneficently from the fake Roman balcony atop the Rock Circus. The red double-deckers. Beetlish black cabs. Motorscooters with flea-engines. The holographic rainbow of advertisements revolving above wave after wave of people in sanitary masks or respirators flowing around the green-black statue of Eros, pouring in and out of the Underground tunnels, surging across the street, coursing up Shaftsbury and down Regent and toward Leicester Square.

And Ben simply opened the door and stepped out.

A nanosecond of peace followed.

Then horns began blaring. Someone raised a shout. Brakes engaged. And metal ground against metal.

He dimly registered Mondo clambering from the Rolls somewhere behind him, shinnying onto the Audi next to it, lumbering across carhoods toward him.

Ben shouldered into the crowd, trying to run, but people pressed him from every side. He pushed ahead, only the throng wouldn't give. He jostled, bunted, feeling Mondo heave through the crush, knocking pedestrians aside, quickly closing the distance between them.

The acrid grit in the air seared Ben's lungs. He began coughing hard like he'd just taken a long swig of whiskey. He raised his forearm to cover his nose and mouth, using the fabric of his shirt as a filter. A fleeting gap opened before him and he drilled through.

Soon he was dodging amid the mob on a side street, serpentining down a sparsely-populated mews into a small cobblestone courtyard lined with trashcans, out again onto a lane curving at an illogical arc. Its sidewalks were hyper with displays of counterfeit designer Levi's, pseudo-antique jewelry, Kevorkian machines, blackmarket fruit-and-vegetable carts. Rotten apple rinds and lettuce stuck to the slick dark pavement. Peanut-oil fumes rising from wok stalls mixed with the sweet smell of pastries, diesel exhaust, and cig smoke. On the left, plateglass storefronts advertised Punjabi cuisine and Virtual Reality arcades. On the right, three-centimeter-thick layers of ripped posters concealed sooty red brick walls. The posters, many of them in the Cyrillic alphabet, followed everyone everywhere around here, telling people what to save, what to avoid, how to wash, where to go, who to vote for, why to care. Over them gang members had spray-painted orange and yellow graffiti, most of it sexual in nature.

Disoriented, Ben paused. He had the impression he'd begun moving toward Piccadilly Circus again. Yet when he began to backtrack half a block he felt he was drifting in Mondo's direction.

Businessmen salmoned around him. It was lunchtime and they were on their breaks, mostly over from the financial district. They'd tubed or cabbed here for an hour's holiday. Some strolled into inexpensive ethnic restaurants or milled around cramped stalls. Most ducked through beaded doorways above which appeared signs for LIVE BED SHOWS. Many of the signs were neon, some just stenciled white letters on brick. All were accompanied with a price: 10 CRD., 60 CRD., or 80 CRD. Ben watched the men walk past women with violet fingernails and facial ringworm hawking from the entrances, and decided he could lose himself real easy in the Chinese puzzle of bars and sex parlors unraveling beneath street level.

Choosing a doorway at random over which batted a blue sign for CANDY STORE, he entered.

The shadowy staircase was so narrow that if two people met one would have to retreat to let the other pass. At the bottom was a cramped alcove with faded tile and a polished door where Ben waited till he'd caught his breath. When he cleared his throat he brought up a clot of blood the size of a small tooth.

Through the door was a gloomy movie theater, eight rows of torn chairs bolted to a tacky floor. Where the screen had once been was now a spotlit waterbed on a plywood stage. A naked oriental flesher, eleven or twelve, played with herself lethargically on it while voicing unconvincing moans at mechanically regular intervals. The air smelled like a belch. A couple of streetpeople slept in the back row, four or five teenagers—all women—made out with each other in the mid-section, and just behind them slumped two elderly businessmen with green ducktails. Ben took a seat down front.

A topless waitress, quite possibly Candy herself, showed up to take his order. Her tubular yellowish breasts lay flat against her stomach. Her arms were unnaturally short and lacked elbows. She wore her magenta hair cut long on top and short in back in a contemporary version of the turn-of-the-century version of the 1980s version of the 1930s. Ben asked her for a Choline Enhancer and settled back in his seat to work out what to do next.

He needed to stay low. Real low. Maybe he could tuk-tuk to one of the outlying shanty districts, get a cheap shed for a few days, and then, when he was sure he was safe, make his way to a phone to let somebody know what kind of crap he'd got himself into. But who? He didn't know a single person in Britain. And the London cops were the *last* people he'd want to have a chat with right now. Not only would he be at a loss about exactly what to tell them but he also knew whoever had the kind of power it took to haul his ass from New Seattle to London, private transportation, body guards, and all, sure had the kind of power it took to keep an odd hacker's eye upon the BritPol CompuSystem.

The waitress returned with the drink and Ben gave her his Visa slab.

On stage the flesher was extracting something from between her legs. At first it looked like a strip of tinfoil. Then Ben realized it was a string of double-edged razor blades.

Dobie, maybe. Maybe Mitzy. You could usually count on the gang at Beautiful Mutants to help you out in a jam. Mikki was always a possibility. She had enough credit in her account to bring him home several times over, even after she'd bought all the toys she wanted for herself this week. Except they hadn't talked to each other in—what was it?—months. Still, family *was* family, more or less, at least when it came to emergencies, sometimes.

Only one prob: contacting *anyone* involved a phonecall. And every phonecall involved entry into the matrix. And every entry into the matrix involved raising an electronic red flag on that odd hacker's screen somewhere if, that is, someone was hacking on him. Which was a fairly good assumption, given the circumstances. Now there *were* always the blackmarket radiophone systems that moved above, below, and around the official matrix, but they were expensive as hell to use. He'd be good for like a three-minute call and then utterly broke. And even if he *could* find his way to a clocker to lead him in turn to an underground sender, say, which wouldn't be easy in a city he knew only as a series of images in rock vids, and even if he *could* contact someone he knew back in the States, which looked like an increasingly dubious proposition given his current choices, what could a person back in the States do for him here, in the middle of the Candy Store, in the middle of Soho, in the middle of London?

"Sorry, sir," the waitress whispered, back again. "Seems we got a little difficulty here."

Ben blinked.

"A little difficulty?"

"Yeah. Seems like your slab's void."

". . . ?"

"Afraid we need another means of payment, if you don't

mind."

On stage the flesher had picked up a piece of newspaper lying by the waterbed. She chose one of the razor blades on the string and flicked it through the sheet several times to prove it wasn't dull.

"But I used it just a couple of days ago."

"Whatever."

"Maybe you like keyed in the wrong ID or something."

"Ran it twice."

Ben looked down at his drink, then up at the flesher who was bowing. No one applauded. She shrugged, picked up a silver bikini she must've been wearing at the set's start, and walked off the stage.

"You got some cash?" Candy asked.

"All I got's the slab."

One of the elderly businessmen with the green ducktails shooshed them.

"Fuck off, mate," Candy said. He fucked off. Immediately. Then she said to Ben: "You want I should get Chick?"

"Chick?"

"Chick. Yeah. Only maybe I should tell you first. Thing is, you don't want I should get Chick."

"Look. Someone pulled the plug on me. I don't have any cash. All I got's the slab. You gotta give me a break here."

"Pity," she said blandly, standing.

"Come on. You gotta give me a break."

"Hey, *Chick*."

A Bigfootish shape stepped from the wings onto the empty stage, bent down, and picked up the string of razor blades lying on the waterbed where the oriental girl had left them. Instead of a nose, he had twin pits between his eyes. His translucent hair was done chemo-style.

"Chick likes shiny things," Candy said. "Hey, Chick, someone forgot to keep some credit in his account. You want you should talk with him?"

Chick didn't have any vocal cords either. A childish grin split below his nose pits. He wasn't wearing sunscreen. The spotlights shone off his face, producing a color found only on the rubber skin of dolls.

A large white hand appeared suddenly over Ben's shoulder and passed Candy an unmarked gold credit slab.

"It's okay, luv, innit," the voice attached to it said. "I got the lad covered, like."

Chick stopped.

Candy looked at the owner of the chip, then at Ben. She rotated the slab in her hand.

"And take a little something for yourself, too. And for the big fella."

"I'll do that," Candy said as she turned and walked away.

Chick trotted behind her.

Soon the theater was deserted. Even the street people in back had left. The hand found the muscles at the base of Ben's neck and squeezed.

"Got that out of your system now, mate?"

"You cut off my fucking credit."

Mondo laughed.

"Know what's fookin' great? Know what's really fookin' great?"

Ben made an attempt to rise but the hand weighed on him like Rhode Island.

"IBM is fookin' great. Panasonic. Compaq too."

"What?"

"Computers, mate. They take all the guesswork out of the day-to-day. Give order to the unorderly. And you just can't say enuf bout their time-saving capacity. Tidy. Efficient. Predicable. That's what they are. Fookin' predicable. Ultimate smart drugs. Know why? Cuz you can bloody count on them. You know what you're getting for your credit."

"You knew where I'd be."

"But you know what's even more fookin' great than computers? People, mate. Cuz people act just like people are supposed to act. They listen to their chemicals."

"You knew before I stepped out of the Rolls."

"Kenwood, Commodore, Technotron. Sanyo, Vologda, Chrysler-Georgio. Fookin' genius machines." He ruffled Ben's hair affectionately. "No need to lock the bloody doors, was it, in actual fact. You would've just gone and kicked out the fookin' window."

Mondo rose behind Ben, knees cracking.

"Which means maybe there's a little lesson in all this for us today, innit, if we search ourselves real deep, plump the depths. Maybe we can find a moral in all this, eh? Like maybe you can get all that fookin' freedom shit out of your system, clean all the fookin' pipelines of all that bloody freewill bilge."

He stepped into the aisle and strolled toward the emergency exit without looking back. Ben watched him go.

"Take a couple of minutes to pull yourselves together, 'less you want a bit more of the old heart-to-heart. Bit more of the old *tête-à-tête*. I'll be in the car when you're ready, mate."

Laughing, he pushed open the door and stepped into the spoiled intergalactic rays beyond.

13

D ecreasing expectations mean increasing speculations,'"
Helmer Skelter chanted to himself, quoting verse 33 from
Pathways to Lessness, a crinkled dog-earred piss-stained
page-torn copy of which bounced on his groin as he careered
south through sepia landscape down Columbia's State
Highway 95 on a pilgrimage to New Meadows, Idaho, where
he would pick up 55, which would take him to Boise, where
he would pick up 84, which would take him by Twin Falls,
where he would pick up 93, which would take him through
Jackpot on the Nevada border and into the desert, where he
would ride till there was no more traffic left, no more one-
horse towns, barely even a road, at which time he would park
on the shoulder, shrug into his backpack, set his vehicle on
fire, and start the long hike toward singleness, paring away
the extraneous as he went, honing, jettisoning, trying to locate
that resplendent point of selfhood burning in the dun
mucilaginous gunk of existence, which was a paraphrase of
another quote from *Pathways to Lessness*, verse 87, he was
pretty sure.

He was jangling down the two-lane highway in a stolen
desert-camouflaged US Army surplus Jeep Hellhound without
roof or shocks, used only by two aged colonels in the pampas
during the South American war, which he'd kind of borrowed
from his boss, Julian Twemlow, at Les Schwaab's, without, exactly, Julian's knowledge. The theft wasn't premeditated or anything. It wasn't like Helmer'd come prepared to do Julian dirty
and then cut out. Helmer didn't have a bad gene in his body. In
fact, he'd assumed this was going to be a fairly ordinary day:
change some oil, fix some flats, tinker with an engine here or
there, and then go home to his *real* passion, music, the heavy

bump of the bass as important to his life as those little blue-and-white Tokyo Exchange readouts along the bottom of tube screens were to insider traders.

Only halfway through this one tire-balancing job something had popped, his fears'd suddenly raised their welt-bespeckled heads and, jabbering, struck. The underbelly of the Nissan he was fiddling with started smelling funny, maybe even a little like a Mexican restaurant, which fragrance spelled nothing if not disaster. The car's owner, an armadillo in a backwards Twin's baseball cap stared at him a little too long through the waiting room window and (if Helmer wasn't mistaken) briefly flashed some fangs in his direction. But, worst, the box he'd been listening to had played the same song, the *same song*, an eerie ballad called "Look Behind You" by Frank Sinatra's great-great grandson, twice in a row. When it came up a third time, Helmer just put down his electric lug wrench, turned, and walked out. That was it. There was, after all, a limit to this sort of bullshit.

The Hellhound had been waiting in the employee parking lot. Helmer'd just climbed aboard, hot-wired the ignition, and toed the gas. Last thing he'd seen, or thought he'd seen, as he'd shot through the gate onto Sprague, was the armadillo smacking Julian on the back and laughing, each three centimeters tall in his rearview mirror.

He hadn't stopped till he'd reached Riggins early that afternoon and pulled over long enough to stock up at an outfitters. But the stink of the Mexican restaurant followed him—enchiladas mostly, though some refried beans, salsa sauce, tamales too. So did The Look, except now it wasn't coming from the malevolent armadillo. It was coming from the landscape itself. You could see it everywhere. *Everywhere.* In the ominous roll of the hills and frightening jut of the mountains, poisonous as a cobra's glare. In that monster cloud shaped like some divine eyeball that kept churning up in front of you. In every tree along the roadside, tamarack or poplar or ash, every bush on every rise when you weren't quite paying attention. You just knew it. The river seemed to boil with whirlpools that vanished as soon as you turned your head. Triangular fins appeared in Payette Lake. Indian headdresses bobbed in fields of wheat. The blades of grass along the roadside—ach, the blades of grass.

Normally at a time like this he would've aimed for the nearest phone and punched 1-800-PARANON fast as his finger could work, and someone on the other end, his or her own voice shaky, teetering on some unspeakable brink, would've then tried to talk him down and, normally, would've succeeded. Back they'd go to Helmer's loveless childhood in a Berlin public housing project, to all that German angst pounding within words like *mustard gas* and *The Wall* and, gradually, ever so gradually, Helmer would've come down, savvying the steps he heard behind him, the shadow that darted up an alley, were nothing more than his past come back to say *wie geht's* and scare the shit out of him just one more time.

Only what town could he trust now, what ominous telephone? Where wouldn't They be waiting?

"'Keep moofing,'" he quoted. Verse 52. "'It's always harder to hit a mobile target.'" Sicher. That's the one concept Uriah forgot that night, having become too complacent to guard his periphery. That's the one concept Andrea forgot as she calmly reclined in her dentist's chair, unaware of the allergic reaction hovering at the tip of that needle.

And you know, you just *know*, it was the concept Ben forgot as well, somewhere out there, you just didn't stop to give that man in the Mercedes directions, enter your apartment without first checking to see if that piece of scotch tape near the knob had been tampered with, slow to give that slightly cross-eyed fan with the posture of a jumbo shrimp an autograph.

You kept moving.

You always kept in motion.

You always kept shedding your belongings and your addresses, your relationships and your credit. Because, when it came right down to it, existence was nothing if not a process of conversion, differentiation, and adaptation. You had to ride it like a madman a never-ending rollercoaster, verse 189, keep all that human contact stuff to a minimum, seek the singleness within each of us, seek the lessness, except —

Except—

Except what *was* that ahead on the side of the road?

His white flag of hair walloped his face, obscuring the object of his interest. So he scooped it back in a ponytail and, as he did so, beheld the sexiest woman he'd ever seen.

She was standing on the shoulder just south of Pollock, razzed legs parted and right arm extended and thumb pointing at the pewter sky, decked in these breathtakingly tight faded

1001s with frayed knees and thighs and butt, flimsy Rachino powder-blue-lace bra, and lobster-red Rush knapsack, skin the color of brown sugar, long polychromatic beaded dreadlocks to just roll over and die for.

Even at a hundred meters, Helmer could make out those dark nipples forming large stains beneath the blue.

So he jammed down the brake and went into a skid.

It was true, he admitted to himself, the Hellhound crunching onto gravel and beginning to slide sideways, he followed the dicta of *Pathways to Lessness* faithfully, felt sure, deep within his being, that Joey Taboo could well represent the new Messiah of late capitalism, believed without a doubt the sole avenue to transcendent peace involved a gradual whittling away of earthly bonds, including things like good food and rich human relationships, because when you leave your carry-ons in the airport locker you don't have to keep checking under your seat in the plane (verse 47), but it was equally true he saw no particular problem with a quick box-springs-grinding one-night stand.

He had space in his consciousness, he told himself, the Hellhound lurching into a 180 as it just kept on heading for the edge of that ravine, for several apparently contradictory impulses, this not being evidence of weakness, hypocrisy, or bad faith, but of the undeniable fact that contradiction was part of the human condition, opposing forces being what made the human mind the human mind.

Though if you really thought about it, Helmer was quick to add as he came to a dusty halt twenty meters beyond the hitcher, tweaked off the radio, and threw the Hellhound into reverse, there really wasn't a contradiction between simultaneously not wanting a rich human relationship and yet most emphatically wanting a box-springs-grinding one-night stand, the latter involving the essence of Joey Taboo's philosophy: no commitments, continual movement, and a religious quest for reduction in all its forms.

And paranoia, in all its brooding grandeur, was nothing if not the psychological equivalent of the Unified Field Theory for, in paranoia, there was space for everything. In paranoia, everything was connected to everything. Contradictions amounted to nothing but a subspecies of myopia.

So "Hop in," he told the hitcher cheerfully, having screeched up to within four centimeters of her toes, which at the moment were housed in a pair of nazi lobster-red high-heeled Implied techno-sneakers.

She chucked her knapsack in back with Helmer's and scooched into the bucket seat up front.

"This's real nice of you, man," she said. "Been standing here for like two hours. Thought everyone'd given up on fossil fuels. How far you going?"

Helmer smashed down the gas pedal.

A peacock-tail of gravel arced and the Jeep sprang onto the highway, tires shrilling, while Helmer tweaked on the radio again, twidgeled the knob, and searched the airwaves for something appropriate, settling after a time on some nice Burroughsian cutup smorgasbord of zoom-core punk, industrial stomp, avant-reggae, double-time circus jazz, and acid-fried heavy metal from a week-old group out on the Arista label called the Rectal Dyslexics.

"Nefada, I think," Helmer shouted over the thunk of the baseline, which he'd cranked way up. "Though Death Valley always holds some honest appeal."

"Deserts."

"Pintwater Range. Sheep Range. Stonewall Flat. I'm into some quiet space right now."

"Quiet space?" she yelled.

"Unpopulated zones."

The hitcher looked straight ahead for a minute, computing, then turned toward him and said: "I don't know if this exactly, um, meshes with your larger plans. But I'm heading down to Phoenix and I got a little credit. How 'bout you and me joining forces for a day or two?"

"Mega," Helmer said, adjusting the volume up on the radio for no particular reason. Large shiny green beetles splattered upon the windshield. "You from around here?"

"Long story."

"We got nothing but time." He pushed the washer button. Azure cleaning fluid spritzed up, wipers clucked. "My name's Helmer, by the way. Helmer Skelter."

"Belinda Santos. Glad to meet ya, man. Call me Lindy."

"Lindy. Okay. Nice name."

"Thanks," she said, sliding toward him in her bucket seat, slipping an arm behind his shoulders, and asking brightly: "So, tell me: what's a Helmer Skelter?"

14

Staring through the tinted windows, Ben found himself thinking he'd give just about anything to hear Uriah's keyboards and Andrea's drums and Helmer's bass again, just about anything to be able to finger the frets on his acoustic, yellow-brown lacquered casing smooth as ice, strings taut as radar beacons. Only at some inexplicable instant back in the Candy Store this had ceased to be a possibility. His prospects had skittered through the exit doors when Mondo had opened them and vanished up the smoggy mews.

He took a hit of Vassopressin and watched the tidy hologram galleries, West End theaters, and quaint French cafés on Charing Cross blend into the seedier pawn shops, tattoo parlors, and grungy Japanese hymen-replacement joints on Tottenham Court Road. The Rolls moved from the tourist quarter into turn-of-the-century office buildings that'd been made over into public housing tracts for the homeless, low-slung glass structures becoming increasingly modern and flimsy, soot clouding their orange and blue windows, clotheslines dense with dirty laundry webbed between top stories. Overpasses and railroad trestles replaced Georgian and Victorian facades. Pubs morphed into bars and the bars became shabbier, fitted with blacked-out windows, tarnished signs for on-site betting, supermarket doors. Derelict cars along the curb lacked tires or windshields, and some had clearly once been set aflame, Ben seeing where fire had lapped their flanks, meringuing paint, charring metal, melting plexiglas.

It occurred to him this was the part of London—by far the largest part—that you never saw in the vids. This was the part where the Londoners in London tried to work, the part where the Londoners in London tried to live. This was the hunchbacked, twelve-fingered doppelgänger of the real thing which wasn't the real thing at all but a television version of a television version of what certain executives and ad men believed the tourists believed the Londoners believed the tourists believed the real thing should look like.

Turning a corner, they entered the biotech district. More oxygen booths slid by. Home of London's Walt Disney Zoo with animal creations combining the talents of genetic engineers and cartoon artists picketed by a handful of Back-to-Reality Kommandos, or BARKS, fed up with replicas and looking for something really wild. Lloyd's Gene Bank of England where embryos were stored in vaults of liquid nitrogen, indexed, and referenced with photos and details of their genetic progens, ready for purchase by savvy shoppers who wanted a clear say in their children's physical and intellectual development. The ConservoFem Complex, recently bombed by the Gynorads, where the old guard produced babies untouched by male hands by artificially combining a woman's genes with the genes from a body-cell of that woman's woman lover. The Thorburn-Harding MaleBond Center down the block, where Malists produced babies untouched by female hands by fertilizing an egg in a dish, implanting it in a man's abdomen, and waiting for the growing embryo (nourished by a series of hormone injections) to develop a placenta with which it would attach itself to the inside of the abdomen, acquiring a blood supply, gestating, and ultimately being able to be delivered via Caesarean section. Bobbies in flak jackets lined the streets here. They carried P53s and mace canisters. The entrances to the buildings were blocked with concrete barriers to prevent frontal assaults from the East-European-based RomanCaths, the Scottish-based AnthroRads, and other assorted Radical Gender Groups.

At New Euston Station the Rolls eased into the loading lane. Mondo opened Ben's door and escorted him into the great limestone Neo-Egyptian edifice through a side access, down a luminescent passageway, and onto a seldom-used platform where a private speedtrain's bullet-shaped engine thrummed.

The cool interior was decorated flashback Victorian. A mahogany dining table surrounded by massive tall-backed chairs, seats upholstered in authentic leather, dominated the room. In one corner hulked a grandfather clock with a gold face, in another an elaborately carved rolltop desk. A narrow four-poster bed with dark red velvet canopy sat near the door leading to the engine, and three luxuriously corpulent leather armchairs (again authentic, from what Ben could tell) squatted near the windows. The cabin was lit with elegant oil lamps and lined with burgundy carpet, velvet wallpaper, and leather ceiling tiles. Delicate blue-and-white Chinese porcelain plates and dolls, decanters, elegant snuff boxes, ivory pipes, a wooden bird cage fashioned after the Crystal Palace, and stacks of late nineteenth-century magazines littered various shelves, cabinets, and sidetables. Ben flumped into one of the armchairs and tugged back a thick drape.

Soon they were flying through the flat industrial wastelands north of London. Black silhouettes of auto factories seethed smoke and flames into the rusty sky. Junkyards strewn with thousands, tens of thousands, of crushed cars and dead machinery shot past. A deserted nuclear power plant. A grimy redbrick town at the edge of a steaming pond. Small herds of emaciated sheep, white fur stained gray by lead, lifted their heads in pastures of withered clover. The dingy sprawl of Birmingham bulked up, abandoned crumbling warehouses and hotels, bonfires in the streets, argon lamps burning even by day. Passing through the broken station, the train slowed enough for Ben to read the air-quality alert signs posted at intervals along the tracks, then accelerated again so that soon the blasted landscape became no more than the blur you see through the viewfinder of an out-of-focus camcorder.

They rocketed by Derby, Alfreton, and Sheffield; Barnsley, Wakefield, and Leeds. The scene remained desolate, tinged with a mineral ocher, though people increasingly began to figure in the picture, riding along shoulders of roads in tuk-tuks, strolling through commons with children, siphoning gas out of wheel-less cars neglected on the shoulders. All wore government-issued respirators, most pretty old models from what Ben could see. Some wore goggles as well, some rubber gloves, and some even the astronaut-like LaCrosse biohazard boots suggested by the World Health Organization for life in England's midsection.

Near Harrogate, Mondo disappeared into the engine compartment and returned with a silver tray piled with a couple of farm-shrimp-and-soybean sandwiches and a plastic bottle of vinegar and pint of warm lager for Ben, then went back to his reading, which consisted mainly of thumbing through crumbling-paged magazines till he happened upon a photograph of a scantily dressed woman, whom he savored in a languid sort of way for the better part of seven seconds, tonguing his wet harelip and fingering the gap where that front tooth should have been.

Ben tried to engage him in conversation but it became clear Mondo was all talked out. He'd given all his opinions on all the topics about which he had opinions. He had nothing else to say. He knew how to gab. He knew how to wait for lulls in another's monologue and lengthily insert his own, which he tended to filch from sleazy tube talk shows featuring spokespeople from various vigilante organizations and minor dart champions with interesting halftruths about more important dart champions' love lives. This he considered in-depth research. But listen? Respond to new and unexpected data? Oi. The best he could muster was a less-than-sincere "So where's the fookin' beaver, eh?" from time to time as he skimmed, ever more hastily, through those grizzled zines.

Ben therefore ate in silence and inspected the ornate compartment around him, dimly sensing the hot breath of his twenty-second birthday panting over his shoulder like the cinematic psychotic hovering, knife poised, just off screen somewhere in the darkened living room. And he thought about how *old*, how just plain *old*, he was getting.

Everyone was getting.

All the time.

When he finished his first sandwich he leaned forward and, balancing the lager on his right knee, tugged back the drape again. This time he saw something he hadn't seen in years: rain.

Actual rain.

Hard, steady, ash-gray rain.

It angled diagonally down the window in thin threads, jittered across the man-made lakes in the fish-farm district along the Scottish border across which they now sped, vibrated on the tin roofs of the power plants that sent massive electrical charges through the lakes to harvest the shrimp, plaice, and eel grown in them, trembled in puddles on the misty green and lilac moors, coalesced into foggy wisps obscuring the tops of the rolling treeless hills, spangled on the black raincoats of the farmers hurrying back and forth between whitewashed cottages.

Ben nudged up his glasses on his nose and grinned.

He remembered how, during his progens' month-long sabbatical from Diacomm when he was five and Mikki eleven, his family had driven this company Orsha mini-van north along Highway 1 and into the Salmons. For two nights they'd stayed in decrepit motels, circa 1995, one room for his progens and one for Mikki and himself, who surreptitiously watched television well into the early morning hours so they were always tired the next day and missed most of the scenery because they were busy conking out in the backseat.

As they moved past Willow Creek, however, they began camping, pulling onto logging roads at dusk and breaking out the Jansport two-person tents and sleeping bags, foam padding, miniature Camp7 gas oven, Igloo cooler, sitting around the fire, sparks wafting into the charcoal sky, spinning ghost stories as the moon enlarged on the horizon.

One cloudy day they hiked into the wilderness, ascending a difficult switchback trail through dense pines toward the summit a park ranger had told them would provide a magnificent view. They stopped for lunch by a small waterfall and unpacked a fancy picnic of soybean salad, Yakutat bottled water, and a blackmarket apple each. As they ate, it began to rain. It was Ben's first, a light drizzle that dampened his hair and moistened his face and made his heart race.

While his progens and sister ate, he stood, closed his eyes, and ran with his spidery arms stretched out at his sides as if he were trying to take off, cool droplets trickling down his neck, pungent earthy fragrance suffusing his mind with pinecones and humus and grass.

When he opened his eyes again he saw his sister, mother, and father sitting around the picnic blanket under a tree by the stream, laughing, and it occurred to him that he'd never really *seen* them before, never really *looked* at his family. Mikki, thin and tall and slightly stiff, a gender-negative of himself. His mother, moppy hair already graying, large green tortoise shell glasses shrinking her face and making her look like she walked around in some kind of scuba mask. His father with those amazing yellow-green eyes, that salt-and-pepper beard, those Diacomm trademark zeros and ones etched in his crewcut, cheeks and forehead blotched with brown spots and creased where he refused to wear sunscreen on the grounds it was treating the symptom and not the disease.

Years later, on a different camping trip somewhere near

Mount Starr King in Yosemite, as his field trainer shook him awake at that time just before dawn when the news you hear is never good, Ben thought about that picnic. He couldn't recall if they'd made it to the summit or not, if he'd seen that magnificent view he was supposed to have seen. And he couldn't recall any of those details a simple two-dimensional photograph would have supplied him with: what Mikki was wearing, what color the mini-van had been, whether his mother already displayed that slight stoop in her shoulders Ben would inherit as he moved into his unwieldy teens. The only thing that stuck from that moment, the only thing he could take back with him, were those bright faces drifting under that dark spruce, that white waterfall rushing over those black rocks, that wild exhilaration in his chest before that sweet scent in the late summer air.

After, his ability to remember anything about himself dissolved like a clump of sandstone under a faucet. He didn't have any problem with global events, with the chronology of wars or the order of tracks on major albums. But important events from his childhood evaporated, events every kid should be able to bring to mind, his favorite color, his favorite games. Next went his adolescence, his early teen years, all the specifics about his emancipation from Diacomm, his decision to travel north, his first meeting with Uriah, Helmer, and Andrea, his interview for the job at Beautiful Mutants.

Now someone'd ask him what he'd done over the weekend, and he'd realize he just couldn't say. Someone'd wonder what his current stroke-number was, and his mind'd go blank. There were times when his window of remembrance opened upon a span less than six minutes wide. He couldn't bring back the plot of the vid he'd just seen, the last order he'd taken, the last song he'd played.

It was like his consciousness had decided the past tense didn't count anymore, that the past was past, outdated, an obsolete model. The present tense was the razzed one, always hovering as it did on the cutting-edge of the future-perfect. It was as if the rest of his organs had gotten together and, like those ancient Egyptian doctors during mummification rituals, just couldn't figure out precisely what the brain was for and so threw it away.

He jerked awake.

It took him a while to understand he'd been sliding along the glassy edge of sleep, relaxing his grip on one dimension and skating warmly toward another.

Mondo was still sitting across from him, picking his ear in yellow lamplight and examining photos of starving naked-breasted African women in a dilapidated *National Geographic* which he held sideways and at arm's length as though it was a *Hustler* with a sexy centerfold. Through the window the sky purpled with twilight. A low clinging fog had replaced the rain. Craggy gray-green mountains jagged from the undulating barren moors. And an incandescence welled into view: the train was slowing down, pulling into a station at the outskirts of a tiny coastal town.

Mondo unlatched the door before they'd come to a complete stop and hopped down. Ben followed him—past the ticket booth, through the waiting room with a wooden bench and portable gas stove in it, and onto a brief main street curving along a tarry bay chipped with whitecaps.

The scent of burning coal bittered the cool salty evening. Ben took a deep breath, the air soothing his scorched lungs. He noticed sores had blistered around his nostrils: they'd show up on his tongue before long.

Gulls perched on telephone wires, circled lazily over the water. Stark whitewashed houses and shops with slate roofs lined the landward side of the cobblestone road. On the seaward side extended a cement barrier, a two-meter drop, then a pebbly beach where the deserted remains of the original pre-melt village used to be. Mossy weeds, rock pools, olive and yellow bladderwrack, the glint of medical waste, and eight or ten red-on-white NO SWIMMING signs were scattered among caved-in walls and empty foundations.

Initially Ben was surprised there were no boats. Then he spied the scaffolding of several oil platforms towering out of the Minch four or five kilometers off shore. Around them winked strings of red and yellow lights warning ships away from an area where oil-eating bacteria had gotten out of control after a spill and emptied the wells.

Nearer sloped the outline of a rough desolate island maybe a kilometer in length.

Up the beach two- or three-hundred meters among the remains Ben could just make out a military assault hovercraft. It was toward this that Mondo steered him. As they approached, floodlights snapped on. Machine guns in the turret above the cockpit rotated in their direction. Mondo kept ambling, raising his fat arms over his fat head in the glare, crossing and uncrossing them while he went. The turbos whirled to life and the chain-mesh skirt around the base of the hovercraft began to inflate. Ben deciphered the words HMS STANLEY stenciled in white below the narrow porthole.

The hatch near the cockpit swung in and a chain-link ladder dropped and Mondo took hold of it.

"Up you go, mate," he shouted. "Watch the feet."

Ben climbed. The hovercraft vibrated so heavily he had to grip the rungs tightly to keep his balance.

Then it struck him Mondo wasn't bringing up the rear. He looked over his shoulder and caught sight of the henchman's massive form retracing its steps across the beach, almost lost beyond the perimeter of the floodlights. Ben thought briefly about hustling down and pursuing, but someone in the hatchway was already waving at him, reaching out to help boost him up.

At first Ben took the guy to be an aged dwarf in a black three-piece suit, just over a meter tall, hair short-cropped gray, rimpled facial skin the color of clay, eyebrowless eyes bulbous and pink, thin-membraned bat-wing ears the size of someone's palms. But there was also something very undwarfish about him. His limbs, torso, and head were all in proportion, for one thing. His legs didn't have that bowlegged jointless appearance Ben associated with the Epidemics midgets he'd seen walking the streets of Spocoeur. His right hand, which he extended as Ben stepped aboard, had long soft fingers.

"I trust your trip was as painless as such things can be, Mr. Tendo," he said. His voice had a diminutive squeak to it. He smiled and added: "Progeria." It sounded like an explanation, not a name, and it crossed Ben's mind he was staring. "Not to worry," the little man said, moving around him to draw up the ladder. "Happens all the time. You get used to it, really."

He soon became winded with the strain and bent from the waist, hands on knees, catching his breath. Then he looked up.

"Lazar. Lazar Peewee Zorilla. Delighted to meet you. You're bang on time."

He sealed the hatch and ushered Ben through a hot congested engine room into a bare two-by-three-meter cabin aft where the swaddies would have sat during an amphibious assault. The bench running along the walls and the walls themselves were made of reinforced steel plates. In the ceiling were two small air-filtration ducts, a line of biolight strips, and a speaker which sissed with static.

"Belt up," a voice on it said.

Ben sensed the hovercraft beginning to crawl across the beach and sat unsteadily. Lazar strapped him into an uncomfortable harness and took a seat next to him.

As he strapped himself in, he said: "Premature aging."

It was hard for Ben to turn his head in the harness which in part acted as a neck and spinal brace.

"What?"

"Progeria. Premature aging. You're wondering. It occurs quite frequently in this vicinity, particularly among our team. Take a guess. How old am I? I shan't be offended."

Ben thought for a second.

"I'm blank," he said.

"Go on."

" . . . . "

"Take a shot."

"What, sixty?"

He was trying to be generous by a decade or two.

"Close," Lazar said. "Nine, actually." He chuckled. "Oh, my, how time flies. For me more than for some, of course. Every month I live a year. It's like doggie lives, isn't it? But I'm quick for my age."

The hovercraft struck those choppy waves Ben had seen and it rose slowly, then smacked down, bucking. The engines jerked. Ben's saliva thickened. He had the image of his stomach sloshing among his lungs and intestines.

Seeing his discomfort, Lazar reached over and patted his leg.

"Won't be a minute," he said.

"How far are we going?"

"You've been a sport in all this, you know. Don't think we won't take that into account. You noticed those oil platforms?"

"Sure."

"Before them was an island. In the dark it's sometimes hard to make out."

"Yeah. I saw it."

"Gruinard. Ring any bells?"

It did, but it took some time for that face on MTV to come back to Ben with its clicking nose stud, chain, and earring.

"Smallpox testing or something. During World War Two. Right?"

"Anthrax, actually. Very good."

"Part of the, what, MBR. MRB."

"MRE."

"Churchill's Microbiological Research Establishment. Jared Marîd was interviewing this guy on the news. Doctor, um, Doctor Something."

"I'm impressed."

"Only it's supposed to've been contaminated really bad."

The hovercraft picked up speed, turbos whining. Ben held on to the front of his harness for support.

"That's where we're going?"

"Yes, well. Afraid all that contamination rubbish is a bit of a joke, really."

"What sort of joke?"

"On the media, primarily. Quite amazing what one believes when it issues from the lips of a scientist."

" . . . ?"

"Chills, fever, dysentery, convulsions, sudden death, long-range infection, all that. A government official says it and what do people do? They take it for granted he's lying. A fairly obvious reaction, of course, given that he's usually lying. But put the same words in the hallowed mouth of a scientist, and you know what happens? People *take notes*. They write things down. The assumption being that scientists don't lie. Which is ever so helpful, when you need a good liar."

"You're saying that guy was working for you?"

"Oh no. But I imagine he's working for some people who are working for some people who are working for us. In a rather vague sort of way. Oh no: he was telling the truth. Which was, in this case, a lie. Though not from his perspective."

"You're saying he's working for a university? Which, at least in part, is working for—who? The government?"

Lazar pulled on his ear.

"You're being needlessly literal here, Mr. Tendo. Lines of influence aren't as clearly demarcated as they once were."

He cleared his throat, trying unsuccessfully to free the squeak. Ben noticed the incisions at the base of his skull where the biochips must have gone in.

"One-to-one correspondences just don't pass muster as in the ancient days of six o'clock this evening."

Ben tried a different tack.

"You said progeria occurs a lot around here, especially among 'our team.' What's 'our team' mean?"

"Power centers aren't very centered in the current geopolitical landscape. The idea of 'center' is getting rather tricky at this stage of the game."

"You don't know what 'our team' means?"

"What 'our team' means when *you* say 'our team' or what 'our team' means when *I* say 'our team'?"

"What 'our team' means when you say 'our team.'"

"It means different things at different times. We're in a fluid state."

"A fluid state?"

"In a manner of speaking. Yes."

The scream of the turbos dropped an octave as the hovercraft began decelerating.

"What did you mean by 'our team' when you used it in the sentence 'Progeria occurs a lot around here, especially among our team'?"

"Ah. Well. Right," Lazar said, looking up at the air-filtration ducts. He thought. "I don't remember."

"Any guesses?"

"I should imagine I meant the 'our team' that's been expecting you for some time. The 'our team' that's almost as happy as you that your travels are almost at an end. We've been looking quite forward to getting to work."

"Work?"

"In a sense. Yes."

"In what sense?"

"Several, actually. But primarily in the one that means 'you're almost home.'" He checked his watch. The hovercraft was back on land. "Let me share one more tidbit with you. The idea of coincidence?"

"Yeah?"

"You might think of it this way. You've just entered into a region of the planet that rather discourages the notion of serendipity."

"Scotland?"

"The global region," Lazar said, beginning to unfasten his harness and wiggle his way out. "The biospheric region. You've just moved from one time zone to another. This new time zone is rather, well, extensive."

"What's in the time zone I've just entered?"

"Oh, lots of things. Many people, for instance, who would very much like to meet you. Your future."

"Debarking," a voice on the speaker said.

Lazar stood and began to undo Ben's harness.

"The rest of your life," he said. "The way things will turn out."

"How will things turn out?"

"Well, it's rather hard to put it succinctly."

"Try."

"In a word?"

"In a word."

Lazar's pink eyes were fissured with red veins like over-fired pottery. He grinned.

"Viva Bonni Suicide, Mr. Tendo."

"Viva Bonni Suicide?"

"In a word. Yes," he said. "Viva Bonni Suicide."

Part Four

VIVA BONNI SUICIDE

15

Ben stepped out onto a dirt track and stopped while his eyes adjusted to the darkness. Lazar stood beside him, cracking his knuckles and waiting. The hovercraft, running dark, revved its turbos and began creeping backward toward the water like a huge mechanical crab.

"You ready?" Lazar asked after a minute or two.

The landscape took on a pearly fluorescence under the sky distended with clouds. Boulders, patches of scree, and thick chunks of long silver wind-blown grass spotted the island. There were no trees and most of the scraggy bushes were less than half a meter tall.

"I guess so."

"Right, then. Let's go."

They began to walk. Ben heard a high-pitched hum, like a shopping mall's security system. He snuck a peek at Lazar, from whom the sound seemed to emanate, and squinting saw him fidget with a malfunctioning hearing-aid in his left ear.

A white sign with red lettering cropped up announcing MOD RANGE. DANGER! Just past this began to appear the remains of sheep bones curling from the undergrowth. Tufts of dirty wool clumped near stones, trembling in the breeze. Skulls were often still intact, mummified skin crinkled across parts of decaying snouts and gathered around eye sockets.

The two passed a battered, weather-beaten sign that read GOVERNMENT PROPERTY. KEEP OFF! and another several meters farther on that said CONTAMINATED AREA. BIOHAZARD. PROCEED AT YOUR OWN RISK. Other signs were printed in Russian, French, and Gaelic. But there were no guards, no barriers of any kind.

"Where's all the security?" Ben asked.

"Oh," Lazar said, short of breath, "it's all around us. You're looking at it, actually. The bones. The signs. Sometimes less is more."

"Yeah, but there's nothing like stopping someone from just taking a boat out here and having a picnic or something."

Lazar boosted himself onto a boulder wedged into a narrow cleft, helped Ben up, and hopped down the other side. He tugged the sleeves of his suit and straightened his tie, then noticed the wet circles on the knees of his pants.

"Blast," he said. "Cripes. Nothing to be done, I suppose. Bloody rocks. Security? Right. The media stops would-be tourists. The media's our security system. No one would dream of picnicking on a well-known chemical warfare test site, would they?"

They crested a hill and Ben saw the ruins of a small stone cottage. Its roof had caved in, as had two of its walls. The only structure remaining in one piece was the chimney. The cottage sat within a rocky field of minuscule white flowers surrounded by the remnants of a stone fence. Behind the fence rose another hill which blocked the view of this area from the mainland. It struck him the island was much bigger than he'd at first thought. Inside the ruins they had to step over slabs of slate and rotten charred beams to reach the chimney. A rusted nineteenth-century plow was turned upside down in a corner. Wrist-thick vines grew toward the diffuse moonlight. Behind an upended table, a meter-wide steel cap was set into the cement floor.

Lazar kneeled, felt along the wall, and pressed one of the smooth stones nearby. Hydraulics creaked, a latch snapped, and the cap rose sluggishly. Beneath it gaped a solid black hole.

"Incredible," Ben said.

"We've learned everything we know from B-movies. All those intrigue jobs. Except, of course, how to keep these bloody things well-oiled. After you, Mr. Tendo."

"I can't see."

"Lower yourself slowly."

"Where?"

"Half a meter in you'll find the upper rung of a ladder. Hold on tight. It's a long drop."

That's when Ben heard the scrapes and slurping noises behind them. He turned. Four tekked Doberman-tiger chimeras had entered the ruins, eyes replaced with glowing infrared camcorders, sensors down their backbones, lips curled in snarls though no sound issued forth.

"*Shit*," Ben said, instinctively lowering himself onto his haunches.

Lazar remained unfazed. He matter-of-factly poked his hand inside his suit coat and pressed something on his belt. The chimeras dispersed instantly.

"Laryngectomies," he explained.

"No noise."

"Their claws are removed as well. You never see them before they see you. Their sensors are jacked into the monitors below. They've probably been trailing us since we landed."

"Jesus."

"Yes. Well. That you're worrying is a good sign."

"What do you mean?"

"I mean they weren't taking us very seriously, were they? Had they been, we shouldn't be discussing the matter at the moment." He inhaled and exhaled, hearing-aid squealing. "Right. Well. Down you go now."

The cap skreaked closed and it was pitch dark. Though Ben knew Lazar was descending somewhere above him, he couldn't see a thing. Before long claustrophobia began to nuzzle in.

The well seemed a kilometer deep.

Two.

He heard his own labored breathing, his heart muscle whomping inside his chest. His lungs started burning again and he fought the urge to cough.

Halting, he stuck out his arm behind him. There was nothing there. No wall. No ledge. Nothing.

So he continued, concentrating intensely on each rung.

His sense of time unhinged. He couldn't tell whether he'd been at this one minute or ten, ten minutes or an hour, an hour or a day. He tried finding solace in familiar images. He pictured Mitzy back in Beautiful Mutants, sitting at her Sanyo monitor, decked out like Dale Evans in her bluejean blouse and rattlesnake-clone boots, prognosticating hypertrichial cataclysm for Dobie.

But Uriah's image kept sailing up at him, lying there in his hospital bed, Andrea in the chair beside him, Helmer pacing the floor as those expressionless suits looked on.

Next came Joey Taboo's face blooming on that screen, light pouring out of his eyes and mouth.

He stooped beside Lazar in a small concrete chamber lit with a single bluish biolight strip and pushed his glasses up on his nose. In one wall was a heavy smooth iron door next to which was a black glass square the size of a note pad.

"Step up to the analyzer," Lazar said, "and place your right palm on it. You'll feel a little tingle."

Ben did as he was told.

"It's taking information from your hand." Something bleeped. "Right. Now step back."

Lazar approached and went through the same process.

After another beep the iron door retracted revealing a resplendent corridor whose glare hit Ben like a magnesium bomb's explosion. It seemed as if the walls themselves were the source of illumination.

"Welcome to The Hole," Lazar said, stepping through. "This is where it all happens."

"All what happens?" Ben asked, following.

"The whole show. Hook, line, and sinker, as you Americans say. Come on. Let me show you some things."

They came to a red panel-door which hissed open as they neared. They walked through into a jumble of activity, people wheeling carts, jogging by, strolling in twos and threes, talking, arguing, laughing, some dressed in labcoats and jeans, some in sleeveless gray flightsuits like Emma and Mary, some in plaid robes pushing IVs before them. A few had on copies of Lazar's clothes, others Mylex uniforms. A trace of chlorine and formaldehyde tarted the processed atmosphere.

A sexy female computer voice was reading announcements over the intercom. "Doctor Bakker please report to level six," it said. "Doctor Ma'at to level four, please. Shift seven will begin in one hour. Shift seven in one hour."

"It's like a hospital," Ben said.

"It is, in a manner of speaking."

"How could you pull all this off without people on the mainland noticing? They had to see the construction work going on, start asking questions."

They passed several rooms busy with computer consoles. People in headgear, rapt with concentration, were working there.

It reminded Ben of his old job.

"Good things take time. You remember those oil wells?"

"Yeah."

"We started years ago. Decades. Set up the front company. Got the permits. Built the drilling rigs. Ran the wells long enough for everything to appear legit. Then, of course, manipulated that spill. Released the experimental species of oil-eating bacteria engineered to mutate and run amok after several days. Shut down the wells"—he fiddled with his hearing-aid, trying to adjust the volume, unsuccessfully—"meanwhile following our real plans beneath the Minch, tunneling in from the platform, making the whole operation look like tankers taking on cargo, cleanup ships scouring the area, EPA monitors checking damage. We dumped our waste on the sea floor, where no one would be the wiser." He flicked the hearing-aid with his fingernail and it let go a knifing keen. He paid no attention. "The entrance on Gruinard was the last thing to go in. An emergency evacuation exit. We dug it from the bottom up."

"And the town we were in. Nobody there noticed the hovercraft we used or anything?"

"Oh, by now there are very few original inhabitants still living in Little Gruinard. Place's been almost completely rebuilt. And those remaining still believe the military is involved in biohazard recon out here. Nor do they think that's such a bad thing, given the fact we keep their economy going, in one way or another."

"But the credit to pull off something like that must have been—"

"Massive?"

"Yeah. Massive."

"It was." They passed a radiology lab where technicians were busy readying a frail man missing the back lobe of his skull for a CAT-SCAN. A luxurious gym with row upon row of lifecycles, VR helmets resting on seats. Six squash courts with plexiglas walls facing the corridor. "Although, from a certain perspective, you might think of us as moving into a post-credit environment." Through a doorway Ben caught a glimpse of an elderly woman inside an iron lung against which leaned a frilly pink parasol. "Credit, in the old sense, doesn't exactly carry its weight anymore where we're concerned."

"No credit?" Ben said, surprised.

"Don't get me wrong. The concept of credit still works on a limited scale, in limited situations. But when you step back far enough from the picture, begin to deal in large enough amounts, credit begins to lose its clout, becomes an unhelpful metaphor for what's actually going on, what's actually changing hands."

They entered a room bare except for a translucent examination cubicle, the size and shape of one of those antique British phone booths still used this far north, in the center.

"We're working with the knowledge metaphor here. With data, access to data systems, the *appearance* of credit can be generated. A kind of post-credit reality results. You don't buy with credit, a metaphor of material wealth. You buy with knowledge, a metaphor of post-technological wealth."

"Sounds like you're running a self-contained country here."

"Oh, no. I shouldn't want to think in such restrictive terms." He changed his tone. "Let's see. If my memory serves, you haven't had a checkup since your Diacomm days. Correct?"

"Yeah. I can't afford luxury items."

"*Couldn't*, Mr. Tendo. *Couldn't*. Past tense. Why don't you shed your clothes and step aboard? This won't take a minute. I'll be outside if you need me."

Lazar left and Ben entered the cubicle. The translucent door shut behind him. It was like standing inside a cloud. He stripped, put his clothes in the clear plastic box at his feet, and that sexy computer voice returned.

"You are currently undergoing a routine physical examination," it said. "Please remain stationary."

A sliver of intense blue-green light shot from the ceiling and sizzled across his head. He felt a slight sensation of heat and closed his eyes and tried not to move.

"Please remove your glasses."

Ben removed his glasses.

The light tracked across his face and then trailed down his neck, shoulders, chest.

"Please answer yes or no to the following questions. To the best of your knowledge, do you possess any physical disabilities?"

"No."

"To the best of your knowledge, have you come into direct contact with an Epidemics carrier in the last twelve months?"

"No."

"Have you acquired an Epidemics blood test in the last six months?"

"No."

"Have you acquired a Government Vaccination Booster-Shot Series within the last two years?"

"No."

"To the best of your knowledge, did you acquire Primary Government Vaccination Shots as a child?"

"Yes."

The blue-green light twitched out.

"Please step up to the wall and insert your right bicep into the aluminum clamp."

It tightened like a blood-pressure unit and a volley of pinpricks flittered beneath it. An immediate liquid warmth suffused his muscles.

Next, a violet mist filled the cubicle and a strobe began pulsating.

"Please inhale," the computer said. "Good. Hold. Release."

A fan sucked the violet mist from the air in less than two seconds. The strobe ceased.

"To the best of your knowledge, are you aware of any genetic abnormalities in your family's history?"

"No."

"To the best of your knowledge, are you aware of any psychiatric abnormalities in your family's history?"

"No."

"Thank you for your time. Please watch your step as you exit."

Ben slipped on his glasses and dressed. The door opened.

"Looks like you're in fine health," Lazar said when Ben emerged. "Except for a case of mild nearsightedness and the pollution sores, you're in top shape."

"I was in Soho without a mask."

"Oh, right, *that* business," Lazar said, waving it away as they began walking again. "Well, you've been given a shot of antibiotics, among other things, and the air in The Hole is clean. You should be fit as a fiddle by the end of the week."

They entered an elevator that dropped them six more levels—two, Lazar said, where research was conducted, one for banking, two for hydroponic farming, water desalinization, and purification, and one for living quarters. Below them, Ben no-

133

ticed, there still remained twelve more.

"Do you know much about addictions, Mr. Tendo?" Lazar asked as they came to a halt.

"I don't. No."

"Good." The door shooshed open. "You're about to learn something, then."

A gum-chewing V-shaped black man in a shocking pink silk zoot suit met them. His left nostril was slit to the tear duct, divulging salmon-colored membrane, and he wore peroxide-blond eyebrows and a peroxide-blond mohawk.

"Marco," Lazar said. "So good to see you."

"You as well, mon," he said, bowing slightly from the waist. "You as well. How you gettin' on dese days?" Then he glanced over at Ben and a wide chameleon-smile broke across his face. "And dis must be de famous Mr. Ben Tendo, eh?" he said, extending his hand.

"The man himself," said Lazar. Then to Ben: "I'd like you to meet Marco Polydor."

Marco's sharp fingernails glisked in the artificial light.

"*Marco Polydor?*" Ben said

"Excellent to finally meet you, Ben mon. I want you to know straight away how much I admire your work. Your sweet spots are white lightnin'."

"As in the Marco Polydor of Air Pyrate Muzzik?"

Marco's white eyebrows arched.

"You heard of us, den?"

"Who *hasn't* heard of you? You're the outfit who pretty much discovered like every major band in England, America, and Russia for the last ten years. Tricia's Nightmare, Flummox, Strange Angels, Beaver Head and the Chicken Pips, Mayday Mayday Mayday —"

"Don't forget Kama Quyntifonic and Dr. Teeth," Lazar said.

"And Kama Quyntifonic and Dr. Teeth. Yeah. *Everyone* in the industry's heard of you."

"I'm flattered. Flattered."

Then he jabbed out his purple tongue as if trying to snatch a mosquito birring two centimeters to the left of his split nose.

The corridor, this time pistachio, was much less active than the one they'd just come from. A series of security cameras on metal perches followed the progress of a stray lab technician speaking Spanish to a couple of teenagers in white body suits and bound feet.

"I was telling Mr. Tendo something about addiction," Lazar said as they began to amble.

"Wild subject," Marco said, clasping his hands behind his back.

Something in his gait reminded Ben of vids he'd seen of the elderly King, a certain stiffness in the spine, an inherent sense of elegance and dignity in the stride, both of which were underscored by Lazar's squat-legged padding.

"You see, Mr. Tendo," Lazar said, peering up at Ben, "each one of us holds the possibility of addiction within us. Although most would predictably deny it."

"Individual volition and all dat sort of ting, you know," said Marco.

"But all you have to do is dig down deep enough and, bang on, there it is."

"Just have to feel 'round for it. You'll find it."

They came to another door. Lazar stood on tiptoes and pressed his palm against the analyzer. The door whooshed open and they entered a tight plexiglas-walled observation deck.

Below them stretched a small lead-gray artificial pond. Around it, far as the eye could see, sprung a nineteenth-century English park with rich green trees, colorful shrubs and flowerbeds, mathematically trimmed lawns, elaborate rock grottoes, wrought-iron benches and lamps, a cement fountain, even an ornate white gazebo. Tiled paths led through covered walkways, by terraces, along streams fluttering with water lilies. Armless statues of athletes in togas dotted the landscape. Above it all arced a ceiling lighted to mimic a clean, clear, cornflower blue noonday sky.

"Most addictions are psychological in nature," Lazar said. "The familiar example being the fellow who continually employs a given chemical substance, but not *too* much of a given chemical substance, as a means of surviving various unpleasant situations. Candy, let's say. Red Devils."

"Which substance is usually thought fun to use," Marco said, "tank goodness for us."

"But then there are the physiological addictions."

"Which is where tings start gettin' int'restin'."

Exquisite birds bulleted among branches of counterfeit bayberry and spruce. Swallows. Larks. A yellowthroat.

On the pond, a naked teenage girl in a VR rig floated in a blueblack innertube, body tanned, breasts the size of small cupped palms, lower lip unnaturally puffy. She'd clearly had some plastics to make her nose appear broken at the bridge. The silver VR rig, no larger than wide-band mirrorshades, covered her eyes and ears, and a wire ran down from it to what looked like a Walkman balancing on her sternum. Her head was tilted back, almost touching the water, long chartreuse hair trailing like a swath of seaweed.

She was masturbating leisurely.

"The fellow in our example continues to employ a chemical substance as a means of surviving various unpleasant situations," Lazar said. "But as time goes on his body comes to tolerate greater and greater amounts of that substance. His cells start thinking for his brain, looking forward to the substance in a reflexive way."

"So our fellow, he need more and more of dis shit to attain de desired magic."

"And, if you take the substance away from him, his cells go on strike."

"Dey stage a mini-revolution."

"And physical withdrawal sets in."

"Which ting is awful to behold. Awful."

"A nasty business indeed."

Marco reached into his suit and pulled out another foiled stick of gum. Ephedra. He unwrapped it and lay it on his purple tongue which he slowly retracted. It soon became apparent he had some difficulty breathing through his split nostril. From time to time he stopped chewing and opened his mouth for extra oxygen.

"First," he explained, "de worst case of insomnia dat fellow ever know jumps him. Den come de tremors and de muscle spasms sneakin' up from behind when he ain't lookin'."

"A horrid feeling of free-floating anxiety sets in," Lazar continued, "followed by a physical and psychological sense of utter weakness."

"Which is paradise, Ben mon, compared to de nausea. Just paradise." He took a couple of smacks. "Makes dat fellow feel his intestines are boilin' wit' eight-hundred liters of molten steel."

"There's the sweating, too. The hypertension."

"De convulsions dat make dat fellow look like he be some kind of spastic's puppet."

"The confusion."

"De snakes-flyin'-out-your-eyes hallucinations dat make him want to flee to a convent 'n' start prayin' on his knees won't somebody just go ahead and shoot him in de brains and get it over wit'."

"And, of course, with *certain* chemical substances, a rather bad case of, well —"

"Mr. Death, mon."

"Right. Well. Mr. Death."

Lazar nodded in the direction of the gazebo. Inside, a pale thin shirtless man with lavender lips and a pudgy belly was shooting up, right arm tied off with a rubber hose. The needle caught the manufactured sunlight in white astonishment.

Next to him crouched a woman whose face was a raw sheen of acne. She wore a turquoise halter and frayed Levi cutoffs trimmed to accentuate the scarred muscle grafts on her biceps and thighs. The soft inner part of her right arm was splotched with thumbnail-sized plumish stains.

"The old paradigm believed almost exclusively in terms of *tangible* substances," Lazar said. He slicked back his short gray hair. His hearing-aid had quieted into a low whistle. "Substances externally introduced through syringes and bottles and pills and so forth. Pharmaceuticals, for instance. Inhalants."

"But de new paradigm, mon, it believes in dat and much, much more."

"With surgical procedures we've been researching here we've been able to produce a variety of biochemical alterations in the brain."

"Readjust a gland here, reorder a cluster of synapses dere."

"And the result has been the creation of a rather more— what's the word?"

"'Intangible'?"

"Quite. *Intangible* range of substance addictions. Our procedures can tease out various fears and desires in their biochemical forms."

Marco eyeballed Ben and between short gasps said: "Instead of addicting someone to heroin, mon, we can addict dem to de idea of hope. Or order." The chameleon-smile returned. "Or dat sense of well-being dat make everyting seem okay on a Sunday night when you're lyin' in dat nice warm bath."

"You name it. We can induce it."

"Cleanliness. Wholeness."

"Happiness. Joy."

"Or de inverse, mon. Dat fear of darkness you had as a child? We can bring dat out in your skull so bad dat dat poor fellow we're discussin' would break down walls and swim through fire to get away from it."

"Tap water."

"Spiders."

"Marriage."

"Afternoon moons."

Lazar nodded in the direction of the teenager in the VR gear. Now she was tugging her nipples between her thumbs and forefingers. Her head rolled from side to side.

"A case in point," he said. "You recognize her?"

"Uh-uh," Ben said.

"Dat be one Vida Venni. Hottest backup singer and lead guitarist 'round dese days. She heaven to hear. From de California club scene. Way down sout' where de surf is up and everyting's new beachfront property dese days, you know."

"You operated on her?" Ben asked.

"We operated on her." He cleared his sinuses. Ben realized it was Marco's version of a laugh. "She really nazi, eh?"

"Mega. Yeah."

"What you tink she be clickin' on, Ben mon?"

Ben ruminated.

"Porno. Some pretty heavy stuff, from the look of it. Someone at the Pentagon? Big Russian auto manufacturer?"

"News footage from de South American War."

" . . . ?"

"And not just de standard fare, neither. None of dat shit. Dis here is CIA footage. Classified images."

"Torture scenes, mostly," Lazar clarified.

"Hobblin'. Electrical nodes on de genitals. You know de kinda ting. She also partakin' of some first-rate bombin' runs. Napalm drops. Smart-bomb strikes. She love dat kinda shit. She really do. Mmmmm-hmmmm."

"She just can't get enough," Lazar said, scratching where his left eyebrow should have been.

"She *live* for violence, mon," said Marco. "She do *any*ting to see it. You want Vida climb Mount Everest? You give her a police vid on de gangs in Detroit. You want her play dat guitar of hers like a cosmic angel on God's very right hand? You give her a little someting on de death penalty. Easy, mon."

"Except that now we're reaching a little impasse on the VR angle," Lazar said.

"An impasse?" said Ben.

"Our researchers seem to be under the impression that the concept of the VR unit might be rapidly becoming rather dated for Ms. Venni."

"She don't want de real ting no more," Marco said.

"What does she want?"

"She wants the *real* thing."

"She be wantin' to move into *administration*, mon, if you know what I'm sayin'."

"And I shouldn't want to think what would happen if she wasn't able to get her way."

"And the two in the gazebo?" Ben said. "They're just regular drug addicts?"

"You'd tink so, wouldn't you?"

Marco pushed back his sleeve and consulted the time on his baroque gold Capri wristwatch with a carbon digital face.

"I suppose in a manner of speaking they are," said Lazar.

"In a manner of speakin'. But not in de ways you might imagine. See, you lookin' at Mikhail Bactine and Ferret Fawcett."

"He's one of the top percussionists in the Ukraine."

"She de primo bass player in New York. Great grand-daughter of dat comic guy."

"Bill Murray."

"Bill Murray. Yeah."

"You know the work on Hitler Fateh Habib's *Mlah Mlah*?"

"Sure," Ben said.

"Mikhail and Ferret's grooves," Marco said. "Razzin', mon. Pure razzin'."

"So if they're not drug addicts, what are they?"

"They're rather taken with the notion of sex," Lazar said.

"Not wit' each other, mon."

"No. Nor with themselves, really."

"Holoporns?" Ben guessed.

"Uh-uh. Dey be into someting far more powerful than dat, mon. Dey be into de chemical by-products of the process. Generous doses of de hormones produced just before and during orgasm. Very generous doses. *Very* generous, you see."

"*Unnaturally* generous doses." Lazar sounded quietly proud. "They'd kill for them, actually."

Marco opened and closed his mouth as if he were popping his ears.

"*Have* killed for dem," he said. "Actually."

"Oh, right. That."

He ran a palm over his white mohawk, remembering. It was a pleasant memory. "You see de guy in de bushes over dere?"

"Where?"

Marco pointed.

"Over dere, mon. Over dere."

Ben strained to make out the form huddling among shadows in a moist rock grotto covered with moss and ivy vines beside a meter-high waterfall. At the base elegant swans slid on a nickel brook through a stand of weeping willows whose plastic leaves shone under the cornflower blue ceiling. In the trees hung stereo speakers, though he couldn't hear what, if anything, was playing on them. Several cement cherubs hid among lady ferns down by the bank.

"Kwasi Elroy Modem," Lazar said. "Cutting-edge keyboardist from Tokyo. Used to play in the Gluons."

"*Heat Death of the Universe*," said Ben.

"*Heat Death of the Universe*. Right. But the Gluons have had their fair share of trouble, financial and otherwise. As have Hitler Fateh Habib and Ms. Venni's band, Synaptic Stigmata. All of which are currently JTed. Sad to say."

"Terrible ting."

"Absolutely. Anyway, we've had a bit of a problem with Kwasi's dosage."

Ben didn't ask.

"He suffers from severe anthophobia."

"Fear of flowers, mon."

"Which, in his specific case, somewhat extends to trees and grass. Natural and unnatural. And shrubbery. Even high pollen counts can set him off."

"But what with all that stuff you told me," Ben said, "you could operate to take away his fear, right?"

Another sinus clearing.

"You a jack a minute, mon," Marco responded. He stepped

closer to Ben and lay a hand on his shoulder like an old friend, then stage-whispered: "We operated to *generate* de fear, mon. To *generate* it."

"His addiction is to the antedote," Lazar explained.

"Ting is, our researchers are still experimentin' wit' de right dosage to keep him happy. Another week or two, and he be jammin' wit' de best of dem, you see."

"He's just having a rather bad day," Lazar said.

"Which is lastin' maybe a mont'," Marco added.

They all drifted into silence for several minutes while they contemplated Kwasi, Mikhail, Ferret, and Vida. Then the sexy-voiced computer came on and announced dinner was now being served.

"We took the liberty of putting together a little something for you," Lazar said. "Some local dishes. I think you'll like them. You must be famished after your journey."

They turned to leave and Marco asked: "So what you tink, mon?"

"About what?"

"About de band."

"They're good," Ben said. "I'm impressed. You got some amazing talent working for you there."

Marco grinned.

"Dey ain't workin' for me, mon. Dey workin' for you."

"Me?"

"Been yours for months."

"Everything's in its place now, Mr. Tendo. Everything's ready to go."

"What do you mean 'everything'?" asked Ben.

Lazar spun on his heels and gestured down the corridor.

"Shall we?" he said. "I'm afraid our meal's getting cold."

16

L et me ask you someting," Marco said as he passed Ben a bowl of peas and then leaned back in his chair at the head of the table. "How many notes and half-notes you got in your musical octave, eh?"

Farther down the corridor had been another door behind which was the replica of what 1930s Hollywood might think a medieval banquet hall should look like. A seven-meter-long bare oak table, chipped and dented, stretched the length of the damp room whose walls were fashioned from large, smooth, uneven stones slick with moisture. Seven carved oak chairs with tall straight backs and elaborate headrests ran up each side, and another perched at either end. At intervals along its surface burned thick white candles whose light tinseled upon a busy silver constellation of cutlery, chalices, saucers, mugs, plates, pitchers, cutting boards, and gravy boats that were constantly refilled by a troop of male and female progeric dwarfs dressed like court jesters.

In the cavernous fireplace blue-orange gas flames belly-danced among three cement logs dimly illuminating suits of armor propped in the shadows, a mace, a double-headed ax, a fan of spears, and a dark tapestry which, when he studied it closely, Ben realized didn't depict a mythological scene as he'd assumed, but the diagram of the double-stranded helix configuration of DNA.

"Eight full," Ben answered, scooping a spoonful of the peas onto his plate. "Five half." He reached for his mug of lager, the taste of which he was starting to get into, and drank. "Why?"

Marco slipped a chunk of lamb into his mouth. His lower eyelids glissaded up.

"On de button, mon," he said. "On de button." He wiped his

greasy lips with the back of his hand, wiped his greasy hand on the lace napkin balled on the table next to his plate. "Now let me ask you someting 'bout dem notes. How many combinations you tink you can make wit' dem?"

"I don't know. Lots."

"Yeah, mon. Lots. What you tink, Vida?" he asked, turning toward the guitarist. "Big number? Small number? What?"

Vida, apparently, didn't think much of anything. Now clothed in a navy blue and white silk kimono, she sat extremely erect in her seat, palms flat on the table, full-bodied chartreuse hair overflowing her shoulders, still wearing her metallic VR rig, riveted by wild shots from another universe. Her plate remained empty.

Marco shifted his gaze down to Ferret and Mikhail who occupied the chairs next to her. Bloodless and silent, they sluggishly stirred their food. Portable drug dispensers with plastic tubes leading to their arms were strapped to their belts. They pressed the release mechanisms every few seconds.

Marco sighed and asked the former Gluon keyboardist: "How 'bout you, Kwasi mon?" he asked. "What you tink?"

Kwasi didn't look up either, but it wasn't because he was out of tune with his surroundings. In fact, he was very much *in tune* with them. With his *immediate* surroundings, that is. Currently free of flowers, he was scoffing away like nobody's business at a plate stacked with lamb, mashed potatoes, stewed carrots, a cluster of grapes, a slab of buttered bread, some kind of whitish sauce, and a salad of fresh iceberg lettuce and red onions drenched with gluey pink thousand island dressing. Clots of the sauce, the dressing, and the stewed carrots clung to various parts of his greenish sunscreened face, maroon hair pigtailing out the sides of his otherwise shaved head, and front of his red t-shirt reading in metallic gold letters PHARMACOLOGICALLY YOURS, the name of his favorite hypertext, a subculture best-seller which dealt with, among other things, a chemist addicted to the sperm of mutant eels called Muglas which he injected directly into his brain through his eyeballs.

"Mr. Modem," said Lazar, propped atop three encyclopedias at the opposite end of the table, "Mr. Polydor just asked you a question."

Kwasi munched away for the count of five, wet sticky sounds issuing from his gullet, then spoke without raising his head.

"Big number," he said.

He nabbed the gravy boat and doused his fruit as well as his meat with brownish-yellow liquid and dove in again.

Lazar stared at him and blinked.

"Well," he said. "We're certainly not ribald conversationalists this evening, are we?"

He looked around for something else to comment upon and noticed one of the jesters replenishing Ben's supply of vegetables.

"Part of our research efforts," he said.

"Hydroponic gardening?" asked Ben, forking a lettuce leaf.

"The potatoes, yes. The grapes. The lettuce and onions were grown on the surface, on another of our islands several kilometers northwest of here."

"You grow your vegetables in the middle of the ocean?"

"New strains we're manufacturing that are resistant to adverse conditions. Yes. Not just natural pests and so forth, but also environmental pollutants—acid rain, high concentrations of carbon dioxide, sea salt. The lamb comes from a private farm on the mainland."

"I've never had real meat before. It's great."

"Very British, you know. The pursuit of fat and cholesterol is our national pastime. For those who can afford it. Second only to our disregard for dental hygiene. But the general public would be disappointed. This stock has been bred to be as healthy for you as a farm-shrimp burger."

A female jester, skin the rumpled surface of cold cream-of-mushroom soup, rose on tip-toes next to Ben, waiting for him to lower his mug so she could refill it. She wore a green fool's cap with bells on it and colorful harlequin tights and blouse. Her cod piece was made from transparent plastic, disclosing her bald withered Mons. Ben put his hand over his mug.

"No thanks," he said, "I'm fine."

She looked at him dully and then cocked her head to one side. Her eyes were coral-pink.

"She can't hear you," Lazar said. "None of them can. They're deaf. Children in Edinburgh when neo-meningitis hit. Even worse off than me, I'm afraid. Can't speak either. Never learned how."

His laugh sounded like a dolphin in distress. He signed to the female jester who shook her head and moved to Marco.

"And the carrots?" asked Ben.

"Ain't no carrots," Marco said, watching the jester pour.

"No?"

"Just look dat way."

"Product of tissue cultures that reproduce the taste and vitamins of carrots. The natural color, which in fact is unnatural, has been added. Same with the butter."

"And this?" Ben asked, touching his fork to the white sauce.

Kwasi unleashed an ox-belch that brought the discussion up short. Everyone stopped talking and eating till it became clear another wasn't imminent, then Lazar continued.

"Mixture of SCPs," he said. "Single-cell proteins. We convert methane gas, which has no protein content, into biomass full of protein. We mix it with a fungus fed on cheap sterilized glucose syrup. The fungus, which grows as a fibrous mat, can then be processed into material which inexpensively duplicates the textures of other products. White pudding, in this case. Bread. Thousand island dressing. Gravy. All you need are some flavor enhancers and you're ready to go."

Ben inspected the white goo spreading on his plate, shiny mole-gray clots floating in it.

"It isn't real, then?" he asked.

"Well, that depends on your notion of reality," said Lazar.

"It be real in de sense dat fungus and methane are real."

"And it's certainly real in the sense that it tastes, feels, and smells like what it looks like."

"And it be real in de sense dat it be *real* profitable."

"You see, we've begun marketing it, in addition to the biotechnology that produced the carrot tissue cultures, to Japan and the United States of Africa, both of whom, as you know, have had some difficulties keeping food production on par with the pace of population —"

Lazar caught Marco's eye and halted in mid-sentence.

"Good lord," he said. "Where *are* my manners? You'll have to forgive me. I love all these biotech affairs. Really love them. Amazing business. Could talk about them for hours. Do go on, Marco. Please."

Marco reached for the loaf of bread and yanked off a fistful.

"I was just sayin'," he began with a full mouth, "I wonder how many mixtures you tink you can make wit' dem notes, Ben mon. And you was sayin' lots and lots."

"Yeah," Ben said. "A real lot."

"Now let me ask you someting else. How many of dem mixtures you tink is goin' to be worth listenin' to, eh?"

145

"I'm not sure I follow you."

"Okay. Tink of it dis way. You got all dese notes to pick from, yes?"

"Yeah."

"And you got all dese *mixtures* of notes to pick from."

"Right."

"Okay. But a whole bunch of dem mixtures is just goin' to be fingers-on-chalkboards to your ears, ain't dey? Ain't goin' to add up to nothin' but noise. Ain't goin' to have no pattern, no rhythm, no harmonics. Right?"

"I guess so." Ben reflected. "Sure."

The door breathed open and several jesters wheeled a low wide cart in front of the fireplace. They hoisted the wooden box comprising the body of the cart onto the floor. Next they unsnapped a lock and unfolded the box so it formed what looked like some kind of game board crisscrossed with numbers. Then they began setting up a low mesh fence around it.

"Okay," Marco said, observing the construction. "So what you're sayin' is dat lots of dem sounds basically ain't goin' to count in our algebra, are dey?"

"Right."

He took another bite of bread.

"So what *dat* mean?"

Without lowering her head or removing her VR rig, Vida reached down and changed cartridges, fingers agile as those of a blind man. She kept a supply of disks in the ammo belt around the waist of her kimono.

"I guess it means there're only so many songs you can write," Ben said, startled by his own discovery. "An incredibly large number, yeah, but not an infinite one."

"Bingo, mon. A *finite number.*"

When the flustered cackle of chickens arose in the corridor, Ferret and Mikhail exchanged looks and Mikhail asked if they could be excused in order to take an evening walk through the park before going to bed. After conferring with Marco, Lazar nodded his assent.

After they'd gone Kwasi asked if there was going to be any dessert. Marco signed to the jester with the transparent codpiece and she disappeared and reappeared with a topless male jester balancing a platter fanned with marzipan-substitutes shaped like four-centimeter versions of computer parts, a telephone modem, an old-time memory tube, laser printers, VDTs, all the same watery blue as plastic ice packs used on swellings.

Kwasi cupped two handfuls and began jabbing the pieces into his mouth till his cheeks distended like a Japanese squirrel's. Momentarily content, he passed the skimpy remains along to Ben, who helped himself to a miniature keyboard and antique floppy disk.

"Den you got yourself another complication," Marco continued, "if you be a rocker."

Ben nibbled at the keyboard, considering. The taste of almond paste rilled across his tongue, stinging his pollution sores.

"You do?"

"Most surely. Lots of dem songs you might be tinkin' of writin', dey ain't goin' to be rock songs. Different rhythms. Different arrangements. Different expectations for you and your listener. You got your Beethovens, your Manellis." He nipped a laptop in half. "You got all dem songs dat *ain't* rock songs. Noh Wave. Country-Shroom. Leisure-prop. You name it. All dose tings dat ain't what you been meanin' to do." He stuck his pinkie between his lower front teeth and freed a cusp of aqua mush. "See, you got yourself dis fence. Barbed-wire fence. Kinda rusty but okay. And you got yourself dis herd of sheep. Mangy bastards, you know. Barely wort' de feed you buy to keep dem alive. Stupid too. Always leanin' 'gainst dat fence, always wantin' to wander off, though you bet your ass dey don't know why or where dey go if you let dem. Your job, you got to keep dem in de fence. Elsewise dey go and join somebody else's herd. And den, you know, you lose everyting."

Two male jesters with unnaturally large flesh-toned dildos strapped to their crotches entered. Each carried a cage inside of which flapped an indignant chicken.

Other jesters began collecting empty dishes and withdrawing from the hall.

"And you should keep in mind that your herd, Mr. Tendo, is nearly a century old," Lazar said. "No one ever dreamed it would last so long. If you take a moment and go over and look, however, you'll find your sheep are all rotten in the teeth. Hides balding, hooves turning into pulp."

"Rock becomin' an old geezer wit' a bad prostate."

"Which isn't necessarily a liability for us."

"Means we can *recycle* a certain amount of material. Borrow a chord progression here, a certain texture dere, maybe even a couple notes when you ain't lookin', and nobody be de wiser."

"Audiences don't have the attention spans they once did."

"Audiences can't remember what color dere *shoes* be wit'out lookin'."

The two jesters set their cages beside the game board. In a hurricane of feathers and flabbergasted squawks, the one on the left freed his chicken.

"You ever hear of chicken droppin'?" Marco asked.

"No," Ben said.

"You in for a treat, den. Little bettin' game, speciality of my homeland."

The jester turned his chicken toward him and tucked its head under his arm. His cohort withdrew a foot-long straw from his belt, lifted the chicken's bottom, and, after some prodding, inserted the tip of the straw into its anus, puffed gently, then withdrew it. The first jester quickly set the chicken down on the board.

"Sixteen," Marco called.

"Seven," called Lazar.

Kwasi, mouth full, called four.

The chicken stood dazed for several seconds, then began dashing wildly back and forth, chattering.

"You can only recycle so many patterns so many times before they start feeling, well, *recycled*," Lazar said as he looked on.

"See, only got yourself x amount of combinations. Only got yourself x amount of time. After dat, got yourself nuttin' but declinin' returns." He reached into his pocket for his pack of Ephedra and began to peel a stick. "Elvis done *done* his ting. Beatles, David Bowie, and Morph Allah G too. All de good seats, dey already taken. Piece of gum, Ben mon?"

"No thanks."

The chicken halted abruptly in the square marked six, ruffled its feathers, and defecated a pile of molten greenish glop.

"Hah!" cried Lazar.

"Close, mon, close," Marco said, snorting and clapping his hands.

The jester plucked up his chicken and crammed it back into its cage while his cohort released his.

"Imagine thousands of musicians, tens of thousands, all over the planet, writing thousands and thousands of songs every hour, every day, every week, every month, for a hundred years," Lazar said. "That's three hundred sixty five days each year, roughly eight thousand seven hundred and sixty hours. Nearly nine-hundred thousand in a decade."

"Pretty soon you goin' to get dis eerie-cold feelin' slinkin' up and down your spine like a bad dream dat everyting's beginnin' to sound de same."

"Which won't be half as alarming as the realization that everything *is* beginning to sound the same. Musicians are running out of things to write about and running out of ways to write about them."

"Simple matter of numbers. Bein' at de wrong place at de wrong time, from a historical perspective."

The process with the chickens was repeated. On each occasion, the chicken, after a crazed waltz and operetta, shat on an unpicked square and was lifted and shoved back into its cage. After the fifth round, Lazar detonated his knuckles in irritation and Marco announced: "Enough, mon, enough. De luck don't seem wit' us tonight."

The dwarves quickly scooped up their cages and left. Five more jesters appeared, took down the board, and wheeled it away while a progeric in a wizard's costume showed up and began juggling three silver balls beside Marco.

"No matter what you do, Ben mon, no matter where you go, you can always hear Laurie Anderson and Zazz Smythe and all dem other ghosts clankin' dere chains behind you," Marco said. The balls multiplied and became skulls, musical notes, miniature naked men and women. Ben figured the wizard was working a holounit beneath his robe. "Whisperin' in your ears how it's gettin' bad, *real* bad, how you can run tryin' to keep ahead of de pack, but no matter what you do it's goin' to get harder and harder to dredge up someting outta dat backbrain of yours dat people will notice for a week maybe, maybe if you lucky even hum a couple bars of while you worry 'bout how many *other* talented musicians out dere, how few companies launchin' dem, how much pressure on dose few bands dey *is* launchin' to succeed financially, how dere is only one ting harder to do dan bring out a first album, and dat's bring out a second album, and only one ting harder dan dat, and dat's to bring out de next."

The diminutive silver men and women began copulating in involved oriental positions as they circled above the wizard's head. Lazar climbed down from his chair and pattered off into the shadows, returning with a crystal decanter with chestnut liquid and three glasses on a silver tray. Marco's face relaxed with pleasure when he saw it. He leaned back in his seat like a huge rubber doll in the process of deflating, plucked his gum from his mouth, and thumbed it under the table.

"So as a musician these days you can't write," Lazar said, setting down the tray next to Ben and opening the decanter.

"And you can't write 'bout not bein' able to write," said Marco.

"And, of course, you can't *not* write, given your constitution. Some amaretto liqueur? Sweet afterdinner drink, in this case enhanced with a mild sedative that will help you sleep."

Ben held up his hand to signal no and said: "So tell me. What are you supposed to do?"

"You sure? It's extremely high quality."

"I'm fine. Really."

"Marco?"

"Just a bit. Please."

Kwasi perked up.

"I'd *love* some, man," he said.

"I'm sure you would," Lazar said, "but I'm afraid it's time for you to call it an evening. You've had a long day."

"I'm wide awake. I feel great."

Lazar and Marco regarded each other.

"Ten minutes" the former said at last. "No more. And no liqueur. Extra drugs could give us false readings in the morning."

"But how come —"

"Agreed?"

Kwasi hesitated, calculating. He looked at Lazar. He looked at Marco. He looked at Vida sitting straight-backed and unmoving as a mannequin in mirrorshades. And then he huffed.

"Agreed."

"Fine."

Lazar faced Ben. Nearby the silver skin began peeling from the pixies till they became skeletons performing fellatio, cunnilingus, and sodomy among themselves.

"Well. Not that we've actually *reached* this state of full creative entropy yet," Lazar said. "Not today at any rate. Most likely not tomorrow, either."

Marco sampled his liqueur. The scent of alcohol broadcast through the hall.

"But soon, mon. Soon. *Dat's* de ting you got to understand. Sure as a cat slinkin' up on a mouse before de pounce, it be on its way."

Ben had never even *thought* about thinking of music this way till now, especially not about *his own* music. It had never even *occurred* to him that through a different pair of glasses you could see time and choices chugging away like a tank of gasoline in an old Caddy. It gave him the jimjams.

"So what do you *do*?" he asked.

"What indeed, Ben mon," Marco said.

"That's the big question," said Lazar. "And it's a question that's been on the minds of music executives for quite some time."

"Scenario goes like dis: no new music means no new albums."

"No new albums means no new vids."

"And no new vids means no new anything—concerts, advertisin' revenues, playin' cards, holographic photos, songbooks, posters, keychains, mugs, pseudo-bootlegs, doll spinoffs, buttons, t-shirts, pens, plates, erasers, bumperstickers, clothin' lines, technologies, you name it."

"And that, in a word, means the collapse of an industry," Lazar said.

"Collapse of an entire *economy*, an entire *culture* so vast and once so *powerful* it make your head spin like you ain't got no bones in your neck."

Now the skeletons stopped spinning, lowered onto the wizard's head, and began chewing. A sublime smile unfolded across his lips.

"We're talking no less than the death of a way of life, Mr. Tendo."

"End of a mythos. End of a legend."

Lazar shifted and hunched forward on his frail elbows.

"*If*, that is, we don't begin planning alternatives well in advance," he said.

The head dissolved, then the neck and chest.

"But what alternatives are there to plan in advance *for*?" Ben asked. "I mean, from what you're saying, sounds like there's not a whole bunch anyone can do to stop all this from happening. Right?"

"Exactly what we thought," Lazar said, "in the beginning."

"But our computers, dey thought differently. See, turns out we been tinkin' 'round 'n' 'round in one big loop."

The torso dissipated, leaving only the legs behind. They fell over onto the floor and vanished in a puff of smoke.

"We couldn't see beyond what we were already accustomed to seeing. No doubt creative entropy is nearly upon us. No doubt we're exhausting content in music. But here's the thing. Our computers pointed out that content is only *half* the equation."

"...?"

"De other half bein' *form*."

"We'd been thinking in terms of the form *of the music itself*. Our computers are thinking about the form *of the musicians*."

Ben realized it was suddenly very still. All the dwarves were gone. The Mussorgsky he'd unconsciously registered playing in the background on hidden speakers had fallen silent.

"Of the *musicians*?" he said.

"Dat be where you come in, Ben mon."

"Me?"

"You," Lazar said. "You see, rock music is, well, all rocked out."

"But de idea of *fads*, mon, dey live forever."

Kwasi rose and moved to Vida's side.

"Guess this is where I cut out," he said, tapping the guitarist on the shoulder. She nodded vaguely and he helped her to her feet.

"You're leaving us?" Lazar said.

"Looks like you folks're doing just fine without me," Kwasi said, steering Vida, still hooked to her VR unit, across the hall. "Nighty-night," he said. He met Ben's eyes. "And sleep tight."

Marco, Lazar, and Ben watched the couple go. The door swished shut behind them. For a moment no one spoke.

"Everybody loves a trend," Lazar began. "But, like the music itself, trends have a brief half-life. So what we need to do is take a quantum-leap in trend-setting."

"We need to redefine de very idea of 'trend.'"

"And our computers tell us you're just the person we need to do so. You're the last lines of our blueprint, Mr. Tendo."

"Exactly de right age, demographically speakin'."

"Right height. Right build."

"Right psychological construct." Marco yawned. His eyes grew liddy. "And you got de kind of talent dat, wit' a bit of enhancement here, bit of enhancement dere, 'll be world-class, mon, world-class. Got someting else, too, dat's goin' to make everyting flow easy as water."

". . . ?"

"Tendencies toward an addiction," said Lazar. "Tendencies that, given your circumstances, will be as effortless to feed as —"

"Steakmeat to de dogs," Marco finished.

"Exactly. You see, Mr. Tendo, you love the idea of fame almost as much as we do."

"Can almost taste it, can't you, mon? All dat glamor. All dat stature. Sweet and rich. Saw de real ting for de first time back in Seattle with Holy and Elektra and it looked *good*."

"You're ours, Mr. Tendo."

"You goin' to wake up every mornin' cravin' it like Vida craves her VR rig. You never be able to get enough. And dat's okay, cuz dere always be more. Your body, mon, *it* goin' to be dat ting teenage girls all over de world finger demselves to sleep wit' every night tinkin' 'bout."

"And everyone, everyone everywhere, Mr. Tendo, is going to love you."

17

With that, an enormous grinding commenced behind them.

Ben swung around in time to see a rectangle of uneven stones below the tapestry of the DNA diagram retract into the wall, divulging a one-by-three-meter portal. Through it, he could make out a spiral stone staircase lit faintly with biolight strips.

"Answer's through dere," Marco said, taking a last taste of his liqueur, violet tongue probing the bottom of the tiny glass, then retreating.

"Tomorrow's waiting, Mr. Tendo," said Lazar.

Ben scanned one, then the other.

"You're assuming I'm like just gonna *do* this thing, aren't you?"

They smiled fondly at him. Lazar's large ears made him look like a mouse. Marco folded his hands on his chest, a happy monitor lizard, tongue just splitting his lips.

"You will, Ben mon," he said amiably. "You will."

"What if I say no?"

"You should hurry," Lazar said. "You're expected."

"What if I say fuck you and fuck your whole rucking outfit? What if I say I'm fucking *fading*?"

"We'll say goodbye for now," Lazar said, "but we'll see you again."

"I'm gone," Ben said, pushing back his chair and crossing toward the door to the corridor and the elevator, conscious of the fact that this move was absurd.

"You've come too far to get upset with us now, haven't you?" Lazar called after him.

"Ain't like you, mon," Marco added. "Ain't like you at all."

"Fuck you both," Ben said.

Marco set down his glass.

"Computers, dey told us to remind you 'bout someting. Told us to remind you 'bout how many, many days you sat at your console at Beautiful Mutants —"

"More bored than you could ever imagine —"

"Waitin' for someting, anyting, to change dat dreary little life of yours —"

"To make your existence slightly more interesting, slightly more bearable, than it was before, even if just for a little while."

The door swashed back. The corridor was empty. Ben could see the elevator waiting at the far end. The security cameras hummed awake and rotated to take him in.

"Told us to remind you of dat warm feelin' you get in your belly when you standin' on de stage playin', everyting smooth as a baby's asscheek —"

"Told us to remind you that that feeling will be increased tenfold, twenty, if you just take those stairs down."

"All you got to do, mon, is turn 'round."

"Think of all those people across the world who don't even know yet that they're going to be your fans. The talk shows, the album deals."

"De backstage parties dat'll make de biggest, wildest, most head-crunchingest crazy party you ever been to look like eleven am on Sunday mornin' in your local Luth'ran church."

Ben stepped into the corridor.

"And," Lazar added, "the computers told us to remind you about something else. That what you'll see at the bottom of that staircase won't be wholly *unfamiliar* to you."

"Won't be wholly strange at all, mon."

Ben stopped.

"What you talking about?" he asked, eye on the elevator.

"We're talking about the fact that someone's waiting for you down there."

"Someone you know."

"Someone you once knew very well."

"Someone who's given up a lot for you."

"Perhaps more dan she bargained for."

"Come back, Mr. Tendo," Lazar said.

"You know you can feel dat desire diggin' itself in your muscles like a bad case of de flu."

"We're speaking about fame here."

"Not just de two-bit pussy bullshit of Club Foot. Not some *garage* to jack off in wit' your friends on Saturday afternoons."

"We're talking the kind that will make the world look new to you every second of every day for the rest of your life."

"You walk out dat door, mon, and you walk out on your future."

"Turn around," Lazar said. "Your destiny is behind you."

The staircase was steep, the walls oily with mildew. There was no banister for support and the steps were so uneven Ben often had to brace himself against the stones. When he pulled his hands away they smelled briny with decay.

On the first landing he discovered a wooden table porcupined with rusty needles, iron clamps for arms and legs, and beside it on a rickety wooden bench what looked like an assortment of ancient obstetrical instruments.

He came across a pile of junk on the second landing: box springs, old stuffed leather chair, ceramic animal-shaped cookie jars, bubblegum dispensers, coiled rope, clown costume, stacks of newspapers, dusty emerald vials, and several large paintings stacked against the wall which he sorted through, eyes straining in bad light, some sort of fungus gnawing across the canvases, rotting them out like a hot bulb behind a strip of celluloid. POPEYE was neatly lettered over one, a silhouette of the cartoon character surrounded by stars. Another had formerly been a pinkish silkscreen of an electric chair, a third the smoking fuselage of a crashed plane.

At the bottom of the staircase was a long gothic hallway which opened onto some umbral stageset out of a Frankenstein vid, large bronze globes atop thin accordioned iron rods fizzing with static electricity, beakers splipping with red liquids on long aluminum lab tables, dense sausage-links of wires, gauges, valves, oscillators, amplifiers, and transformers packed row upon row along fake instrument panels, man-sized levers protruding from what appeared to be a titanic spark plug that almost reached the vaults twenty meters above Ben's head.

The only thing that looked like it actually *did* something, though, like it actually *worked*, was the colossal glossy mainframe stretching down a wall as far as the eye could see. Attached to it with heavy high-voltage cables like thick black blood vessels was a one-by-three-meter plexiglas coffin filled with thick white vapor through which Ben could just make out the rough outlines of a human form: a naked woman, skin spotted as if she'd been lying in a sauna for a long time, large erect nipples terra cotta red, short bob and pubic hairs pink as her glazed eyes staring through Ben toward the ceiling. Her lips were barely parted, revealing a golden front tooth.

A minute passed before he understood he was examining his sister.

He knuckled the plastic. She didn't respond. He went over to one of the lab tables and picked up a metal rod and tried cracking the plexiglas but the rod just thumped off. He swung three or four times and then stopped. Winded, he began coughing.

"Coughs are bad things," a woman's voice declared.

Ben raised his head. It hit him that this was the same sexy computer voice that'd been reading announcements over the intercom.

"They're like Christmas, only in reverse," it said. "You can't argue with your scrapbook."

"Who's there?"

"We miss them all so much. Elizabeth Taylor. Brigitte Bardot. The Waldorf Astoria."

"Who are you?"

"And, then again, we don't." Pause. "It takes half a day to get uptown and half a day to get downtown. So there's no time in between to be aesthetic." Pause. "I think I'm missing some chemicals. The last time I saw Paris... Peter Sellers... I wish I was a waiter, don't you? A waiter already knows his lines."

Ben walked among lab tables, searching for the source. He wandered toward the shadows, following components of the mainframe.

The voice changed from a sexy woman's into a little boy's.

"I live in the future. When I start eating a box of popcorn, I always look forward to the last piece. Watches mean you literally have time on your hands. They can always get worse. They can always escalate."

Ben stopped and listened, trying to orient himself.

"Where are you?" he asked.

"They came to me on my death bed and asked me for my aura. They said they wanted my aura." Pause. "Where is Lou Reed? Basil Rathbone? He could solve problems like no one else." Pause. "I'm a commercial for waiting in lines for movies... A slick, colorful bauble of entertainment based on the Broadway adaptation of Anita Loos' venerable story. Two people kissing always look like fish."

"Who wanted your aura?" Ben asked.

Silence dilated.

"Do you ever think about crowd scenes in old movies?" the voice said, flat and genderless, strumming with an electronic edge. "Every single person in them is dead. Time off, time in, time card, time lapse, time zone, meantime, good time, bad time, beforetime, time out. Time out."

In the back wall, almost lost among darkness, was a small portal so low Ben had to crouch to get through. On the other side was an imitation crypt lit with biolight strips. Cells had been carved at meter intervals into the stone and inlaid with parts of human bones. Some were filled with skulls, others with hipbones or ribs. All were covered with cobwebs which, Ben saw when he stepped closer, were really thin strands of fiber optic threads.

"Empty-space is never-wasted space," the voice said. "But junk is important too. It gives us something to do. It gives us a reason for cleaning."

Initially Ben thought the wall in front of him was bare white, the widest screen wide-screen television he'd ever seen, then he realized it was transparent glass forming the face of a huge vat. The liquid it contained was thick and pearly. A mop of yellow hair fanned out like a sea anemone below which two rust-colored eyeballs bobbed on the ends of pinkish muscle-strands leading to a brain stem and six or seven vertebrae. Around it drifted ten or twelve other brain stems.

The eyeballs tilted up and focused on Ben.

"We need to talk," the voice said.

18

The crypt smelled like wet hair. Hundreds of votive candles formed static waterfalls of melted wax in crannies along the walls. The fiberoptic cobwebs quavered in a faint breeze generated by an air vent sunk behind a stack of hand bones.

"Did you hurt her?" Ben asked.

"Her?"

"Mikki."

"My favorite wife would own her own television station and lots of albums. She would have a complete collection of Beatles records and all the scripts from the original *Star Trek* series."

"Answer me."

The top halves of many of the skulls crowding the cells were missing.

"I believe in low lights and trick mirrors. I believe in plastic surgery." Pause. "She's with us now."

"'With us'?"

"Everybody ends up kissing the wrong person goodnight, Crash."

"Ben."

"You've changed. We all have."

"Let her out."

"You think you're the same person at seven o'clock at night that you were at seven o'clock in the morning."

"Let her go."

"When I was dying I had to sign autographs."

"I'm not doing what you want till you wake her up."

"Looking is no fun unless you can buy." The eyes at the end of the stalks rolled back toward the ceiling. "Otherwise all you're left with are memories." The voice became Mikki's. "I'm so cold."

"Mikki. Where are you?"

"Everything is ice. My heart's pumping frozen water."

"What've they done to you?"

"Everything you can imagine."

Then Helmer Skelter was speaking.

"This is what your dream looks like, nicht? Her last thought
. . . was of the stock market." The eyes swiveled quickly to meet
Ben's. "We love her. We love her so much. Being famous is watching MTV and knowing everyone you see on the screen. She'll be
with us as long as you decide to be with us. She'll be the commercials between your rock vids."

Helmer's voice became an electronic cloud fizzling with dis-
tortion.

"They came to me and asked me for my aura. They said they
wanted my aura. I said, 'I don't have an aura. I don't have a personality.' But they said they wanted it anyway."

Ben stepped closer to the vat. A three-centimeter packed
layer of dust gathered on the floor of the crypt. The eyes jerked
back like a pair of skittish fish, the vertebrae beneath them
spasming.

"Who *are* you?" Ben asked.

"What's left."

"Of what?"

"Game shows. What you end up with after syndication."

The plastic wall looked at least eight or ten centimeters thick.
Ben tried to imagine the mass of one of those thigh bones heaped
in that cell nearly within arm's reach, feel the heft of it in his
hand.

"What's left of me . . . Us. Anwol. They asked me for my
aura. I said, 'The people who have the best fame are the people
who have their names on the fronts of stores.'"

Ben lowered himself onto his haunches, thinking. Something
from his childhood, something from California . . .

"You're that guy," he said finally.

"That guy?"

"That artist guy."

"The most beautiful thing in Tokyo is the McDonald's."

"Went into the hospital for some operation. Gallbladder deal
or something."

"The most beautiful thing in Hong Kong is the McDonald's."

"People still talk about what you did. We learned about you
in school."

"Tibet doesn't have any beautiful things."

"Story was you final-dined all of a sudden. Only there was this mystery about how it all could've gone down the way they said. Pieces didn't fit together. Investigation afterwards didn't turn up anything. There was this big auction, then the whole thing sort of just faded. You're him."

"I'm a Timex."

"What's left of him."

"Transplants, virus-exposures, media manipulations. It's miraculous. I never fall apart because I never fall together."

"And they added all these other consciousnesses to yours to—what? Keep you company? Build on what you already knew?"

"I'm not myself anymore. But, then again, who is?"

"You were *so* famous."

"It was time to become something else."

"And now you're everywhere."

"Thanks for using AT&T."

Ben pondered, nudging his glasses up on his nose.

"Everyone must have been in on this thing," he said.

"There are so many art lovers around the world."

"Biologists, lawyers."

"One day we stopped agreeing with each other. We grew in separate directions."

"Virus?"

"Eighty-three percent of marriages end in divorce."

"Sabotage?"

"Some of us began speaking to you." Ben massaged the blisters around his nostrils, trying to take this in. The voice shifted shapes again, accruing aspects of Kama Quyntifonic's. "People are beautiful because they're just like computers, only softer," it said.

"People made you."

"We make people. Buy one, get one free. Michael Jackson. Pontius Pilot."

The density and smoothness of those thigh bones.

"The biological phase of intelligent existence is only a brief one belonging to more primitive epochs." Pause. "You know who possessed the most angelic voices in all history? Three hundred years of flawless purity?"

The tensile strength.

"Farinelli . . . Pacchierotti. La Zam-bin-el-la. Kama needed an occupational reorganization. Her career needed . . . restructuring. We like plans. We have some for you."

"Like what?"

"Compusystems' computer-generated lyrics. TechLabs' voice-synthesizer implant. Diacomm's new enzyme formula. Disney's —"

"Diacomm emancipated me years ago."

"They continue to maintain an interest in your development."

"I have my emancipation papers. It's legal. It's done."

"They own ten percent of your value."

"No."

"They've invested wisely, kept a diversified portfolio. You know Monteverdi, Vivaldi, and Mozart wrote leading roles for them?"

"Who?"

"The hyperstars of the seventeenth, eighteenth, and nineteenth centuries. No singers were more highly prized, none with more money. You have so much to look forward to. They performed in the Sistine Chapel. They performed with Handel in London. The Prince of Wales paid one of them two-hundred guineas to sing a single aria. If you can't believe this's happening, just pretend it's a movie."

"*Who?*"

"The last European castrato was named Alessandro Moreschi. He died in 1922 at sixty-four. Though there were sightings in villages throughout South America well into the late twentieth century, all the way up to the war . . . There's a recording on a wax cylinder. It's the saddest thing you'll ever hear."

Knuckles cracked behind Ben.

He was in the process of turning as the first dart pinged into the flesh below his left shoulder blade, springing his legs out from under him, bolting him into the vat wall.

Blueness scintillated through his brain.

"You will be so famous," Anwol was saying. "The surgeons will make you into a franchise —"

The second dart snapped into his neck.

Then he was lying on his back, looking up at Lazar's shadow framed against the weak radiance of the biolight strips.

"Right," he said to someone else Ben couldn't see. "Wet himself, didn't he?"

"I can't breathe," Ben said.

"Shat himself as well."

"Fook," said the other voice. "What a pig."

"I'm suffocating," Ben said, his body beginning to quake.

"All got our problems, don't we now, mate?"

In the background Anwol discussed plans for a new restaurant chain called CRASH-MATS, the idea being people would get their food at computer-monitored cafeteria vending machines and take their trays to booths where they would watch television, on which would be two hundred and fifty channels, each depicting different kinds of people eating different kinds of food.

"Airports are my favorite places," he said as Ben's legs began to move by themselves as if he were climbing a wall. "They smell like the present. They look like yesterday." Pause. "My favorite Life Savers are cherry."

19

Behind the ballerinas with spikes through their heads rose a large gutted redbrick housing project whose windows were boarded with sheets of charred plywood. Ben slowly made his way toward it, shinnying over human-sized hunks of concrete and around snaggled screens of iron mesh. Though he couldn't tell for sure, he had the impression it was late afternoon, the green sun hanging like a round lime low in the purple sky, just brushing the air-conditioning units atop the building.

On the stoop, flanked by cement statues of reclining lions, stood his sister, a trickle of blood centipeding out her right ear and down her jaw, disappearing in the frilly lilac folds of her tutu's neck. A blood-bubble swelled under one nostril.

"Mikki?" Ben said.

"It's winter," she replied. "We never even saw it coming."

Ben looked around. He hadn't noticed the clots of gritty snow waved along the curbs, in patches across the parking lot, upon the corpses.

When he turned back at Mikki she was no longer his sister.

Dreadlocks spiralled halfway down her back. Her irises were rust, her skin darkening as he watched. She touched the tribal scars notching her forehead and cheeks, astonished as he was by the translation taking place.

The deserted hallway belonged to a dwelling from the 1950s. Flat mousey paint husked off the walls in seven- and ten-centimeter scales. Amber fishbowl lamps, most splintered, ran at two-meter intervals along the ceiling. Gelatinous crude oil dripped from the ventilation ducts and plopped onto the hazy blue linoleum floor tiles.

Ben and Jessika took several flights of stairs in near darkness, the banister wobbly, the must of old dormitories rich in the air. Sections of plywood had been ripped out of a window in a room on the top story and powdery white light swamped the iron-framed bed and bare mattress, olive green chest-of-drawers, seatless toilet in the bathroom globbing over with more crude oil that had already formed a four-centimeter layer on the floor and now oozed toward Ben standing near an empty doorless closet. Jessika stood at the window and gestured for him to join her.

Instead of the parking lot and other redbrick projects, he saw a glacier extending to the horizon. White ripples of snow, sawtooths of bluewhite ice, a small black dot advancing toward them.

It took hours for it to grow into a human form and then suddenly there was a noise behind them in the hall and a guy in a black leather jacket, black jeans, and black steel-tipped motorcycle boots stepped through the door. His hair was greased back like a Teddy Boy's and his jacket was open, a ragged whitish-yellow undershirt beneath. His face was a tone that said from the moment of birth he'd been raised in a room with artificial lighting. Blue-green moles reminiscent of the surface of a piling clogged with barnacles crusted his cheeks and neck. He never stopped moving. He walked straight at Ben.

The switchblade appeared from nowhere.

Before he could even raise his hands to deflect it, Ben heard it crunch through the cartilage of his voice box.

Jessika was placing a derm on his wrist. He was in a hospital bed, a fistful of thumbtacks stuck in his throat.

"Hey, Crash, how ya doin' man?" she asked.

Ben tried to nod but a surge of nausea rolled through him. Jessika produced the bed pan.

"One down, two to go," she said.

Only it wasn't ice and snow.

It was a desert of styrofoam pellets.

Their feet creaked several centimeters into them with each step they took. They'd been hiking across it for days, sky blanched and sunless, terrain barren and flat as a foundation slab. The temperature was steady and bland. Jessika carried high-protein, high-carbohydrate, high-moisture army rations in small unmarked aluminum cans in a black knapsack she wore over her right shoulder. The goo in the cans was grayish and fibrous and reminded Ben of the gristle left on his plate when he was done eating lamb. Every few hours Jessika'd stop. She'd take out a jar of Sterno, squat, light it, heat the cans. Often they'd eat in silence. Sometimes Ben would try to start a conversation.

Every day her eyes glowed a richer shade of orange. Rust to copper red. Mandarin to yellow carmine.

Then they weren't eyes anymore, but pinpoint ember-sites on a laser rifle.

Then she ceased blinking all together.

He was staring up into a doctor's face. The guy was wearing a lab coat and Canon mirrorshades. His flesh looked like bad cheese.

"You know where you are?" he asked.

He was American.

Ben opened his mouth to speak. His throat was swollen. He shook his head yes.

"You've been gone a while, Crash. What's the last thing you remember?"

He handed Ben a computer note pad and electronic puck.

"The snow," Ben printed.

A nurse in a saffron mop-cut was fidgeting with his pillow, fluffing it up, humming to herself.

"Help me," Ben whispered.

"Wot?" the nurse asked.

"Help me," Ben repeated.

She laughed.

"You're the kidder, now, ain't you?"

"You had a couple of rough days, man," Jessika said.

She was squatting next to his bed.

An intravenous trailed from his arm, a catheter from under the sheets.

He was numb from the waist down.

"I'm all right?" he asked.

His voice sounded funny to him, a mechanical quality to it he couldn't put his finger on, some change in pitch.

"You remember just asking that?" she said.
"Asking what?"
"Lie back, man. Relax. You got some R-and-R coming."
"I'm all right?"
"Depends what you mean by 'all right,' you know?"

On the fifth day they came across a chest-high pyramid of lava stones on the white plain. Inside was a new-born baby attached to a portable life-support unit. Moist transparent plastic had replaced the baby's skin. Scarlet liquid jerked through its veins and around its greenish-blue organs. Jessika matter-of-factly stooped, unplugged the equipment, picked up the infant, and offered it to Ben, who accepted it awkwardly. The warm wetness from the plastic skin began seeping through his t-shirt. He cupped its head and held it against him for a minute, rocked it back and forth. It didn't cry, didn't make a sound, just breathed steadily. But when Ben tried to give it back to Jessika he couldn't pull it away from his shoulder. The thing had burrowed into his neck with a tongue like a lamprey and begun feeding on him. Ben tried to tug it free, careful not to rupture the veins beneath his skin, only it began to growl and twitch its head side to side. So Ben shook it, gently at first, then harder. It fastened on more tightly. He felt its tongue slither beneath his skin, locate the jugular, and begin gnawing through. Panicking, Ben tried to holler but tendrils shot off its tongue and clogged his throat, cobraed down his esophagus, shot into his bowels. Eyes glowing, Jessika watched him struggle and then turned and began strolling away, black knapsack slung over her right shoulder. When Ben tried to follow his legs buckled. He tried to crawl but discovered he'd lost so much blood he no longer possessed the energy. So he lay on his side, shaking, listening to the thing feed upon him.

" . . . happens and you just don't know it."
Mikki was holding his hand, whispering something to him.
"Sorry. Really. Only you gotta see *my* side of things, you know? You gotta see things from where I'm standing. It's not all me, me, me. It's not like that, okay?"
Ben tried to open his eyes but they were taped shut.
His head was bandaged.
"The credit, Crash. Oh, *man*, the *credit* . . ."

The green sun.

The purple sky.

They weren't colored contacts but actual prescription Toshiba iris-implants that turned the browless eyes lemon yellow. A concentration camp ID number, circa the South American war, was tattooed vertically from the left temple to the earringed jawbone. And the hair—the hair was this incredible white, like angels' wings, and spiked short. Rather than shaving the scalp in patches, they'd genuinely burned off small tufts, so pink thumbnail-sized scars glinted through the quills. Glossy fire-engine-red lipstick shimmered on the lips lopsidedly injected with collagen. And he'd know those teeth anywhere. They were Kama's teeth, no doubt, filed to keen points, except for those upper central incisors which must have been Nosferatu inserts. Where the Adam's apple used to be rose a shiny black cube.

It took Ben nearly a full minute to figure out he was examining himself in a mirror.

"Hey, Crash, steady man. Steady. What the fuck are you *doin'*, man? Settle down . . . settle . . ."

Reclining in a hot tub, waterjets frothing, he remembered his first bath in Seattle. That sense of contentment like warm margarine in his veins.

Lazar was reading an old-fashioned newspaper in a deck chair nearby while the nurse with the saffron mop-cut adjusted gauges on a Hitachi control panel across the room. Ben closed his eyes and tried to concentrate his memory into a fist-sized ball of light that he could rotate like a miniature quasar.

Something bobbed up next to him, whitish-yellow and wrinkled, then was sucked under again.

He tried to fix on the images of the simulated Roman villa, the marble pillars, the tapestries, the mosaics, the amazing scent as he lowered himself into the sugary blue water that night, but another swatch pitched and disappeared.

Uneasy, he tried standing but he was strapped into some sort of therapy chair. The chair was alive, its surface slippery flesh, its restraints bristly tentacles, at its hub a toothless gumming mouth. He tried to call attention to his situation only he was missing his tongue.

Preoccupied with her control panels, the nurse didn't hear Ben's worried grunts. Lazar continued to flip pages of what Ben now saw was *The Sun*.

More wrinkled yellowish strips heaved among the boiling water. They were pieces of Ben's skin.

The water was too hot. His epidermis was peeling off in shreds. It didn't hurt, which surprised him. Miraculously, there was no pain at all associated with this dissipation. Yet Ben knew pretty soon his muscles would shed like bark. His toenails and fingernails would pry off. His organs would soon be tugging at the ends of sundry tubes and blood vessels. And then he would simply scatter. He would become somehow less than himself. He would become nothing more than these body parts floating in a hot tub.

Only it didn't much matter to him. He wasn't scared. He wasn't even apprehensive. Interest was more what he felt. Inquisitiveness.

He didn't know something like this could happen. Till now he didn't know this was a possible end for a person. Car accidents, yes. Planes falling from the sky. Electrical shocks. But breaking up in a hot tub, becoming human soup—it had just never occurred to him.

So he tried to make himself comfortable.

He tried to open himself up to what was transpiring as he might to any other new and potentially edifying experience.

And then his right arm fell off.

He awoke in bed next to Jessika, having slept so hard his hands fizzed. Naked, she'd curled back into him like a living semicolon. Her hot skin pressed against his flank, her wire-sponge hair barely grazing his shoulder. The bright red numbers on the Pioneer digital clock-radio on the side table said 3:32. When she felt him stir she rolled over.

"You kept trying to stand, man," she explained groggily. "Kept ripping out your IV, saying you had places to be. They tranked you pretty mean, put you in restraints. Can't have you fuckin' with that new body of yours, can we?"

"What've they done to me?"

Jessika sat up and unthinkingly hugged her knees to her chest. Her breasts, plump and pert-nippled, flashed and vanished under the sheets.

The clock-radio flipped to 3:33.

"What haven't they done to you is more like it," she said. "You're a new person. Earned yourself a fresh life, one you always wished for. They didn't do anything you didn't already want."

Ben stared at the ceiling, reflexively fingered his new voice box.

"What if I want the old one back?" he asked.

"It just feels like that at first, man. Common enough emotion. Just gotta give it some time. Get acquainted with it. Live with it a while."

"What if I want it like it was?"

"You won't, man. You won't. Not once you get a taste of this stuff..."

" . . . Crash? Yo, Crash? You with us?"

"*Jesus*. Hold It *down*, hold It *down*."

"Gonna ruckin' tear a suture if It don't watch out."

"Hit It wi' the morph."

"Right. Hold It . . . Hold It . . ."

"Who the hell took off the restraints?"

"Fuck if I know. Tha' should . . ."

Propped in a wheelchair, groin aching, Crash watched the M Technology HDTV mounted to the wall of his hospital room while Jessika and Mikki slumped on a couch in the corner eating pepperoni pizza-substitute.

The camera must've been fewer than ten centimeters from Joey Taboo's face, which became something closer to a point-blank cubist collage of gold wire-rimmed reading glasses, plastic goggles, black derby, bushy beard, and black pores than to any mug Crash'd ever seen. And those unblinking eyes—ugh, those unblinking eyes trembled on just this side of decorum and sanity.

"I'm thinkin' rock star," he was saying. "I'm thinkin' *idol, icon,* workin' class *he-ro.* I'm thinkin' someone simple as rain and good as gold who's gonna change the way you see.

"You know the one I mean. You know the one I'm talkin' about. Close your eyes. Go on. Lower your head... And *look*: you can see him too.

"Yes you can.

"You can see him plain as day. Hair white as Bahamas sand. Lips swollen roses. Sign of the victim, sign of the outcast, singed across his face.

"And his voice? Oh, his voice, his voice . . . pure as a cut diamond, folks, sweet as the skin between the fingers of a baby's hand.

"And you know what he's doin' *right now*? At this very moment he's tunin' up in some garage. At this very moment he's rehearsin' to enter your lives and transform you utterly.

"*Listen to him.*

"*Listen good.*

"You know why? You have any *idea* why?

"Cuz that boy, you see, that boy's strikin' up the chords that're gonna usher in a new bein'-in-the-world for you. Here comes tomorrow, friends, and it's howling fast as a speedtrain through a tunnel, loud as a locomotive in your bedroom.

"You tell me he looks like he's pluggin' in his amp. But I say you're wrong.

"You tell me he looks like he's gettin' out his pick. But I say he ain't.

"I say, he's pluggin' in your *souls*, folks.

"He's turnin' on the juice that's gonna galvanize your hearts.

"He's a walkin' electric chair. He's an amblin' nuclear reactor. He's a meltdown comin' to get you.

"And all you got to do is feel that energy. That wattage. That high-voltage superconductor oscillatory-discharge *power*.

"And let's send that boy some credit to help him on his way up the popcharts of life. Let's send that simple young man who wants nothing more than to change the basis of your bein' a little financial assistance.

"Let's buy him a bigger amp, friends.

"Let's buy him a finer Fender.

"Oh, yeah . . ."

Crash was alert and erect in his wheelchair.

"Hey, you hear that?" he asked. "He's talking about *me*, you guys. Oh, *man*, what a kick."

But no one answered.

They couldn't.

Mostly that was because Jessika was busy slipping her tongue between Mikki's lips. But partly it was also because

Mikki's palm was busy cupping Jessika's pudenda under the pizza box and polishing it.

Crash looked over at his sister, and then at his one-date girlfriend, and then, embarrassed, back at the HDTV.

"*Halle-praisetheLord-lujah!*" Joey was shouting into the camera. Crash noticed an ugly whitehead festering in the crevice between Joey's porous nose and hairy left cheek. "*Praise His mightiness and grace!*

"*Our phones are startin' to ring!*

"*Our switchboards are a-lightin'!*

"*They're turnin' into a Norwegian CHRISTMAS TREE! They're turnin' into the technicolor arctic sky at midnight!*

"*Oh YES!*

"*Oh holy-mother-of-god YES!*"

"One," Crash said, right hand sheathed in an ebony Atari electronic glove poised over the strings of his new Erato guitar, headphones on, taking Marco's signal from the control room behind the window in the studio.

"Two," Ferret said, face a radiance of carbuncles, Apollo bass slung across her scrawny chest.

"Three," Vida said, still behind her wide-band mirrorshade VR rig, this time hooked into a camcorder run by Lazar who was already busy steering among the instruments, music stands, cables, and sound gear, so she could experience herself playing in simulated 3D, Fujitsu guitar hooked via a long thin wire into the Baldwin synthesizer and sound drum.

"*Four*," Mikhail said, slamming down his sticks on the Diacomm percussion plates as if on a wad of nitrocotton, Kwasi coming in a microsecond later with a gabble of static from his Samson keyboard and a ray-gun of pulses that Vida echoed with a speed riff and Ferret with an eardrum-scrambling bass line.

And they were *on*, stunningly on, as though they'd been jamming together like this all their lives, grown up side by side on the same city streets, run with the same Pomo Pogo gangs, slunk through the same tight-assed high school corridors on their way around the same metal detectors and out the same back door, done this gig for years and years in every alley-club from here to Moscow and back again, agile and hot, erotic and angry, grungy and absolutely cranium-stompingly simpatico.

Marco smiled behind the window, happy as a boa after that

172

baby pig just trotted into view below, tongue sliding forth to see what all this noise was about.

The sampler whirred as Crash's hand dropped for the first chord, chatter of babies' half-language, crackle of a highrise in flames, feral growls, and seraphic swoops, all against the background digital loop of John Lennon's tossed-off slur from "Strawberry Fields," more mistake than intention, more afterthought than premeditation... *I bur-eed Paul, I bur-eed Paul, I bur-eed Paul*... while Vida started the spiral climb up the neck of her Fujitsu, fingers an insect blur, toward the neo-baroque preamble to the computer-generated lyrics of "Hysterically Blue."

And then the infinitesimal lull, the microscopic moment of suspension, the hover, the halt, the airborne skier just off the ramp.

And the plunge—

The voice.

That voice.

That crystalline ghost-ridden eeriness expanding through the studio.

Even Vida had to tilt her chin toward the ceiling and cock her head to one side behind those silver shades to listen to this hoodoo. Even Lazar had to stop filming and peek out from behind his camcorder to see what perfection looked like in the flesh.

It was the loneliest, most immaculate, most innocent, most inviolable, most blameless tone you have ever heard.

It sounded like sadness.

It sounded like dreams.

Part Five

HYSTERICALLY BLUE

20

Hysterically Blue" premiered on MTV two months later.

Joey Taboo cycled his by-now famous "I'm Thinkin' Rock Star" spot every three hours the last thirty days; Diacomm a series of saturation promos featuring Plugheads, Post-Verbalists, Überthrashers, and Guerilla-Brutals; Air Pyrate Muzzik unheard-of hundred-and-twenty-second infomercials on all the key trade-video magazines.

And at midnight Greenwich Mean Time television screens around the world darkened for the count of three. Impulses were coded, transformed into a haze of computerized garble, and shot into the sky toward the Hendrix I twenty-two thousand miles above Nairobi.

When those signals ricocheted back to earth, and those screens flooded with data once more, the result was electrostatic, some cyber-shaman conjuring oracular spirits from the consensus wetdreams of Noisyland: documentary images of Crash's surgery (gleam of scalpel, crack of bone) intercut with Viva Bonni Suicide recording *Tonguing the Zeitgeist* in that studio somewhere down in the gut of The Hole while Marco Polydor's head, ever-present grin upon his narrow lips, levitated behind Crash and the others through that plate-glass window.

Viewers were instantly enraptured. The special effects were nazi, they said, pure nazi, the operations so mega, the layers of fat and blood so rucking, rucking *authentic*.

Critics said the juxtaposition of metaphoric abomination with musical flawlessness was a gift.

But it was that voice, that phenomenal electroshock-therapy-of-a-voice, that ultimately thrilled them. It was that voice that made people envision the most poignant things that'd ever happened to them as children and imagine the moment of their own deaths when everything would turn white and half their brains would believe they were beholding nothing less than soul-expanding revelations from another world while the other half would know all too well it was just oxygen deprivation, chemical imbalance, carbon monoxide poisoning.

Nearly two billion spectators sensed their lives change at 12:01 GMT in one vast collective hallucination, though each subculture understood that change in different terms.

Adolescents understood they'd just witnessed the advent of novel fashion. Teenagers heard a band that made them feel part of something larger than their own beleaguered affectless selves for the first time in months. People skewing helplessly into their twenties recollected experiences that'd never actually happened to them, teen years that belonged to television flashback-images of what teen years should have been. People already in their thirties found someone fresh to hate. Asians, drug addicts, Gynorads, gays, the handicapped, the divorced, Moscovites, and cadmium babies discovered unprecedented role models.

Spiked white skulls appeared in high schools and on college campuses the next week.

Lines began to form in front of seedy tattoo parlors for a run on certified concentration camp ID numbers indexed to those worn by inmates at Belsen, Auschwitz, and Caracas.

At 12:12 GMT, following the first flood of phone calls and faxes, MTV slated "Hysterically Blue" for frequent rotation.

The next evening video magazines started carrying top-story profiles about VBS. No one quite knew where they'd come from or where they lived. Some said Taiwan, others Istanbul, still others Mexico City. They'd been good buddies all their lives. They'd just met a year ago. They'd been struggling for almost a decade. They were an overnight success.

One journalist claimed to have discovered where Crash'd gone to high school, yet when he went to look up the hyperstar's records, camcorders at the ready, he found Crash's file empty, erased from the mainframe.

Another said there were clues Mikhail had been in the Navy for two years, but the building once housing his recruitment papers had burned to the ground. Vida'd been involved in a satanic cult, in the recent civil rights movement in China, in a real-estate scam down in Belize. She'd been a Buddhist, a Wahabi, an undercover cop. She'd been none of these things. Ferret was really a man, Kwasi a woman. They were married to each other. They were members of American Abstainers and had never touched a person of the opposite sex nor, for that matter, of the same sex. They were hermaphrodites, shrimpers, Shiites, paranoids, rat-exterminators, born-again Mansonites, cyborg prototypes. To scrape by during the lean years they'd worked in a vegetarian bakery in Seattle, starred in live flesher shows in New York, raised dogs for blackmarket meat in Odessa.

Crash'd majored in physics at Cornell, never completed sixth grade. His internal organs were synthetic. He had a fetish for eight-year-old boys. He was still a virgin.

The operations on the vid weren't staged.

Lines began to form in front of cosmetic boutiques for a run on lopsided collagen lip shots.

The day before *Tonguing the Zeitgeist* was shipped to stores, Viva Bonni Suicide's stock began to sell on the Tokyo Exchange like a psycho-killer in a sorority house.

That night a team of Anti-Abortionists raided a warehouse in Hoboken, New Jersey, killing one guard and injuring two others, heisting more than eight thousand copies of the album in order to finance their activities in the Northeast through the illicit profits.

Devotees of VBS queued up outside digital cassette stores from Rome to Melbourne, Ulan Bator to Rio de Janeiro, hours before the doors opened.

Fights among jockeying fans erupted in Montreal and Berlin.

Riot-police squelched a ruckus in Cape Town.

AJAKS picketed Tower Records in London, protesting Crash's unstable sexuality and disfiguring surgery. VBS admirers showed up in counterforce with their own pickets advocating gender ambiguity and cosmetic freedom. Although bobbies tried to keep the two groups apart, a fracas ignited and a car was set on fire, windows shattered, traffic at Piccadilly muddled almost half a day.

Within an hour of the album going on sale, one hundred and

twenty-seven people worldwide were hospitalized.

But all this was nothing compared to the reaction to *TTZ* itself, an hour's worth of ravaged weather, a squall of sampling, a blizzard of trance music and raunch, a typhoon of crystal-meth velocity and razor-heat sound-collage, all playing backdrop for a sonic clarity that seemed as if it came from some choirboy singing solo in a Viennese cathedral.

Here was an album that said *be more extreme*, that announced *rock'n'roll isn't over yet*, that proclaimed *listen to me, fuckhead, and I'll make you weep*.

The theme, critics pointed out, *if* the album could be said to have one (the metalogical computer-generated lyrics being what they were: a vortex of surreal visions and unhinged syntax), was metamorphosis, the ability of humans to mutate into what they needed in order to survive.

In addition to "Hysterically Blue," a song about a guy who gets dumped by his tekked partner only to transform into a deranged chemo-fiend who infects him with the New Virus, there appeared pieces like "Scar Love" (about the infected partner's revenge), "The Dead Can Dance" (about necromantic cabals in Boston), "Saving Face" (about elective surgery getting way out of hand), "Microwave Your Mom" (about your worst nightmare: becoming your own progen), and "Dissolution Planet" (about getting along after the Big Toxic Storm some scientists had begun predicting would hit the Pacific Coast any day now), as well as less obviously related tunes like "Passed Normal" (about the ups and downs of a zoophiliac corporate executive), "Hardwired" (about a kid dreaming of sporting bio-software that induced hallucinatory bliss akin to megadoses of pure coke), and the grand finale that took up fifteen minutes on the second side, "Tonguing the Zeitgeist" (about making it in various unwholesome ways with Mr. Death himself).

If the critics were breathless, the fans were convulsive.

TTZ sold out by the end of the first week in a firecloud of speculation about a tour.

But Anarchists for Jesus the Annointed King and Savior was back again, scrambling for media attention to combat the contamination of youth by moral degradation, erotic perversion, and biotechnical repulsion. They broke onto the airwaves, inserting illegal ten-second video-graffiti announcements into *Wheel of Fortune* and *Stretto*. They lobbied the Rock Commission, demanding VBS's album be banned. They approached principal congressmen and women and asked for legislation that'd make cosmetic castration a federal crime.

And then they marched on the Capitol, decked out as various states in the union, every hundred yards or so falling together to form an outline of the USA in order to suggest the solidarity of the silent majority. They were soon joined by Mothers Against Grindcore, the neo-conservative KKK splinter-group, dressed in signature robes and hoods; Heterosexual Union Machine, the new Protestant denomination, outfitted in paramilitary camouflage; Bikers for Jesus, the ancient evangelical organization, garbed in leather and studs astride their Harleys; and various other tribes who felt disenfranchised and humiliated in a country that embraced androgyny, auto-disfigurement, cacophony, buggerdom, anarchic rebellion, schizophrenia, cruelty, electronic pharmaceuticals, and anti-corporate sentiments.

Followers of VBS found the march beneath contempt and decided to forego a counter-protest. Which in retrospect turned out to be a mistake.

Fueled by images of the human flood surging across the Washington Mall (some said in excess of one hundred and fifty thousand well-disciplined souls), high schools and churches in New Haven and Boston burned VBS effigies for the networks. In Kansas City a radio station refusing to ban "Hysterically Blue" was bio-bombed and four employees contaminated with yellow fever. Canisters said to contain the New Virus were detonated at a pro-VBS rally that finally materialized outside the state buildings in Portland, though no New Virus cases were actually reported among the fans.

The Rock Commission responded by mandating warning labels for *TTZ* as well as fifteen-second announcements preceding each airing of "Hysterically Blue" stating the contents of the vid may be offensive to some adults and inappropriate for viewing by minors.

In a gesture of support for the music industry, President Redford invited VBS to the White House on the American leg of their tour for a gala bash involving a banquet and dance attended by the entertainment elite, essential business brass, and remnants of the Kennedy clan.

Album sales tripled.

Clone bands, sniffing the ambrosia of trickle-down revenues and surrogate notoriety, emerged overnight.

The VBS sound, now dubbed *technoguerre*, thundered across the planet. Russian garage bands played it and Austrian cover bands, tired old Zulu bands and jazzy young Filipino Neurocore ones.

Blitz, lead singer of Malfunksion, an ailing group out of Atlanta that'd seen their heyday nearly two years before, staged a public self-castration in Times Square. The two surgeons supervising the procedure couldn't stanch the bleeding caused by some slatternly switchblade moves on the rocker's part who, before the ambulance arrived, drifted into shock. Malfunksion's stock missiled up for three weeks straight as footage of the incident looped on international tube stations.

In Tucson, God Fodder Too garnered rave reviews when all four of its members began sporting expensive electronically enhanced voiceboxes. Some journalists in the biz said Yoko Ono Enterprises was behind the move, others the alternative music company Military-Industrial Kompleks. In either case, GFT was clearly bound for success till its tour bus hit a landmine on a desert road just outside Las Vegas late one night, killing three members and crippling two more. The police inquiry which followed lasted slightly less than forty-eight hours and concluded clueless.

Vampire My Vampire, a group out of Iowa City, tried to mimic VBS by studying *TTZ* closely and then copying its songs on an Erato guitar with an Atari glove, Fujitsu hooked into a Baldwin synthesizer, Apollo bass, Diacomm percussion plates, and Samson keyboard. The night before their first national MTV interview they fried in a hotel fire in Miami. In an exclusive, which gained the station three ratings points over *Crime Deterrent Digest* carrying a death-by-lethal-injection execution of another Cannibalist in Oregon, Jared Marîd reported that investigators discovered the door to the band's rooms on the thirty-fourth floor had been wedged shut, the sprinkler system turned off.

King Charles hosted VBS in a media extravaganza at Buckingham Palace. Joey Taboo was in attendance, as were leaders of the United States of Africa, British Diacomm VPs, a Fleet Street entourage, a senile Queen Mother, Holy Ryder in her first public appearance since she and Elektra Geestring dropped out of sight nearly four months ago (and since the latter had turned up, minus her reproductive organs, in the backseat of a Ford Ada in a Hoboken, New Jersey warehouse), a full hour of fireworks in the heavens above St. James Park, music by the old bubbles band Public Image Ltd., and Marco Polydor himself.
Everyone who was anyone was there.
Except, that is, the members of Viva Bonni Suicide.

They were somewhere over Greenland, en route to America, and the instant their Mantra 3000 touched down at JFK bedlam broke loose, an hysteria of press conferences, talkshows, hotel rooms, photo sessions, guest-VJ spots, limos, sponsor-promos, political parties, autograph sessions, vid-shoots for "The Dead Can Dance," and then, somehow without warning even though you'd been expecting it all along, turning around one evening to confront those whitehot spotlights, that holographic image of the naked girl tonguing a skull, that discharge of sound that slammed into your back like hurricane-force winds, the disciples' wild rush for the Touch, the sheer *enormity*, the sheer Promethean *extensiveness*, of the crowds whose lysergic gusto could always get you going, always get you to come back for one more song, be it in Hartford or Boston, Louisville or Memphis, Milwaukee or Detroit, because this is what you always said you'd wanted, this is what you always said you'd craved, and now you were in the midst of it, pumping in its heart, part of it like your eye-color was part of you.

And yet there was something you hadn't expected, something *they* hadn't expected *themselves*, the one variable those statistical computers couldn't foresee.
Those handmade posters screaming SAY NO TO CASTRATION!!!, DON'T DATE DEATH!!!, SAVE YOUR EYES TO SEE CHRIST!!!
At first just two or three, but the thing was there were al-

ways *more*, a group of protesters, a rally, that fullblown goddamn mob in St. Louis, more rumors of more canisters filled with the New Virus in Omaha, and you did what you were told, you kept trying to sing, but the fights started breaking out right in front of you, the body guards outnumbered, the police holding back just an instant too long to see what'd happen, and then there were these angry suits streaking toward you across the stage, hustling you off, white faces pressed against the windows of your limo as you were rushed toward the airport in Little Rock, Jackson, Mobile.

It seemed almost negligible at first. A fluke. But the concert in Boulder got canceled next, and the one in Flagstaff too.

Another bio-bomb threat came over the phoneline in Albuquerque a minute before you left your dressing room.

And the media was always there, sharks roiling around a wounded whale, waiting for the next thing to go wrong, broadcasting the protest in Reno where your sound gear got wrecked, the one in Phoenix where Ferret lost a tooth, the one in Santa Fe where a roadie was beaten up pretty bad. And then the Salt Lake City police chief ordered use of the Diacomm man-ape chimera prototypes for crowd control. Only it turned out, as with the Doberman-tigers, the limited-imprint potential caused some real problems. Thirty fans and nine policemen were killed outright, close to a hundred others hospitalized (most in psych units), and several hundred-thousand credits of damage done.

MTV backed off the next morning. Air Pyrate Muzzik reconsidered its publicity budget. Sponsors released statements to the effect they didn't necessarily endorse the content of the songs or performances.

It seemed almost laughable at first, certainly nothing to get worried about, maybe even something that'd ultimately generate some extra sales. But those stories started running about how it was no longer safe to attend a VBS concert, how your chances of being harmed at one were almost as great as your chances of being harmed in Manhattan during those ongoing food riots.

And everything began changing one more time.

Album sales stalled.

Those stadiums stopped selling out.

And then, at some ghostly moment one night, your band having just wrapped up its Northwest leg, ready to leave the country for South America in the morning, you winced awake with the realization that something had knifed by you in the darkness.

No one had ever thought the impulse would've become this *real*, escalated this *fast*, come right at you fierce as a Seattle gang on speed while you lay there trying to recall the last time you'd seen Marco at one of your concerts, a vid of yours play on MTV, and it hit you *this* was the only instant you'd never imagined before, the only one you'd somehow always managed to forget.

And now here it was caressing you in bed somewhere in Eugene at—when was it?—four o'clock in the morning. Snuggling up next to you like a lover's corpse.

Whispering sweet nothings in your ear.

21

Crash didn't notice the hotel rooms any more. He didn't notice the king-sized waterbeds or the bushes of man-made roses. He didn't notice the authentic cotton towels or the large baskets of hydroponic fruit. He didn't notice that at that second he was in a penthouse that was in effect a huge fish tank you could walk through, a series of corridors puzzling through an immense aquarium illuminated by masses of biolight strips.

Sitting in the living room here you also sat in a bygone Caribbean. Silver barracuda cruised around you. Jewelfish, swordtails, and butterflies arrowed among white plastic coral and counterfeit seaweed. Reclining in the bedroom you also reclined in a Canadian lake stocked with rainbow trout, largemouthed bass, and walleyed pike. The halls teemed with sea snakes, the bathroom with exotic dragon eels that wore their eyeballs on the ends of long optic nerves, sea robins that trundled along the sandy bottom on wormy legs, angler fish that fluttered the lengthy flowerlike growths on their heads in an attempt to attract prey.

He didn't notice the cities, either, the skylines, the around-the-clock rush-hour continually rumbling below. He didn't notice Caracas, Brazilia, on the other side of the living room window-wall. Nor the sunset. Nor the megalithic rays transmuting the smog collecting against the bare rugged mountains into a transcendent nuclear red. He didn't notice the skeletons of the bombed-out public-housing projects from the war scattered through the city center, nor the Cézannesque collage of shanty roofs tumbling toward the sea which had become a plain of gooey catsup ever since the pollution-derived oxidation had gotten a toe-hold and the anerobics had taken over, nor even the multitudinous silhouettes of offshore-wells scragging up like a desert of steel cacti.

It never occurred to him that if he happened to open the sliding doors built into that window-wall and step onto the balcony, a garden of kaleidoscopic glass shards embedded into human-sized concrete lizards, snakes, and monkeys, that the smoke from the smoldering landfills flecking the base of the mountains would make the humid air so grainy he'd taste catpiss.

Nor if he happened to peer over the tarnished baroque grillwork he'd be able to see the ever-present cluster of protesters, at least one-hundred strong, bearing plywood signs forty floors below.

Nor if he happened to glance behind him he'd be able to make out Mikki sprawled on the watercouch shaped and colored like a huge vagina, pale orange derms patching her right arm, mesmerized by what transpired in the aquarium above her; Lazar, bat-ears catching the dying light and defusing it into a pink blush, pacing nearby as he talked in low tones on the wireless phone; Jessika, sporting new sideburn implants beneath her dreads, checking the numbers on her digital Seiko and rising to administer Crash's next round of enzymes and hormones to control his voice, or maybe tranks to keep him lowtekked between concerts ever since that time he'd acted up in Boisie and said he wanted out and wanted out *now*.

In fact, the only thing he *did* notice through the slow fog of estrogen and ludes was the NetFRAME screen half a meter in front of him and, from time to time, the wallet-HDTV propped beside it. This because he was in the process of generating, or trying to generate, new sets of lyrics, an undertaking that had eaten up his entire afternoon.

In theory the process was simple. The only thing Crash had to do was come up with a syntactic schema (e.g., adjective »» concrete noun »» verb »» preposition »» concrete noun »» preposition »» abstract noun) and feed it to the computer which then randomly produced words that matched the pattern (*green headaches thrill through the door of love, rotted knells strangle around the crown of adversity, corkscrewed ulcers whip by the hair of well-being*). The problem, however, was that many of the resulting patterns didn't have the punch of fully-realized lyrics and, even if they did, you still had to crazy-quilt them together to create a coherently incoherent song, which took a lot of time, particularly when your brain stem was aslosh in a nebulous ocean of mones and trancers.

And particularly when something potentially intriguing was going on on that wallet-HDTV, which seemed to be the present case. For a good part of the last several hours the World Health Organization had been displaying dreary public-service Epidemics computer-projection models, swirls of reds, blues, and greens oiling across the globe, blending, recoiling, surging forward. But now a group of unclothed people with interesting bodies were sitting around in beanbag chairs and discussing a subject Crash couldn't make out at first, yet had the distinct impression involved him.

He stopped typing for a moment and turned to see what was up.

A seventeen- or eighteen-year-old blond with surfer-tattoos across her surgically reduced breasts and gold hoops through her pierced eyebrows was explaining something. Her skin had been spot-tanned into an intricate design of squares and rectangles that semi-disguised the scars from her various operations.

Something far back in Crash's mind elbowed his hypothalamus.

"Yeah, they're like virtual," she was saying. "Something totally rige, you know? Newness down the pike of freshness when I see them. Wilco."

"What is it you find so appealing?" asked the announcer, an undernourished black man in his twenties. He wore turquoise nailpolish and lipstick.

"Oh, everything and plenty, everything and plenty. But mostness is the cyberpendages, wilco. It's like, *yes*, we don't have to be *humans* anymore. Like we can be anything we want. Flesh won't stop us anymore. It's just so *senior*, you know?"

Zero Hour, Crash remembered through the bad weather in his skull. Nude talkshow beaming down from Havana. He'd gotten into it a couple of months ago, gotten into lots of television shows a couple of months ago, especially soaps and games based on pain-thresholds, since that post-concert party in London when he'd realized his operations and subsequent doses of hormones had left him, well, had made the whole idea of holoporns and groupies pretty much a moot point.

The blond, identified as Soozy Proviso, a new MTV veejay, continued talking. Crash continued trying to concentrate. But it was a lot harder than you might think.

He'd recently become spatially unstuck, temporally unhinged. Now he was back in that Georgian-facaded flat bordering Holland Park, the thirteen-year-old male flesher with cobalt hair fondling the cosmetically created female twins with copper-capped teeth and pubic mounds Naired soft as rubber while Kool Thing billy-clubbed Jinx in the air above them.

Then he was pushing all of them away, chucking the ashtray at the holographic images, raging from the living room as Jessika and Mikki who'd been making out on the nearby couch till a second ago stopped to look on.

Now he was poised on stage somewhere up north, the dingy Astrodome maybe, maybe the New Palladium, as the first prophylactic packages landed at his feet like pellets of hail while the Diacomm chimeras in the pit below him nipped at the crowd pressing closer.

Initially Crash thought Soozy must have been talking about VBS, she was so into her subject, so *glazed*, and a warm carnation unfurled in the center his chest. Only when the picture cut to the vid he realized it was a different band all together. The lead singer was standing in a flood of green light, a swarm of holographic eyeballs circling his head in a meter-wide retrodelic galaxy—*if*, that is, you could call it standing. Where his legs should have been were dark metal Yugoslavian military prosthetic arms. A child's diminutive prosthetic leg hung from one shoulder, a functioning robotic clamp from the other. Like Crash's, his voice had been electronically enhanced. But instead of radiating sonic purity, it buzzed with acid chatter. His face was a webwork of metal flakes, his nose a ventilator insert.

Soozy Proviso was right. He wasn't just human anymore. He was something else.

Something, Crash had to admit, a whole bunch more interesting.

As much as he wanted to feel differently, truth was he was impressed.

"So you believe My Friend Noo and the Biohazards are here to stay, then?" the announcer asked Soozy after the vid.

"For like a thousand years, wilco," she answered. "For like a thousand years. Time for rethoughtfulness in real time. Time for quality controlledness in primetime. It's more than like music, you know? It's like wearing a new set of brainwaves."

Crash didn't need to turn around to know Jessika was waiting there with another dose of ludes. He stared at the face that used to be his reflected in the tiny blank screen, waiting for the inevitable.

"C'mon, champ," Jessika said.

"I don't want any," he said.

"Hey, man, we already done this number," she replied. "It's not a question of wanting."

"I'm done. I don't want anymore of this stuff."

"Come on, man, stick out your arm."

Crash was sitting next to Mitzy at Beautiful Mutants, typing in an order from Vermont. He was a little boy, running beneath a canopy of pines.

"What's this, then?" Lazar asked from across the room.

"Fuck you," Crash said, swiveling in his chair. "Fuck you both."

Lazar and Jessika exchanged looks like tired parents at three in the morning deciding whose turn it was for the next feeding.

"Are we having a little moment?" Lazar asked.

"It saw the bit about My Friend Noo and the Biohazards on the tube," Jessika said. "It's feelin' sorry for Itself."

"What does It want this time, hmmm? What does It think will make It happy? What'll make It feel good about Itself again? What'll make It stop acting like a *bloody horse's ass*?"

Trying to hold his ground was like trying to cross the street during the Shudder. Crash was already in the Lost in Space, in the Hideous Sun Demon's lap, talking to Jessika on their first and last date.

Sitting there this time, he both knew and didn't know what was going to happen. He both saw and didn't see the whirl of people that'd cluster around him like rapid crystallization. The team of assistants flitting over him from the very instant they joggled him awake every morning, hustled him into the shower, dressed him, packed for him, cooked for him, washed his clothes, shoved him in this limo or that plane, led him onto some generic stage in some generic city and nodded for him to begin, kept that ever-magic flow of drugs heavy and constant right up to the very instant he passed out every night.

All he could see was how cute Jessika was, barely sixteen, with those clicking beaded dreads and white irises. He felt like reaching out right then and there and tracing his fingers along her tribal scars, getting up and walking around the flying-saucer table and hugging her, just hugging her, like a good friend he'd known for years and years.

She'd felt so—safe.

"Let's not start, man," she said.

"I don't want any more derms," said Crash. "I don't want any more shit in my veins."

Lazar sighed.

"We can't always get what we want, can we?" he asked.

"I don't want to be told what to do every rucking second of every rucking day. I want to know where I am."

Jessika looked at Lazar.

"You want me to take care of this?" she asked.

"This whole thing's like living inside a fucking broken VCR or something," Crash said.

Lazar didn't change his expression. He didn't smile and he didn't frown.

And yet at that instant something completely left the contours of his face. That part of his muscles, tendons, and bones connected to Crash just disappeared. Crash no longer factored into the complex equation of Lazar's countenance.

"Fine," he said, pivoting on his heels and pattering toward the balcony doors. "Call me when you're done. I hate the pleading business."

Jessika, features also void, took a step toward the rocker. This was an old vid. He'd viewed it hundreds of times. He wheeled his chair back till it bumped into the computer table, braced for struggle.

Jessika peeled the derm and reached out her powerful right arm for Crash's bicep.

"Wait," he called to Lazar over her shoulder.

Jessika halted.

"Listen, okay? Listen a minute."

Lazar stopped.

"What?" he said without turning.

"Okay. Look. I want to go outside. On the street. Just for a little while. For a walk. Let me do that, then we can do the derm thing." He tried thinking but began sliding toward another space-time continuum. "Come on, it won't hurt anything. I just need some air, is all."

Small back still facing Crash, Lazar cracked his knuckles.

Jessika waited for her cue.

Crash saw her bend and detach the new-born baby from its portable life-support unit in the pile of lava stones. He saw her hand it to him and he saw himself accept it, even though in this replay he already knew what the result would be.

"Half an hour," Crash said.

"Twenty minutes," Lazar countered. "Then It's back again, and the derms are on."

Crash wavered.

"Half an hour," he repeated.

"Look around," Lazar said. "You see any spotlight? You see any fucking gameshow host? We're not on *Wheel of* bloody *Fortune*, are we, you shit."

"Okay, okay. Twenty minutes." He swallowed, added: "Thanks."

He tried to rise and his legs went wobbly.

Jessika chucked her handful of derms on the table and helped him up, ushered him through a sparkle of agitated fish, past Mikki who was still staring at the ceiling as though none of this had just gone down, and into the harsh light of the corridor.

"Have a lark," Lazar called after them. "Have a good fucking lark."

It was a long ride in the service elevator.

Jessika fixed on the display above the doors ticking off their descent while Crash tried to collect his strength so he'd be able to celebrate his tiny victory when he reached the alley.

They'd been through this junk more times than he had the stamina to remember, and if there was one thing he understood by this point it was not to piss off Jessika anymore. She'd had enough of him this evening.

So he stayed mute for the first twenty floors and then launched a quiet apology.

"I'm sorry. Really. Just gets to be a lot sometimes."

Jessika didn't take her eyes off the display.

"I was out of control. I know it. It just happens." He rubbed his lips. "I mean, who the fuck is this My Friend Noo and the Biohazards? Where the hell'd *they* come from?"

She waited several breaths before answering, then her voice came out flat as the EEG of a brain-dead motorcycle-accident victim: "Old story, man. Part of the dance. Everyone does it."

"The dance —"

Jessika glanced over at him, back at the doors.

"Only one in town," she said.

"But I thought *VBS* was gonna be the only dance in town. I thought everyone was gonna love *us*."

"They did, man. They did. For months. Almost half a year. Who could ask for anything more than that? You had the world at your feet. You were a media item. You were *hot*. That's somethin' to be proud of."

The elevator slowed to an air-cushioned stop and the doors glided open.

Jessika gestured for Crash to exit first.

The alley was three-meters wide. The yellow-and-white-graffitied brick wall opposite was lined with dented dumpsters, tops flapped open, an overwhelming stench of rotten fruit and fat saturating the humid dark.

Crash turned toward the vital speed and radiant aura on the street thirty meters away and thought briefly about trying to run, an additional bit of junk he'd been through more times than he had the stamina to remember.

"Six *months*?" he said, walking. "Six fucking *months*?"

"Six months is a long time, man, when you're everything," Jessika said behind him.

The three shots from the silenced slamgun smacked into him in rapid succession and he was down and bleeding from the nose and mouth before his sluggish consciousness had even registered the impact.

He observed the pinkish sky revolve slowly above him. The amazing intricacy of lit windows riddling the side of the hotel. And it dawned on him that, even though he was inhaling, his lungs were no longer inflating with air. He heard a gurgling in his esophagus like coffee brewing.

The first two shots had hit him in the back, shattering a couple of ribs and spinning him around to receive the third shot square in the groin.

He opened his mouth and closed it again, tried to relax and retard his pulse-rate to ease the flow of blood, decided to concentrate on his feet, willing the muscles in them to soften. This seemed to work, so he moved up to his ankles, then his shins, then his knees.

In his peripheral vision he saw Jessika take something out of the pocket of her Versace tank suit, a latex glove, artificial fingerprints, and tug it on her hand. She squeezed the gun handle, the barrel, methodical. She inhabited her own world now, going through motions she'd clearly rehearsed in her mind many times before.

She didn't bother looking up when Crash made a sound like he was gargling.

"Prints'll implicate the head honchos," she said.

Crash couldn't feel anything below his chest but he could smell his own fecal reek. Hear Jessika flip the gun into one of the dumpsters, squeak off the glove, stick it back in her pocket.

She stood over him, her face empty.

Crash tried to figure out if his eyes were open or not, listen if he was still breathing. Instead he heard the noise, gravel on cement, and focused on it.

Tried to steady the sound in his mind, bring it toward the front of his consciousness.

Several seconds passed, but then he understood something.

He realized what he was listening to.

What this was all about, what it had all always been about.

The scrape of Jessika's feet walking away.